THE GAME OF LOVE:

A Stalker's Kiss

KATHY WINSLOWER

DEDICATION

To all the curious minds, young and old,
may this story inspire your sense of
wonder and the joy of unraveling
mysteries together.

Happy reading!

CONTENTS

Chapter One

The night was dark, and my house was like a secret place with lots of shadows. I was sixteen, and my father always had this rule about being home by eight. He thought it was super important for bedtime, but that night, I decided to break my curfew.

I went to my father's study, where it was really quiet. It felt heavy, like there was a secret in the air. The room smelled like fancy wood and old leather, but there was trouble hiding in there.

"Amara," he said my name in a serious way. His eyes were scary, like mine but scarier. I felt really small. "You broke the rules, kiddo."

His words were like a bossy song, and I shivered. I tried to explain, "I was just a bit late, Daddy. I didn't mean to—"

But then he slapped me hard, and it hurt a lot. The sound was like a mean whisper. "Rules don't bend, Amara. They're to make you strong, and breaking them means trouble."

I didn't want to cry, so I didn't show how much it hurt. "I can't live like this. I don't want to do everything you say like a puppet."

He laughed, but it wasn't a happy sound. "You belong to me, Amara. You show off my importance. Rules are there to make you perfect."

I looked at him with more strength. "I'm not a doll for show. I'm a person with my own dreams and wishes."

He got really mad, and his face looked mean. "You have to learn, kiddo. Doing things your way has consequences."

As the door closed in front of me, I felt trapped. But I also felt something brewing, like a little fire. My father got really mad super-fast, and it felt like I was being hit with fists, like hail in a big storm. I cried, but nobody could hear me because the walls were empty. Every time I got hit, I knew I had to get out of the situation before it got worse.

Even though my father's punishments hurt, I was ready to be free and face whatever came my way with a brave heart and a strong spirit. My journey to freedom was just starting, and there were lots of things I didn't know, but I was ready for them.

When the clock hit midnight and my dad was half-asleep in front of the TV, I saw my chance to break free from the things holding me back.

I sneaked away with the cool night air helping me, and my dad's snores covered up the sound. Tears rolled down my face, just like the stars in the sky watching me do something rebellious.

Suddenly, I woke up and took a deep breath. My body was all sweaty, just like in the scary dream I had. The angry feelings towards my father were still with me, like whispers in my head. But I felt so relieved when I realized it was just a dream, a mean trick played by my past memories.

The room felt weird, with the moonlight shining through the curtains. I was kind of confused, trying to shake off the leftover feelings from the bad dream.

Looking around, everything seemed different from the small rental house. Instead, I was stuck in my old childhood bedroom—a place I wanted to forget about. A little bit of light came under the door, shining on the old carpet. I got a shiver as I heard footsteps getting closer, and I started to feel scared, making my heart go really fast.

The door squeaked open, and I screamed really loud, breaking the quiet.

And then, I woke up.

I was in my bed, waking up from the nightmare inside my dream, feeling a sudden jolt of reality. It was like a cool breeze that made me catch my breath. I held onto my sheets, reminding myself that I was far away from the scary darkness in my dreams.

After a bit, the terrified feeling started to go away. I looked at the dim light peeking through my curtains. I was grateful for the sounds of the world outside, a comforting noise that made me forget about my spooky dreams.

But when I closed my eyes again, bits of my scary dream were still in my head, like spiderwebs sticking around. But I knew I was never going back to my childhood home and I felt safe. Even though those memories haunted me, I wanted to make a new story for myself, a life where I'm happy.

∞

When the morning light showed up, London was covered in mist. But it still felt like restricting for a girl who traded one kind of prison for another. My rented house, in a quiet neighborhood, was like a strong castle keeping me safe from my past ghosts.

As my nightmare slowly faded away, I got out of my messy sheets and entered the world of reality. The cold floor stung my bare feet as I walked to the bathroom. The city's distant hum was like a calming song.

Looking in the mirror, my face seemed almost strange, carrying shadows and secrets from my dreams. Splashing cold water on my face felt like trying to wash away the leftover bits of that eerie vision. The London morning said hello through the window, with muted grays and soft promises from the city.

Every morning, my routine was like a dance. It was all set, like a choreographed show mixing quiet moments with regular life. The smell of coffee brewing told me a new day was here, making me feel part of the now. Sipping coffee felt like a small act of going against the rules, pushing away thoughts in my head.

Getting ready for my morning run was like putting on my protective outfit. I wore running clothes, like armor, but only to stay hidden. A wig with chestnut curls covered my real blonde hair, making me look different. Glasses on my nose hid my eyes, the windows to my soul.

My face used to be on billboards a lot, but now they were hiding in secret.

When I stepped outside, the morning air was

fresh. The city was waking up, and my footsteps matched the heartbeat of the neighborhood. Me and the winding streets had an agreement—a promise of freedom and keeping things secret. It was a special connection with the city that kept my secrets safe.

Every day, I enjoyed being anonymous in my new life. The steady pace of my morning run became a comforting habit, keeping me in the present.

As I moved through the city, it unfolded like a secret picture. Every step showed a bit of my hidden life—a dance between keeping hidden and setting myself free. In the quiet corners of London, where nobody knew me, I had silent talks with the people around me. They were part of my secret world, each with a story in the city's fabric. But none of them knew the mysterious chapters that made up Amara Delacroix's secret.

I loved going to the cool park in my neighborhood! It's like the center of our little town, and it's where I get to talk to my running buddies. We chat about the weather, how awesome our city is, and all the regular stuff in life.

Breathing in the fresh morning air, we feel connected, like we're part of something special.

That day, as we jogged along, someone said, "What a great day!" They didn't know I was hiding something, running away from something I didn't want to face. We talked about our running shoes, the different seasons, and how fun it is to jog in the morning. But while we chatted, I kept my real self, hidden behind easy conversations.

It was amazing to be with these friends whom I didn't really know. They didn't recognize me from movies or magazine covers, and that felt good. In their company, I found calmness and peace.

But under the fun talks, there was a strange feeling, like a hidden worry. It was a constant reminder that my peaceful time in the park wasn't really what it seemed. Every chat was like walking on a tightrope, balancing between telling the truth and keeping secrets. These new friends unknowingly became people I shared my thoughts with, mixing their stories with mine in a mysterious dance.

I talked to these people without names, the ones who made my life feel kind of regular for a bit. While the city buzzed with their busy lives, I thought a lot about being close to others but also feeling kind of alone. It was like I was running away and trying to find a safe place in the crowd, keeping my real self a secret as I heard whispers in the streets.

We said nice things to each other, like building a puzzle of who I was. Each word was like a stroke in a painting of the person I turned into – just a quiet part of the city's big sounds. Their laughs, real and happy, echoed in the small streets, making a tune that mixed with my short time here.

Talking to these faces, both familiar and strange, made me appreciate those quick connections – shared laughs, nods, and the everyday sounds that made me feel like I belonged. In those moments, my secrets didn't feel so heavy, and I could enjoy the pieces of a life not messed up by the trouble that made me leave.

But behind all the talking and friendly stuff, I couldn't forget that my safe place was delicate, built on being careful. The idea of my double life hung in the air, a secret shared between the city and me, a dance mixing what's real with what's not.

So, I kept going through the beat of London, pretending to be someone else. Each time we met, felt normal, and every smile reminded me that here, I was both just a regular person and a mystery – a woman with a hidden identity, like a puzzle waiting for people in the busy dance of city life.

As the sun rose high above the skylines, spreading its warm fingers across the sky, it made long shadows that played with the memories of my past, I felt like my safe place wasn't really as strong as I thought. The pretend disguise around me was like a thin wall, not enough to stop the person who kept following me.

So, I started running to avoid those feelings—through small paths and busy streets, acting like I wasn't a famous actress hiding in a small neighborhood. I became like a ghost, fitting into London and hoping to stay hidden. In those quick moments, I wanted to get away from the bad things in my head and just forget for a bit.

∞

When I went into the local bakery, it felt like going into a place where stories happened every time someone baked fresh bread. The lovely aroma made it nostalgic, like a stage where I could do my own little shows.

The old baker, his hands covered in a dusty layer of flour, said hi with a friendly smile while he shaped dough perfectly. "Good morning! The usual, miss?" he asked, sounding familiar.

"Yeah, thanks," I said casually, acting like it was no big deal. As we kept talking, he told me stories about the neighborhood's past. His stories were like a history play, and I was the quiet listener, taking in every detail.

While he spoke about his life, I nodded along, lost in the smell of cinnamon and memories. The aroma of pastries baking was like distraction, hiding the real me who found comfort in the stories he told.

The baker's eyes, showing the marks of time, didn't have a clue about the famous actress hiding in the community. Not knowing the real me, he shared stories about different seasons and how life goes on. I played my part, quietly joining in the flow of his stories, becoming a part of the bakery's old charm.

Another day, I went to this really nice bookstore in the middle of a quiet square. It was like a secret hideout where I could enjoy lots of cool books. The lady who owned the place had hair with silver streaks, and she really loved old stories. When I acted like I was into the newest popular books, she told me about some good ones.

"See anything you like today?" she asked, looking all excited.

I casually grabbed a book, acting interested. As she talked about how great the author was, I got caught up in her words. The bookstore, with all its forgotten stories, turned into a special place where I, pretending to be just a regular reader, felt right at home.

While I flipped through the pages, I heard people talking around me. A kid said, "Mom, can we get this one? It's about dragons and adventures!" The mother smiled and said yes, and they kept exploring books together.

When I went to the counter to pay, the silver-haired lady was talking to an old man. She showed him a book and asked, "Have you read this classic?" The man laughed and shared stories about reading it when he was a kid. It was nice to see people connecting over their love for books.

The air in the bookstore was filled with the sound of pages turning and people talking about books. It was a place where stories weren't just in the books but also in the talks between people who loved reading. With my newly purchased book, I left the cute bookstore, happy for the quiet spot it gave me away from the busy world.

But I felt like I was in a strange situation. Like I was both seen and hidden. I used to be an actress in the spotlight, but now I was like a ghost hiding in the shadows. I wore a disguise to look normal and protect myself from people who wanted to know too much. But I still worried.

After catching my breath and feeling a bit free, I slowly jogged back home. But there was a scary message on my front door that said, "You can't hide." It stood out in the middle of the quiet neighborhood, making me really scared.

I panicked and looked around, trying to find who wrote it. I felt like the safe feeling I had was gone, and I didn't know what danger was waiting for me. I was desperate, so I called my friend and personal assistant

Sarah. She's been with me through a lot, and I needed her help.

"Sarah! Someone figured out where I am," I told her in a worried voice. "I have to move again."

The phone made weird sounds, but finally, Sarah's voice came through, calming me down.

"Don't worry, Amara. I think you should come to my flat right away."

I felt so relieved when she said that. Sarah became my rock, helping me deal with the scary situation. We talked about what to do, and it made me feel better.

But I watched my security camera footage on my phone, hoping to find a clue about who was after me. Sarah's words kept me calm during the uncertainty. But all I saw on the video was me leaving through the front door; there was no sign of the person who had invaded my safe space.

Chapter Two

My heart was beating rapidly as I rushed to pack my stuff into a suitcase. I knew I had to leave soon, and everything I grabbed felt super important. The bedroom was really cold, and I could feel the panic all around.

I looked around, trying to take in the bits and pieces of my life. It was like a puzzle, and I had to grab everything quickly. The energy in the room felt strange, like something big was going to happen. Shadows were moving all over, dancing in the crazy rush.

I remembered all the times I nodded at people I didn't really know and talked to neighbors. Those memories were like special things tucked away in my brain, just like souvenirs from a dream that was slowly fading away.

Out of the blue, my phone rang super loudly, breaking the quiet around me. I grabbed it fast, and Sarah's voice on the line urgently said, "Amara, the taxi's here. Hurry up!"

Sarah, always looking out for me, set up this plan for me to get away – like a rope keeping me safe from all the crazy stuff trying to take over. I held onto my suitcase real tight and rushed to the door, taking one quick look back at the place where I kept my secrets for a little while.

As I quickly stepped outside, the chilly air brushed against my skin, and I felt comforted by the sound of Sarah's voice guiding me through the busy surroundings. "Come on, Amara, we've gotta go," she said, speaking in a calm and steady way.

A taxi was waiting at the edge of the sidewalk, its engine making a soft humming noise. Inside on the back seat was Sarah gestured for me to get in, and her eyes carefully checked the area around us. "Get in and stay down," she told me in a hushed voice.

The yellow taxi, a special kind of car that could help us blend in, was like a promise that we could escape. It smelled like old leather and the air was a bit stale as I slid into the back seat. The taxi driver, with his eyes hidden by the mirror, waited patiently for me to settle.

As we drove away, the city lights and shadows became a blur outside the window. The disguise that hid me from curious people now clung to me like a soft veil, keeping my identity a secret in a tricky dance.

And when we left the quiet neighborhood where I had been hiding, Sarah's voice became gentle. "You're safe now, Amara. We'll figure everything out." Her words were like a warm hug, and I held onto them as we went into the unknown.

Even though we were rushing away, I still felt a bit scared. What if the taxi driver knew who I was? What if my disguise didn't work, and someone found out who I really was with just one look?

I plopped back in the seat and looked out the window at the busy city passing by. Each building and bright sign reminded me of the life I was saying bye-bye to. The taxi driver just drove, not saying a word, and I was happy about that. No chit-chat, just the hum of the car rolling on the road.

While the city moved outside the window, my mind was zooming even faster. I kept peeking at the driver, hoping he wouldn't figure out my secrets. In the quiet taxi bubble, the feeling of not knowing what comes next squeezed me like a choker necklace. The road ahead was like a mystery, and I wondered what surprises were waiting for me.

Sarah's apartment building looked like the perfect hideout in the middle of the busy city of London, lit up by a warm, gentle glow. The taxi rolled to a stop, and I got out, holding onto my suitcase. The familiar smell of the city air surrounded me as I walked toward the entrance.

As I stepped inside, there was a kind of nervous feeling in the air. Sarah gave me a concerned look. "Amara, we need to talk. It's getting worse, isn't it?"

I nodded, feeling the heaviness of the truth settling between us. "The message on my front door, the strange feeling—it was getting more intense. I can't just keep running away. I need someone to help me fix this."

Sarah's eyes showed worry, a quiet understanding that the shadows we'd been avoiding were catching up to us. "Maybe we should get the police involved," she suggested.

"But what if they don't believe me?" I asked, feeling unsure about the idea.

Sarah put her hand on my shoulder, trying to reassure me. "We have to give it a shot. It's the best chance we have to make this stop."

Sarah and I sat close on the comfy sofa in her snug

apartment, talking about what to do next. We finally came to an agreement that involving the police was the only way forward. But I ask Sarah to talk to them, and she agreed.

"Hey, my name is Sarah" Sarah said into the phone. "My friend, Amara and I, we need help. There's something not right going on, and we're a bit scared."

I nodded, feeling relieved that we were reaching out for help. Sarah gave the police all the info they needed. The air in her apartment felt a bit less tense after the call.

"Okay," Sarah said, hanging up the phone. "They said we should go to the police station later and tell them everything."

I nodded again, feeling a bit more hopeful. We planned to head to the station after things in my mind quieted down a bit. It was a small step, but it felt good to know we weren't facing everything alone.

Afterwards, Sarah decided to make a quick meal of hot ramen noodles. We both went over to the little table and sat down. The steam from the tasty broth made us feel all warm and nice, like a big cuddle from the inside.

As we slurped up the noodles, we started chatting about fun stuff, like our favorite songs and silly jokes.

It was like taking a break from all the serious stuff that was bothering us. The ramen was like a magic spell, making us forget about our worries for a little while.

"Hey, have you ever tried making funny faces with the noodles?" Sarah asked, giggling.

I laughed too and said, "No, but let's give it a try!" We both started making goofy faces with our ramen noodles, and soon enough, we were both cracking up.

It was nice to have a moment where everything felt light and happy, even if just for a little bit. The hot ramen turned our frowns upside down, and our little table became a place filled with laughter and warmth.

As we gobbled down our food, I got this feeling like butterflies quieting down in my tummy. "Hey, how 'bout we head to the police station now?" I said, feeling all tough.

Sarah gave me the "I'm a bit scared but also kinda brave" look. "Sure thing, let's do it," she said.

Sarah and I left her apartment, ready to face whatever awaited us. We went through the maze-like police station, urgency in our steps, but the slow bureaucracy hung in the air.

And finally when we talked to the inspectors, doubt reflected in their eyes.

"Many famous people deal with this stuff," one inspector said, not seeming to care.

"Did you ever see the stalker in real life?" another asked, with a mocking tone.

"No," I said, getting a bit frustrated. "But I can feel it—the feeling of being watched. It's real."

Sarah whispered to me, "Don't worry, we'll figure this out together." I nodded, grateful for her support. The room felt tense as the inspectors exchanged doubtful glances. The whole situation seemed unusual for them, but we were determined to see it through.

When the inspectors looked at each other again, it felt like the room was getting smaller. They didn't seem to care much, making it hard to talk to them. One of them said, "If there's no real proof or someone to blame, we can't do anything about it." He said it like it was final.

I felt really mad but also kind of stuck. The system didn't help me against my stalker. "So, what should I do? Just wait until it's too late?"

"Maybe hire someone to protect you. Be careful. We can't do anything without proof." The inspector's idea hit me hard. It was like a cold gust of wind.

Feeling down but not ready to give up, we told the

police everything they wanted to know. They wrote it all down in a report, and when they handed it to us, their eyes kind of said, "You're on your own, guys."

Walking out of the interview room, it got really quiet between me and Sarah. The night felt heavy, like a big secret we had to figure out.

As we strolled into the busy corridors, we realized the red tape we were up against might be even thicker than we thought. But, you know what? A little bit of courage sparked up inside us. We couldn't count on the system to help us out, but we promised each other that we'd figure out a way to face whatever was lurking in the shadows.

∞

Leaving the police station with Sarah, we carried the frustration with us, like that bad aftertaste you get after eating something bitter. The city, which used to feel safe, now seemed like this tricky puzzle without a clear way out. Riding in the taxi, with the bright lights of London passing by, I couldn't shake off the thought of getting a bodyguard—a sort of invisible shield to keep me safe from the creeping darkness.

The city lights played peek-a-boo on Sarah's face in the taxi, and the quietness around us was full of unsaid worries. After the cops acted all uninterested, deciding to get a bodyguard to protect me, felt like something I had to do, even if I wasn't too thrilled about it. It was like admitting I needed some extra protection from the scary stuff closing in on me.

Back in Sarah's apartment, I couldn't hide the way I felt- really scared. The stalker following me was an unknown person, hiding in the world around me.

The city, which used to feel friendly, now seemed like it was keeping secrets too. It was nighttime, and I was alone with my thoughts. I realized that the answers I needed might be with someone I didn't know—a person who could protect me from the shadows that were trying to take over.

"I never thought it would be like this," I said quietly. Sarah and I were sitting on her old sofa.

Sarah sighed, looking worried, just like me. "Don't worry, Amara. We'll get through this. We just have to be strong and face it together."

"But what if the bodyguard can't keep me safe? What if this never stops?" I shared my fears, and the room felt a bit better, even though it was dark.

Sarah put her hand on my shoulder, trying to comfort me. "We're doing everything we can. We won't let fear control us. Tomorrow, we'll find the best bodyguard, someone who can really help."

I nodded, feeling a little hopeful because of Sarah's words. Outside the window, the city was sleeping. Deciding to hire a bodyguard was like starting a new part of my story—a part where I took charge of what was happening and faced it head on.

∞

In the days that followed, the digital world looked like a giant confused network to me. But each click felt like I was taking a step to take control of my life. I checked out the profiles of potential bodyguards on Craigslist, their faces staring at me from the screen. Each one promised safety in all this confusion. But they turned out to be a wild parade of characters - some too excited, some a bit shady, and none giving me the confidence I needed. Even though I was unsure, Sarah decided to organize the interviews.

When Sarah set up the first video call, she winked at me and said, "Get ready for the show, Amara!"

I sat with Sarah on the sofa, staring at the screen from the sidelines, waiting for the first bodyguard to show up. The excitement bubbled up inside me as the call connected.

Then this guy, Jack, appeared on the screen. He had sunglasses on indoors, and it made me giggle.

Sarah pressed the mute button and gave me a look

like she knew something. "Amara, meet Jack, the Sunglasses Guardian!"

Jack got close to the camera and said, "You're looking to hire a bodyguard, well you've come to the right person. I've got a sixth sense for danger, and these shades are my secret weapon."

Sarah struggled to maintain a professional face while asking Jack about his experience and skills. I tried hard not to burst into laughter. Jack's excitement was catchy, even though his sunglasses remained a funny mystery.

∞

The next candidate, Lisa, hopped onto the video call, showing off cool karate moves right from her little room. I was like, "Whoa, that's awesome!" But then Sarah leaned in and said, "Hey Amara, we're looking for a bodyguard, not a ninja!"

As Sarah kept chatting with different people, there was this one dude who believed his pet parrot could sniff out trouble. Imagine that, a bird as a bodyguard! And then there was this lady who was all about disguises, thinking that's the secret to staying safe. It felt like we were on some kind of weird talent show.

Sarah and I just couldn't help but giggle and give each other these funny looks. It was like, "Can you believe this?" and we were both trying not to burst out laughing.

After the last interview was done, Sarah closed the laptop and let out a big sigh. "Phew, that was fun, but we still haven't found the perfect bodyguard."

I laughed. "Yeah, it was kinda funny. Maybe we should look for someone who's, you know, just regular?"

Sarah agreed, her eyes twinkling with a smile. "Regular sounds good, Amara. Let's keep searching. The right one is definitely out there somewhere."

As we scrolled through more options, I rolled my eyes, "What about someone who likes pizza? Pizza lovers are cool, right?"

Sarah grinned, "Totally! A pizza-loving bodyguard sounds awesome. Let's add that to our list of must-haves."

As Sarah and I got comfy in the living room, the serious talk from the night hung in the air. I felt a bit uneasy, like I need to hire a bodyguard immediately.

That's when Sarah spoke up, her eyes showing she cared a lot.

"Amara, what if you get one of those security

companies to help out?" she suggested, looking genuinely worried.

I thought about it, running my hand through my hair. "Sarah, those companies are for super famous people with loads of cash. I'm famous, but not exactly rolling in money. My bank account doesn't scream Hollywood glam."

Sarah looked puzzled. "But your safety is super important, Amara. We've got to find a way to keep you safe all the time."

I agreed, thankful for her caring. "I know, Sarah. It's just that those big security guys cost a ton. And with all the drama around me, getting a good deal or support isn't easy. I need something that's affordable and, you know, trustworthy."

We both understood the importance of trust. My past had messed up my trust issues, and finding security that wouldn't let me down was a big deal. It felt like my problems were getting even trickier as we talked.

Sarah put her hand on my shoulder, trying to make me feel better. "Don't worry, Amara. We'll find a way. My fiancé, Mike, used to be in the army. Maybe he can help. He would know some reliable people," she said with a determined look.

I didn't really care about Mike's history at that moment. I just wanted to feel safe. "Please ask him. I don't care who it is, as long as they can keep me safe," I pleaded.

Sarah, showing that she was determined to help, promised to talk to Mike. But it was late, and Mike was busy being a bartender in a lively pub downtown—a place where people were having fun and dancing their worries away. Wanting a break from all the stress, we decided to surprise Mike at the pub. The taxi outside was ready, waiting quietly for our secret mission under the city lights.

As the taxi zoomed away, the car's hum mixed with the city's nighttime sounds, making a cool melody that felt full of adventures. The disguise, which used to hide who I was, now turned into my special armor, keeping me safe from curious night gazers.

∞

Soon, we arrived at the pub, appearing magically out of the darkness like a convenient hideaway where happiness bubbled up like a friendly stream. When we walked in, the air was thick with the smell of drinks and the steady rhythm of people talking against the music in the background.

The soft lights made us blend into the crowd, and nobody around us knew about the secret conversation we were having.

Sarah and I went to a quiet corner. "Hey, what's the plan?" I asked, my voice hushed.

She smiled and whispered back, "We need to be careful. We're going to talk to Mike, and we don't want anyone overhearing us."

I nodded, feeling a bit like a spy. The pub was full of laughter and chatter, creating a lively atmosphere for our serious conversation. "Got it. Let's keep it on the down-low."

I looked around the pub, trying to find Mike's face in the busy crowd. Finally, I saw him at the bar. Sarah saw him too and guided me through all the tables and people. When we reached the bar, Mike smiled warmly at us. He paused his talk with someone else.

"Hey there! What are you two doing here?" Mike asked, his happy voice standing out in the loud pub.

"We need your help with something," Sarah said, a small smile on her face. "Amara needs a bodyguard, and we thought you might know someone."

Mike looked at me, understanding how serious it was. "Sure thing, I've got your back. Let me make a few calls. We'll find the right person for the job."

In the midst of the low buzz of people talking, the sound of glasses clinking, and the warmth of the pub, I found a little bit of peace. We were feeling a bit thirsty, so we ordered our drinks. The alcohol was like a small escape from all the serious stuff going on.

While we waited for our drinks, the pub turned into a safe place, like a quick getaway from all the things that were bothering me. The sound of glasses clinking and people laughing made me feel better, like a bandage for the worried feelings. It reminded me that, even when everything is crazy, some things can still be normal.

In the quiet corners of the pub, me and Sarah looked at each other without saying anything. It was like we both knew we were on this journey together, a journey now in the hands of a guy who used to be in the military.

The night went on, like a story filled with not knowing what would happen next, but also a little bit of hope. We were getting ready for something big that was waiting for us outside the pub.

As I sipped my drink, a tiny bit of worry popped into my head. What if someone here knew who I was? The disguise that was supposed to make me look different suddenly didn't seem so strong.

I kept my eyes down, not looking at anyone I

didn't know, feeling better in the low light. Even though the pub felt nice, there was still a little bit of nervousness as I sat among the crowd, trying to stay hidden in the busy place.

Chapter Three

It was just like any other night, I was chilling on my old worn-out sofa, munching on a bowl of cereal while watching late-night television. My old sofa and the flickering screen were like my trusty sidekicks during these quiet nights.

Out of the blue, my phone rudely interrupted the calm. I quickly grabbed it to stop the loud ring from ruining my peaceful moment. Guess who it was? It was Mike, bringing a welcome break from my usual routine.

"Hey, John. Ever thought about a job that pays more than bagging groceries?" Mike's voice crackled through the phone, surprising me in the stillness of the night. I was intrigued, so I leaned forward, forgetting about my cereal for a moment.

"Tell me more," I asked, my voice full of curiosity.

Mike, was someone who always came up with unusual idea. He began to share the job details. "It's a gig, buddy, something a bit different than what you're used to. Might be a little dangerous, but I know you've got the skills."

A sense of excitement bubbled up inside me when Mike mentioned the aspect of danger. "So, what's the job?" I asked eagerly.

But Mike took a different approach, checking in about my leg, asking, "How's your leg these days?" He sounded caring over the phone.

I casually touched the leftover scars on my knee, reminders of old battles. "No problems in over many months. I'm good."

Mike, sounding satisfied, said, "Great! I'll set up a meeting tomorrow. Also, dress nice—you're entering a different league, buddy."

Thinking about the new adventure mixed with a bit of danger, I felt something spark inside. After the call, I sat there, pondering the unknown path ahead.

The ordinary bowl of cereal on my lap suddenly felt like a symbol of the extraordinary turn my night had taken.

My weekdays at my boring work place was all about doing regular things, like putting groceries into bags. But now, it feels like those old days are behind me. Something new was happening, a break from the usual stuff that always happened in my life. The television blared on in the background, making shadows on the walls as if they were giving me hints about the danger that was waiting for me.

When it got all quiet at night, it felt like a whole new part of my story was starting. I was figuring out what to wear for this big meeting that might change everything. I felt a little thrill, like super excitement that was more than just the normal stuff.

The night kept going, kind of like a shadowy picture. I did my bedtime routine in my tiny studio apartment with only one lamp. The soft light fell on my old furniture and the marks of a life that's been on the edge.

Every night, I gently put on the cooling gel on my knee, like a special routine I can't miss. This helped with the pain, like a gentle touch to say, "I care." The gel smelled familiar, and for a moment, it took me away from the present, connecting me with memories of the past.

My small apartment was like a comfy hideout, filled with stories from when I left the military. Life wasn't going so great, and it led me to there. The walls had bits and pieces of my journey, like a cocoon that hide me from the world that once knew me as a soldier.

But then there was Mike. He wasn't always there in my post-military days, when I needed a steady friend in my lonely world. But a few years earlier I finally reunited with him, at a support group for veterans. Being with him felt good, like a connection to a life beyond the shadows I've been in.

And, if I'm being real, there was something more than just friendship between us—a little crush that started back in our military days.

∞

My room was always lit kind of dark, like when you're scared of the shadows at night. I couldn't sleep because of my new friend, Insomnia. It came from haunting memories that wouldn't leave me alone, making me feel stuck on my little bed.

I closed my eyes, hoping to get a cozy sleep hug, but the memories doesn't ask for permission. In my bad dream, I went back to a really scary time. There were loud blasts, smelly smoke, and heavy gear pushing on me. I was dizzy and my knee hurt as I lay on the ground. Someone pulled me away from danger, and everything was blurry.

I wasn't sure if I would make it out alive.

The dream got super intense. As I got pulled out of the warzone, and all the scary memories mixed up like a crazy whirlwind. It felt like a sad music concert in my head, replaying all the sad memories and fear I had deep inside.

Then, bam! I woke up in my small apartment, sweat sticking to me like leftover bits of the dream. The room was still kind of dark, but it didn't have the sounds of gunfire from my dream. I was all alone, thinking about how sleep, my escape buddy, let me down again. The nightmare stuck with me, even in the quiet of my room.

It was already morning and the sunlight peeked through my old curtains, making my room all warm and cozy. I woke up from a night of not-so-great sleep, thinking about the strange dreams I had. As I moved around on my small bed, I heard a sound—my phone making a noise. It was a text from my friend Mike.

I grabbed my phone from the table next to my bed and looked at the message. It was from Mike, and he said, " Morning. Secret stuff. Let's meet now at the pub where I work."

I couldn't help but smirk. Pubs are usually quiet in the morning, but they hold secrets and surprises. I felt a little excited, like when you're about to do something daring. Mike always knew how to make things interesting. It was like a dance with danger, and it had become a regular part of my life.

The message made it seem urgent, like something mysterious was going on. I liked that feeling—the idea of not knowing what was going to happen. I got out of bed, feeling the cool air in my room. It was like a sneak peek of the chilly morning in London.

I looked through my small collection of clothes, trying to find something cool, just like Mike had said. A really old leather jacket caught my eye, hidden in the back of the closet. I decided to wear it with my favorite blue jeans, a brand-new white T-shirt, and my tough boots. The whole outfit gave off a strong, outdoorsy vibe—kind of like a style that matched my own world perfectly.

∞

Out in London, where the weather was changing, and winter was on its way, the city felt really cold. I wore my leather jacket like I was part of biker gang, protecting me from the cold and whatever secrets were waiting for me at the pub. As I walked through the streets, it was like the city was showing me all the things that could happen, hidden behind the mist in the morning.

The pub, like a clubhouse for friends and their secrets, looked big and important from far away. Its front was like a book cover with stories and whispers written on it, and it made me want to go closer. I felt so excited, like there were cool things waiting for me inside. I was wearing clothes that were both practical and cool, and I was ready to explore the unknown—a risky adventure in a city that had seen me change from a soldier to someone who kept to myself.

The sunlight made the street's bumpy stones glow softly, like a quiet helper for the special meeting about to happen. I had a feeling that this meeting was going to be secretive, with a hint of danger, making it an exciting mystery.

The pub's door made a creaky sound, and the soft noises of a London morning came in, like whispers waking up the sleepy place. It smelled nice, like old wood and the ghosts of drinks from before. I walked in, and my steps made echoes in the empty room.

Three people stood waiting for me inside, where a mysterious feeling hung in the air. Mike and Sarah were by each other's side, their faces telling a story of a friendship that went way back. Right between them stood a stunning blonde lady, the kind that makes you look twice because she's so beautiful that she grabs everyone's attention in the room.

Sarah, not just Mike's friend anymore but now his fiancée, was beaming with happiness. A tiny bit of jealousy tried to creep up on me, but I quickly brushed it off—like when you sweep away crumbs from a table.

Mike's eyes were shining like he knew something exciting, and we exchanged greetings like old buddies. Our friendship was solid, built on the experiences we had during our time in the military. The morning sunlight streamed through the windows, making the pub look like a place where secrets were about to unfold.

While checking out the three of them, my eyes locked onto the blonde woman. Her face seemed familiar, but I couldn't quite put my finger on it. She had these captivating eyes that looked at me like she was figuring me out. Suddenly, I felt a bit self-conscious in the outfit I wore, thinking it was cool. Her gaze made me feel a little exposed, like when you're on a stage and everyone's watching you.

Mike had a sly smile on his face as he stepped up, breaking the quiet tension in the air. "Hey, John, this is Amara. We gotta help her out."

Amara, a name that echoed in my head, like it was trying to fit into my memories. It made me a bit frustrated, like I was missing something. I tried hard to remember any Amara whom I knew, but my brain felt all foggy. Names of girls were never my strong suit, and I hadn't really been with that many women.

We shook hands, and Amara's hand felt warmer than usual. There were questions in the air, but we didn't say them out loud. Our eyes met, and it felt like there was a story unfolding underneath—a tale weaving us into a web of interesting stuff. Mike and Sarah, watched as me and Amara shook hands, like it was a part of some cool collaboration that went beyond what we knew—a kind of dance with shadows and secrets in the middle of a London morning.

Sarah's eyes wandered around the room casually, finally fixing on Mike with genuine interest. "So Mike, what's this security thing that John does? Tell us all about it," she asked, a bit unsure.

Mike, good at avoiding direct questions, gave me a little nod—a signal for me to jump in. I cleared my throat and spoke in a calm way. "Security work involves a lot of things. I've done some jobs before, nothing too exciting. You know, the low-key stuff," I said, not getting into too many specifics.

Amara turned her attention to me, curious. "And?" she asked, sounding a bit suspicious.

Looking her in the eyes, I shared just enough to seem open. "I used to be in the military," I said, trying to keep it simple. "Private security is actually easier."

There was a bit of tension in the air as Sarah kept looking at us. Mike, always good at changing the subject, jumped in, "Don't worry, Sarah. We're low-key and help out friends when they need it. John's got the skills, and that's all we need."

The atmosphere in the air changed, and it felt like things were going to be okay. I turned my attention to Amara. She had been quiet during the whole thing, just watching. But, there was definitely something on her mind. She looked a bit nervous as she spoke up, her voice shaky in the quiet pub.

"I'm in some kind of big trouble," she said, looking at me like she needed some comfort.

I leaned in, wanting to understand. "What kind of trouble?" I asked in a hushed tone, making sure she knew it was a safe space.

"Someone's following me," Amara admitted, and her words seemed heavy, like there was something really bad going on.

"Why would anyone follow you?" I asked, my eyes wide with curiosity.

She looked at me with a troubled expression, her eyes telling a story of fear. "Because of my movies," she said in a hushed voice. Suddenly, it hit me like a surprise party—Amara Delacroix, the actress who used to be on all those magazine covers, making everyone excited with her work in the movies. A few months back, the news was all about her, from walking on the red carpet at movie premiers to scandalous headlines in the tabloids. But then, she disappeared like a magician's trick, vanishing into the shadows.

I couldn't believe how she managed to stay hidden in a big city like London. She moved around like a secret agent, and nobody knew where she was. No new pictures of her in the tabloids—nothing. But now, someone had found her secret hideout, lurking in the shadows like a mystery.

As she told her story, it felt like I was watching a movie with a surprising ending. Amara Delacroix, who was famous, now wanted to be a nobody. Even though I stayed calm, I could sense that something big was happening in her life. It was like two different worlds colliding—her old life with lights and cameras and the new one filled with danger, right there in the quiet pub.

∞

Amara looked really sad and scared when began to talk about how the stalker found his way inside her London apartment. It felt like there were complications hanging around her words, like invisible bullies. I felt a strong need to protect her, like a hero.

I asked her, "Can you tell us what happened with the stalker who's bothering you?" My voice was soft and kind, hoping she'd feel safe telling us about the chilling things in her life.

Amara, feeling all upset, covered her face with her hands, like she was trying to hide from the person who was bothering her. Sarah, who had been watching

Amara closely, spoke up before Amara could say anything. "It got so bad that Amara had to leave her flat. I found a quiet place for her to stay, but even then, the stalker found her. It's like they followed her everywhere, they could be watching her as we speak."

The words Sarah said felt heavy in the quiet room. I looked at Mike, and he seemed really serious, like he was thinking hard about what to do. The pieces of the puzzle were all over the place, and we needed to figure it out quickly.

I turned to Sarah, my eyes serious. "Who else knows where Amara was?"

Sarah looked worried and a bit frustrated. "Just me and Amara. I was the one who rented the house, and no one knows me. I'm not like Amara, who is always in the spotlight."

That made me realize how risky Amara's situation was. In today's world, where everyone knows everything, staying hidden was like trying to catch a slippery fish. I glanced at Mike, trying to show him how serious this was.

"It's too easy to find info about Amara's assistant with just a few pictures from public events," I said, thinking hard about what we could do.

Sarah seemed to struggle with the idea that it could

have been her fault. She looked at Amara apologetically. "I'm sorry, Amara. I didn't think..."

But Amara interrupted her, determined. "I trust Sarah with my life. But we need another way."

Feeling the pressure, Mike spoke up. "There's a way to draw out the stalker, but it's gonna be extreme."

Amara turned her blue eyes to me and said, "I trust you." It was a big responsibility, and as we discussed our plan to expose the stalker, the pub turned into a place of determination—a safe spot where we joined forces, getting ready for the storm ahead.

Chapter Four

The little pub was super quiet early in the morning, like a secret keeper waiting for the day to begin. Mike and I found a comfy spot at an old table, and our talk mixed in with the leftovers of the nighttime feel. Sarah had taken a really upset Amara home, leaving just me and Mike to figure out our big plan.

I looked at Mike, trying to make sense of the whole situation. "So, how much do you know about Amara?" I asked, keeping my eyes on him. I really wanted to know if he and Amara were like super close friends or just sort of knew each other.

"Um, not that much, John," Mike said, looking kind of worried. His forehead got all wrinkled with concern. "I knew she was hiding from her stalker, but

I didn't get how bad things were until today."

I nodded, feeling a bit serious. "Yeah, today was like a wake-up call, huh?"

Mike agreed, "Totally. I had no idea she was going through all this."

A big secret hung in the air, making us feel like we had to do something right away. I started thinking about what we could actually do. "Did they go to the police?" I asked, not sounding too sure.

Mike looked upset when he answered, "Police? You know they're not much of a help. I don't really trust them."

I nodded quietly, getting why Mike felt that way. Sometimes it's hard to tell if the police are on the same page as us. Our talk kept going, like a plan starting to come together. We had to help Amara, but we needed to figure out how first.

I looked at Mike and said, "So, What's the plan?" My voice was quiet, like when you're sharing a big secret with a friend.

Mike, who's really good at coming up with plans, started telling me lots of ideas. It was like he was spreading a big spider web of possibilities to catch the person who was following Amara. He talked about watching and waiting, like detectives in a movie, and even setting up a sneaky trap. Each idea was like a special move in a secret spy game we had to play.

"I don't think we should treat the stalker as a bad guy," I said, looking right at Mike. "We should try to understand how he thinks."

The situation was really serious, and we had to be careful about how we handled it. We were trying to figure out what to do about Amara's stalker. The pub was like a secret place where important decisions were made. We were like explorers, trying to solve the mysteries around Amara.

As we talked about our plan, you could feel the tension in the air. It was like the quiet moment before a big storm.

∞

The noise outside the pub buzzed around us as Mike talked about his plan to find the stalker who was bothering Amara. But there was a big decision hanging in the air, like a mystery waiting to be solved - whether I was really up for this secret mission. The job ahead seemed important, and I felt it in my gut. The air got thicker with excitement, making me realize that I had a crucial part to play in this mysterious game.

"I haven't said yes to doing this job yet," I said,

making sure my voice sounded strong. The responsibility of it all made me stop and think. I needed to be sure before jumping into the unknown.

Mike, always good at convincing people, leaned in closer, his eyes showing how urgent it was. "Come on, John. We really need you for this. It's not just about Amara; it's also about keeping Sarah safe. You're the best person for the job."

Hearing about Sarah, Mike's fiancée, hit me in a way I hadn't expected. It stirred up feelings I hadn't explored before.

Suddenly, I felt a bit jealous - like an unexpected guest had joined the party in my mind. How did she manage to win the love of a guy I looked up to, a friend I had shared tough times with, in the military?

But even with the jealousy, I pushed those emotions aside. Being practical took over. This could be my chance - a good, steady job that could help me finally get the knee replacement surgery I'd been avoiding for too long.

"I'll do it," I said, nodding my head, thinking hard about what Mike asked me to do.

Mike grinned happily, looking satisfied that I agreed to help. "Awesome! I'll tell Sarah. You can start tomorrow."

Walking out of the pub, the morning air in London felt really cold around me. My decision to help Mike felt heavy, like taking a big step. The next thing I had to do was clear—I needed to go to the corner store where I work part-time. It was time to quit that job, to leave behind the usual stuff in my life for something new and unknown.

As I handed in my resignation, I felt a strong sense of duty. I could have just left the part-time job without telling anyone, disappearing like a ghost. But I believed in doing things the right way, following a code of honor. The path ahead was full of mysteries, secrets, and even danger, but I stepped into it with a strong belief. It was more than just a mysterious adventure— it was about protecting others and finding the stability I've been searching for a long time.

And as I walked through the London streets, the morning mist made everything look like a secret adventure. I left the corner store and wandered through narrow lanes and hidden paths until I found what I was looking for—a secret underground internet cafe! These places used to be all over the city, but now they were disappearing.

When I walked into the internet cafe, it was pretty dark, but I liked it. It felt like a special society for computer stuff. The computers were humming, making a noise that felt like a song I knew. Some people were sitting at the booths, their faces shining from the light of the computer screens. The whole place smelled like coffee, and I could hear people talking quietly, like they were sharing secrets.

I found a seat at one of the computers and started looking for someone super mysterious—the famous cyber hacker in London called The White Panther. In the world of computer wars, she was known for providing unique services. I was excited to see if I could find any clues about her!

As I was looking around, a message popped up on the computer—a special invite to a secret chat room where The White Panther hangs out. I clicked my way through secret codes and stuff, and bam! I was in this digital world where nobody knew who anybody really was.

Suddenly, this character appeared on the screen, all decked out like a white panther. The name alone made me think of someone super sneaky and precise, perfect for someone who's exploring the delicate world of cyber secrets.

A computer voice spoke up, saying, "What brings you to The White Panther's hideout?"

I was totally surprised! Turned out, The White Panther was a woman, and she was hiding behind this cool panther look. In the dim lights of the secret internet place, I was staring at someone who broke all the normal ideas I had about hackers. The White Panther wasn't just a guy—she was a guardian of the online world, smashing all the gender rules.

I began typing, my words making ripples in the online space as I started a conversation with The White Panther, introducing myself. This mysterious online guardian dealt in secrets and shadows. The hum of the café made our discussion feel even more secretive.

Sitting in front of the computer's soft glow, I kicked off the chat that'd help me uncover hidden digital secrets. It was like teaming up for a secret dance in a place where the online world and real life blended together. The internet café hummed softly, setting the stage for our undercover collaboration.

"Tell me about Amara Delacroix," I typed, my words floating into the virtual world.

The White Panther's computerized voice filled the encrypted chat room, "You know the deal, John. Are you ready to pay?"

We went back and forth, negotiating the terms of our secret exchange. In the virtual space, I tapped on my phone, sending the last bit of my savings. It wasn't much, but it was the key to unraveling Amara Delacroix's mysteries.

As the digital money traveled through cyberspace,

The White Panther's fingers danced on the keyboard. Lines of code transformed into a picture of information, exposing details about Amara Delacroix that went beyond what the public knew—a mysterious figure hiding in plain sight.

"She's not British," The White Panther said, the words hanging in the quiet room like a mystery waiting to be solved.

I couldn't believe it. Amara Delacroix, the famous actress from England, had a secret that went beyond her cozy home across the seas. The idea tugged at my curiosity, making me wonder about the real story behind her.

"Where is Amara Delacroix really from?" I asked, my fingers tapping the keys with excitement.

The White Panther's answer was a bit unclear. "I need more time to figure that out."

Feeling a bit antsy, I could sense that the mystery around my soon-to-be boss was getting deeper. The air in the internet cafe got thicker as if it held onto hidden truths. Shadows and secrets were dancing around, making everything more mysterious.

The White Panther, my digital guardian, had the answers to Amara Delacroix's hidden past, but the truth remained a puzzle—an example of the complicated web of secrets waiting for us to uncover.

After what felt like forever, the White Panther finally shared the big secret she had been keeping.

"Guess what?" she typed with a big smile. "Amara Delacroix's real name is actually Amara Wilson, and she's from Scotland."

My eyes got really wide when I learned this simple fact. "Scottish? Seriously? Isn't that the same as being British?"

The White Panther laughed, or at least it felt like she did in the digital world. "Well, technically, Scotland is part of Britain, but it's got its own special identity. It's like being in a big family but having your own room with a cool door."

I thought about it, feeling pretty amazed by this geography stuff. "So, she's originally from Scotland. That's really interesting!"

The quiet in our conversation, which used to be like a silent room, now felt different. It was buzzing with the weight of this new information. The shadows and secrets in the internet cafe seemed to slow down, like they were taking in the news about Amara Delacroix's true roots.

As I sat in the underground internet cafe,

waiting eagerly for The White Panther to share more secrets, the computers hummed around me, making the suspense even more intense. It felt like a mysterious cloak wrapped around me, mixing with the soft glow of the dimly lit room. The whole atmosphere was full of unknown possibilities.

The promise of discovering hidden things was like a secret waiting to be revealed. The White Panther revealed something important about Amara Delacroix's online activity. There was nobody actively stalking her social media profiles on the internet. The revelation left me feeling like I needed to know more, especially with Amara Delacroix's secrets looming over me. To navigate through them, I knew I needed The White Panther's help.

Tapping away on the keyboard, I wrote, "I want to hire you for your special skills."

Curious, The White Panther asked, "Why do you want my help?"

Carefully choosing my words, I replied, "I need to uncover the stalker who's bothering Amara Delacroix, the actress. I think you can find any digital clues they've left behind."

There was a moment of silence from the virtual feline figure. Against the dark background, her white silhouette stood out. Then, with a small nod, she agreed to help me. Our collaboration in the digital world started, promising to blend the real and virtual as we worked together to keep Amara safe from hidden dangers.

A message from the White Panther popped up on my phone really fast, like a champion coming to the rescue. It said, "You can contact me anytime." Those words felt like a guiding light in the web of confusion

∞

I left the underground internet cafe and stepped out into the busy London streets. There were so many people, like pieces of a puzzle all mixed up. I felt kind of invisible in the middle of it all. The secrets I was about to learn were like a heavy backpack on my shoulders, always with me in the middle of the busy city.

As I walked, a yummy smell of Chinese food made my stomach growl. I followed my nose to a nearby restaurant. The streets were full of life, like a big party. It was a nice break before things got crazy.

The Chinese restaurant was all lit up with colorful lights that kept blinking. Inside, people were happily chatting, and the sound of chopsticks hitting plates made a fun beat. I went up to the counter and asked for a box of delicious stir-fried noodles and tasty dumplings to take home. The person at the counter gave me a box, and I could feel the warmth coming through the cardboard.

I left with my bag of warm food, walking through the familiar narrow paths back to my apartment. The tall buildings made long shadows, making the city look mysterious and exciting. On my way, I saw some interesting things and even met some friendly passerby.

As I turned a corner into a dark alley, something surprising happened—I suddenly bumped into a noisy group of teenagers. They were waving around sharp knives, trying to scare me. It was like stepping into a different side of the city, nothing like the online mysteries I had just explored.

"Hey, there boomer!" one of them shouted, the shiny blades reflecting the dim light. The air felt heavy with the demand for money, like a scary tune in the middle of all the city noise.

Caught in this unexpected situation, I had to make a choice—give them what they wanted or figure out a way through the shadows in the tough streets of London. The city was showing me a complicated story, blending the online and real worlds together in a mix of uncertainty. The suspenseful feeling echoed through the alley, mixing with the smell of Chinese takeout in my hand.

"So, what's it gonna be?" another one of them

asked, making the decision even more difficult. I could feel my heart pounding as I looked around, trying to find an escape route. The shadows seemed to dance around, playing tricks on me in the dimly lit alley. It was like being in the middle of a real-life mystery, with the city as the backdrop.

But the bunch of teens, with their untidy appearances, gave off a strong smell that hit my nose. I held my Chinese takeout close, it's delicious aroma interrupted by the unpleasant scent of unwashed bodies. The alley's dim lighting cast shadows on their faces, making them look even scarier. But, my hunger trumped my fear.

I wrinkled my nose and blurted out, "Man, you guys really need a bath. You stink!"

The atmosphere got weird, like when you mix oil and water. Their tough and mean looks turned into confusion, breaking their tough-guy act for a moment. The leader, this skinny guy with a faded tattoo on his neck, gave me a puzzled look. Injecting humor into a scary situation was risky, but I did it, creating a strange kind of peace.

But, my comment seemed to annoy the gang's leader even more. He lifted his knife, its blade catching the dim light and looking super dangerous.

He demanded money, making the whole place feel

tense, like a sour note in a loud city.

"I'm not gonna give you guys any money," I said, crossing my arms and looking straight at them. We were in one of those intense stand offs, and my words sort of just hung there.

Things were getting intense. One of them, looking all tough, started stepping closer, like he was about to do something. But then, out of nowhere, we all heard a police siren in the distance. It was loud, and you couldn't miss it.

The guys, they scattered like birds taking off, darting into the twisty streets.

I turned around to see where the noise was coming from, and I saw a police car lights flashing. That feeling of relief hit me when I saw the officer inside. It was someone I knew, someone I've seen around. Fate works in funny ways, right?

His arrival made things interesting. I had questions, and the whole city seemed like this puzzle, revealing surprises in the weirdest moments.

Life is pretty crazy, with all its secrets and twists.

As the police car rolled to a stop, my brother Ronald hopped out from the driver's seat, his face familiar with laugh lines and the tiredness of being a cop. He walked over to me with a big grin.

"Hey, Bro! You owe me big time for saving you!" he said with a friendly tone, like we always do when we tease each other.

I felt relieved and gave him a friendly slap on the back. "You always show up just when I need you, don't you?"

Ronald shrugged, mischief in his eyes. "Just doing my job, keeping the streets safe. But seriously, what were you thinking, getting into a scuffle with those guys?"

I rolled my eyes, realizing how not-so-smart I was. "I guess I just didn't want them taking my money. Plus, they could use a bath."

He chuckled and slapped me back. "Come home for Christmas dinner this year, John. Mom's been wondering where you are."

I raised an eyebrow, thinking about it. "I'll think about it," I replied, making Ronald laugh. Our relationship was kind of like a seesaw, balancing between family and my love for being alone.

With a final laugh, Ronald gave me a friendly warning. "Stay out of trouble, and seriously, don't end up in jail. I can't keep bailing my own brother out all the time."

He walked away, leaving me alone in the alley, holding my cold Chinese takeout. I thought about getting a microwave – small things that make life easier, especially when it's always so unpredictable.

Chapter Five

Sarah's apartment was the lit by the morning lights from the city outside. I sat on the sofa, feeling all sorts of mixed-up emotions swirling inside me. It was like memories from the past crashing into the present. Sarah, my friend who always listened, hurried around the apartment, looking a bit worried.

The room felt full of things we didn't say out loud as we both waited for John. His coming was a big deal – a crucial step to figuring out who was bothering me. The whole place had this feeling like something important was about to happen.

"Hey, Sarah, do you think John can really help us?" I asked, my voice filled with doubt. I wasn't sure about this collaboration because it seemed kind of mysterious.

Sarah turned to me, her eyes showing she was both sure and worried. "Amara, trust me. Mike wouldn't have told us about him if he couldn't handle it. John must be good at dealing with tricky situations."

I nodded, showing that I got what she meant. This was a big deal, and whether I'd be safe or not depended on this guy John and his ability to sort out the mess I was in.

A buzzing sound echoed in Sarah's apartment. It was like a musical doorbell that told us John was here. The quiet hallways were suddenly alive with the sound.

"Hi, John! Come upstairs!" Sarah's said to the speaker by the door as she buzzed John inside through the building door. She sounded excited, like she had been waiting for this.

I sat on the sofa, feeling a bit jittery. I wondered what was going to happen now that John was here. Was he going to be the hero I needed, or would he bring more issues and make things even more troubling for me? I had so many questions buzzing in my head.

The doorbell rang, and Sarah hurried to open it. John's shadow appeared against the faintly lit hallway, making the whole place feel secretive.

"Hey John! Come on in. Amara's been waiting,"

Sarah said, sounding friendly.

Sarah swung the door wide, and I saw John standing there. He looked tough, like a character from a mystery story. The meeting of our worlds was bound to happen, and as John walked into the room, things got a little exciting.

"Thanks," he said with a nod. As he stepped inside, I noticed his sharp look, like he was sizing up everything and everyone.

The city's soft morning light outlined his figure, creating a mysterious vibe. Each step he took filled the air with a kind of tension you could almost touch. It felt like something important was about to happen, something that could change everything.

∞

The atmosphere in Sarah's small living room felt like it was buzzing with excitement as I motioned towards the comfy sofa, asking John to have a seat. I looked at him for a moment, noticing how tall and tough he seemed, which made me feel a bit more secure in the middle of all this uncertainty. He wasn't exactly the kind of guy I usually befriend, but right now, having him around felt like having a strong anchor during a storm.

"Hey there. Nice to see you again," John said, his

voice kind of rough but with a hidden friendliness. He reached out his hand, and I shook it. His grip felt strong, like he could be someone I could count on.

"Same here," I said, giving a little smile. Without saying much, we all kind of knew that our lives were about to mix up as we tried to figure out the weird stuff going on.

John settled into the seat, and I took a big breath, feeling the seriousness of what I was about to say. "John, I need you to keep me safe. This stalker is making my life miserable, and I can't deal with being scared all the time."

He looked straight at me, like he got how heavy my words were. "I'll do my best to help you find this stalker. But remember, once we're done, we're done. No more hanging out," he said, sounding pretty sure about it.

I felt a strong pull towards him, like a magnet drawing me in. The challenge of the situation clashed with the professional boundaries he was setting. If things were different, maybe I'd be up for the attraction game, but right now, there was a big problem we needed to deal with.

I took a deep breath and said, "John, we really need to be on top of things here. Security is crucial, and I need to know you're vigilant and committed to getting to the bottom of who is behind me."

John nodded, his expression serious. "I hear you. Your security is my top priority. I'll be keeping a close eye on everything."

Encouraged, I continued, "And it's not just about physical security. We need to unearth the truth behind this stalker. I want someone who can dig deep and figure out what's really going on."

He leaned forward, meeting my gaze. "I understand. Finding the truth is part of the job. I'll do whatever it takes to get to the bottom of it."

It was reassuring to hear his commitment. "Good. We can't afford any slip-ups. This is serious business, and I need to know I can rely on you."

John's response was firm, "You can count on me. I'll be by your side every step of the way."

The conversation flowed smoothly, both of us understanding the importance of the task at hand. Despite the magnetic pull I felt, it was clear that we were on the same page when it came to the seriousness of the situation.

I really looked up to this mysterious man, feeling more and more impressed by his strong will that cut through everything. But, I had to be careful. I knew this was a risky game, and I had to keep my feelings in check.

While we talked, John explained his ideas about keeping things safe and how he'd make sure I stayed away from any danger. His words made a promise—a promise to keep me safe and find the truth no matter what.

Sarah joined in the conversation, her voice sounding both worried and determined. "John, Amara's safety is super important. We really need your help to make sure she doesn't have to be scared all the time."

He nodded, silently agreeing with us. The three of us were forming a team, a mix of serious work and emotions, right there in the living room. Outside, the city kept on going, not knowing about what we were talking about inside.

As the night went on, we made plans, talked about strategies, and figured out what we would do in the coming days. It was clear that John was really committed to being my bodyguard, and a small feeling of hope started growing in me—a hope that the dark things in my life would soon be gone.

∞

The city outside the window glowed softly, like a

bunch of faraway twinkling stars. It felt like a secret world beyond the glass. In the midst of all the uncertainty, something important happened - a big change, like stepping out of the dark into a safer tomorrow.

"Hey John," I said, feeling a bit unsure, "You know, the stalker got into my flat once, and I really need someone I can count on all the time."

John looked puzzled, his forehead wrinkling up. "How did the stalker even get past your building's security?"

I looked at John and sighed. "I don't know. I even checked the building's camera, and no one came in," I said, feeling really upset. "This happened again, and I moved away, but he found me again."

I started telling him about the weird things that happened - how the security cameras didn't catch everything, the flowers left inside my London apartment, and the message left on the front door at the house I rented. The stalker seemed to know exactly where I was. John looked just as doubtful as I felt, like we were both trying to solve a complicated mystery about this shadowy stalker.

John just stared at me, like he really understood how serious the situation was. The creepy message from the stalker played over and over in my head —

"You can't hide." It was super scary, and we had more questions than answers. The room felt smaller, like it was squeezing us. We all knew we had to work together not just to solve the mystery but to keep me safe from this creepy person who just wouldn't leave me alone.

I felt like having John move in was admitting that I needed help, that my safe place wasn't safe anymore. Sarah jumped in, trying to be supportive, "Amara, it's the right thing to do. John being close will help us. We'll figure it out together."

I agreed with a little nod, but I couldn't resist testing things out. "John, maybe it's time for a challenge," I said, trying to sound playful. I could see the surprise on John's face; he didn't see that coming.

"A challenge?" he repeated, looking confused.

Sarah sighed, knowing I liked doing unexpected things. "Amara, we can't treat this like an experiment. John is here to help, not for fun."

I felt my face getting a bit red, and I explained quickly, "You know, like being a bodyguard. I was thinking, maybe you could stay with me in my flat." I tried to keep it light, even though I was really curious.

The idea of John moving in with me hung in the air, making the room feel a bit tense. Sarah, always the one to make sense, spoke up. "Amara, I'm not sure about this. Bringing a stranger into your home, especially now, might not be the safest thing to do."

John gave a big nod, showing he agreed without saying anything. "I'm gonna stay with you at your flat, and I'll check all the safety stuff. No one's gonna sneak past me, not this time."

∞

Once John decided, it felt good, I was less worried but still a bit tense. The night turned into talking about how and when John would move. In the quiet light of the living room, we all started to feel like friends, all ready to face the darkness and win. As we got ready for the journey ahead, the quiet city outside kept on doing its thing, not paying much attention to our story. But it was up to us, we needed to work together to face the mystery that messed up my life.

But I couldn't resist a bit of mischief. "So it's decided then. John, welcome to the world of being a celebrity bodyguard," I said, pretending to make it a big deal. "Let's go back to my place. You can stay tonight and check out the security stuff."

The room felt different, like a mix of unsure feelings and a strong sense of wanting to do something. John, still figuring out the unexpected twists, gave a nod of agreement. Getting ready to leave Sarah's place, I had a feeling that this choice would show more parts of the mystery about the person following me.

As the night went on, our talks changed from serious stuff to more personal things. Sarah, always good at making peace, helped the conversation flow smoothly, making us feel like a team. John, in his serious way, started sharing bits of his personal side, showing that he's been through some tough times too.

The living room, now a center for planning and sharing secrets, had a strong pull—like an invisible string connecting our stories while facing challenges. The city outside, with its evening lights, seemed to understand that we were teaming up against the mystery messing up my life.

As we got into the unfolding plan, working with John turned into more than just staying safe. It became a shared adventure into the unknown, a dance with shadows that promised not only to keep me safe but also to solve the mysteries around me. The night stretched out in front of us, full of possibilities and a strong determination to face the stalker who was causing trouble.

∞

The cold London night wrapped around us when we left Sarah's place. John, always watchful, held the door for me, looking around the dimly lit hallway. I liked how strong and quiet he was, especially after all the mess in my life.

Sarah's worries hung in the air like a secret, but I decided not to think about them. I focused on the night ahead. When we got to the street, John waved down a taxi, its yellow light cutting through the dark.

"Here we go," John said, calmly opening the door for me. I hopped in, feeling the warmth inside compared to the chilly weather outside.

John handled my bags like it was nothing, showing off his military skills. While he put the bags in the taxi's boot, I took a moment to look at him. The lines on his face told stories of times and battles.

He shut the boot, got inside, gave a little nod to the driver, and off we went to my apartment. Outside the taxi window, city lights blinked, throwing shadows on John's face. I wondered what was hidden behind that calm look—maybe memories from wars or secret scars.

As the taxi wound through the twisty streets, it felt nice just being quiet with John. Even though I couldn't see the stalker who was following me, having John next to me made me feel safe. The car moved through the city, and I couldn't help but wonder what was waiting for us at home.

Sarah's voice was there in my mind, making things

a bit less scary. But her worries felt like a shield against whatever mysteries were waiting for us in my apartment. The city's sounds played in the background, like music for our adventure into the unknown.

When we got closer to my apartment building, I started feeling even more excited and nervous. I was curious about what John would find out and how the mystery of my stalker would unfold. Little did I know, there were even more secrets hiding in the night.

∞

The taxi rolled to a stop, and a wave of relief washed over me as we pulled up to my apartment building. The city lights were like magic, turning the night into a playground of shadows on the ground. John, my bodyguard, stood next to me, making me feel safe from the scary stuff out there.

We got out of the taxi and collected my bags from the trunk. I stood in front of my building while John carefully checked everything to make sure we were safe. His eyes moved around, looking for anything that might be a problem. I watched him do his thing, feeling more and more like I could rely on him.

It was like an unspoken agreement that, in this dance with shadows, John was the partner I could trust.

We walked up to the front door, and I felt a mix

of being a bit scared and really excited. The security guard at the entrance looked up when we got close. I took a big breath, trying to be cool, and went up to him.

"Hey, good evening," I said, acting like it was no big deal. "I'm Amara Delacroix. We were just going up to my flat."

He looked at me for a second, like he wasn't sure, because I wore my brown wig. This was the big moment. I took off my big sunglasses super-fast, showing my face. The guard's eyes changed, like he remembered something.

"Oh, Ms. Delacroix! Sorry, didn't recognize you at first. Welcome back," he said, going from being careful to being friendly.

The lobby greeted us with a warm welcome, like an old friend saying hello. We hopped on the elevator, and it took us up to the floor where my apartment was. Going up felt like it was taking forever, each floor passing by like a steady heartbeat. Finally, the doors opened, and there it was – the familiar hallway that made me feel safe.

"Ah, home sweet home," I said, almost like a magic spell to keep the dark away.

Getting to my doorstep, I searched for my key

card inside my purse. The hallway was eerily quiet around us. John kept a careful eye, silently reassuring me without saying much. The door made a creaky noise as it opened, and we went inside my home.

The apartment, all lit up with gentle lamplight, felt so familiar. John looked around carefully, checking for anything that might be a bit off. I felt a strange mix of things – kind of nervous about sharing my place with someone almost unfamiliar. But I had to remind myself that John was here as my bodyguard, promising me safety.

"Let's make sure the windows and doors are all good," John said, moving with a purpose. I nodded, thinking his way of doing things was pretty thorough. As the minutes went on, every creak of the floor and the soft humming from the heating made a sort of homey music. It was a mix of normal home sounds, but also a bit serious because of the reason why we were there.

As the clock kept ticking, I was always around John, like a friendly constant. Our small talks, which used to be all serious and business-like, started changing. We didn't need fancy words anymore; just looking at each other and understanding without saying anything made a special link that went beyond the job we were doing.

Finally, when John seemed okay with the

apartment, we ended up in the living room, still getting used to working together. I remembered Sarah telling me to be careful, but the night that was unfolding had a special feeling – like it promised safety, solving mysteries, and maybe even making unexpected friends in the dark.

"You think everything looks good here, John?" I asked, looking around.

"Yeah, it feels right," John replied with a friendly nod. "This place has good vibes."

I smiled, feeling more at ease. "It's nice to know we're on the same page."

"Definitely," John agreed.

As we stood there, the night held the potential for something exciting. I couldn't help but wonder what mysteries we might uncover together in the shadows. The living room still looked nice, with a touch of fancy stuff that reminds me of the good times I used to have. It was kind of like seeing something you were familiar with, but it also felt a bit strange, like my whole world had changed a lot.

"Have a seat, John," I said, pointing to the sofa. "So what do you think of my place?"

John plopped down on the sofa and looked

around. "It's cool, man. You've got some real fancy stuff here. What happened?"

I sighed, thinking about the past. "Yeah, it used to be different. Life was, you know, more elegant. Now, it's like a whole new esthetic world."

John nodded. "I get it. Things change, huh?"

I walked over to the window, staring outside. "Yeah, it's like everything changed overnight. But hey, we're here now, just chilling."

John grinned. "True that. So, what's the plan for tonight?"

I shrugged, keeping it laid-back. "Not much to do for me. Make yourself at home, John," I offered, my voice carrying a hint of gratitude.

As John leaned back onto the comfortable sofa in the living room, I told him I needed a moment and shuffled towards my room, the master suite. The door squeaked open, showing off my room, all fancy and stuff, but it was like a fancy prison. I sighed, feeling the heavy secrets I kept banging against the room's walls.

My bedroom walls were painted with calming yellow shades and plushy furniture. It was like a room filled with my memories, but not the happy kind. When I caught my reflection in a mirror, I noticed the lines on my face that told a story. It was like a story of me running away from someone, trying to hide as someone else.

Then, I heard footsteps coming closer, and I turned around. There was John, just standing in the doorway. His eyes, normally all guarded, showed something different.

"You okay?" he asked, sounding all concerned and serious.

I nodded, feeling kinda grateful that he cared. "Just trying to get used to having someone else around," I said, feeling all open and honest.

John's eyes got softer, and he smiled, trying to be reassuring. "I'll make sure you feel safe here."

As I got used to the feeling of living with a bodyguard, I began mentally preparing myself to deal with all the weird stuff that comes with it. Then I started thinking that this team-up we had might not just be about the mystery stalker. I had a feeling that tonight was gonna spill some secrets hidden in the dark for a long time.

∞

The night kept its secrets close, and as I closed the door to my bedroom, I felt like the shadows were just waiting to spill the beans on hidden truths.

I felt the familiar sensation of being back in my room, like a safe place where I can be myself. The big bed in the middle was like the star, with its super clean sheets that seemed inviting but also knew the stories of many nights without much sleep.

I walked over to the huge mirror that reached from the floor to the ceiling, like a quiet friend who saw everything. My fingers followed the twists and turns of my disguise – the bunch of brown curls covering who I really am, the glasses keeping my eyes a secret. With a sigh, I started taking off the layers that hid the real me. Each piece came off, showing the person I turned into.

"Oh, these fucking glasses! Always hiding my gorgeous eyes," I said out loud, talking to myself as I took them off.

"Yeah, and the wig, they're like my secret identity," I added, holding a strand of the curls between my fingers.

The room seemed to listen as I kept talking to myself, and I felt like I was letting out all the hidden things, just like the night was about to do.

Staring at myself in the mirror, I looked closely at my naked reflection. On my back were scars from the tough times I went through, like battle marks that told stories of fights and healing. The room was really quiet, and as I stood there, a picture popped into my head – John, a tall and tough guy, standing out from the danger around me.

I smiled, remembering how he made the space feel special, like he had this mysterious vibe. But deep down, I could feel he had his own soft side, kind of like me. His eyes were dark and deep, like they understood the same struggles we both went through, without needing any words.

Thinking about it, I realized the road ahead was going to be full of surprises. There was this person following me- my stalker, making everything feel dangerous.

But at the same time, there was this pull toward John- my bodyguard, like a strong force pulling me in.

In the mirror's reflection, I wondered about the choices I had to make, feeling both the weight of danger and the magnetic pull of something different with John.

I put on a soft silk robe and the room felt like it was buzzing with a quiet kind of excitement. I made up my mind - in the middle of it all, I really wanted a special connection that went beyond just being safe. I really wanted that closeness that only comes out at night, like dancing with shadows and sharing hush-hush secrets.

As I stared into my reflection, with a strong, determined gaze, I thought about all the new things that were going to happen. The room was super quiet, and you could hear the city's heartbeat through the windows.

Right then, I decided, no matter what happens, I'm going to be with John.

And together, we'll figure out all the secretive things about our lives that will be all tangled up together.

Chapter Six

Walking into Amara Delacroix's apartment felt like stepping into a charming place full of interesting things. But her place didn't have a lot of furniture, just a few large ones here and there. It looked like she wasn't planning on staying in one place for too long or perhaps that was because of the interior design. The living room was like a treasure chest, filled with modern furniture that made me wonder about the hidden stories inside the walls. It was as if the room itself knew all the special things about Amara's life that she didn't want anyone to know.

As I started doing my job, I felt a strong sense of purpose. I carefully checked everything to make sure Amara's safe haven stayed just that – safe. I ran my fingers over the beautiful furniture, looking for any hidden devices that could cause trouble. The door security system hummed softly in the background, like a watchful guard, making sure no one could disturb the special place that was both a hideaway and a place of battles for the famous actress.

Focused on what I was doing, I couldn't stop thinking about all the conversation that happened in this place. Amara and her buddies must have laughed a lot and told each other secrets here. The air still had bits of those times, and I felt like I accidentally ended up in the middle of the famous actress's personal world.

As I carefully checked every nook and cranny, the memories stuck in the apartment's material came alive. It was almost like I could hear Amara talking, sharing stories about winning awards and facing the rumors in tabloids, and it echoed through the fancy rooms. The walls, with their own stories, made me feel like they were silently telling me secrets.

As I tiptoed through Amara's apartment, the blend of splendor and mystery unfolded with each step, like a magical dance. Her place was a mix of luxury and hidden challenges she kept to herself. The fancy furniture and the fancy security system made it seem like she lived a glamorous life in the spotlight, but there was a hidden side, a private struggle against the prying eyes of fame.

After making sure everything was secure, I couldn't help but think I had stepped into a world not many people get to see. The walls, which were once just quiet spectators, now whispered tales of the actress's life. With my security checks complete, Amara headed off to her bedroom, leaving me alone in the living room, surrounded by the opulence and secrecy that made Amara's life so extraordinary.

As I stood there, I couldn't help but wonder about the events that could have happened within these walls. The plush furniture seemed like it could tell stories of fun house parties and maybe even moments of vulnerability. The security system, with its futuristic beeps, hinted at a constant battle between fame and personal space.

"I bet you've seen quite a lot, haven't you?" I mumbled to the silent walls, imagining the tales they could share. It was like being in a museum of Amara's life, with each piece of furniture and every electronic gadget telling a different part of her story.

The air was thick with the blend of grandeur and secrecy, creating a unique atmosphere that lingered even after Amara had disappeared into her private space. As I considered the mysteries behind those walls, I couldn't help but appreciate the complexity of Amara's extraordinary existence, a life painted with both brilliance and hidden struggles.

I turned my eyes towards the kitchen and got super excited, because I always loved to cook. But

Amara's kitchen wasn't designed just for making food; it was a cool mix of being super useful and looking awesome. Shiny gadgets were all sparkly under the soft lights, making the place feel so different from the comfy vibe around. The big marble countertop looked like it was saying, "Come on, let's make something tasty!"

With the lights softly buzzing above, I headed over to the fridge. It was like the boss of all things delicious. But when I opened it up, no colorful fruits or veggies were in there. It seemed like Amara was always in a rush, and the empty bins showed how she had to give up some things just to keep going.

Instead of the usual healthy stuff, the fridge was full of cool drinks and snacks. It was like a treasure chest of treats, showing how Amara liked to live in the moment. I started thinking about all the fun adventures she must have had, especially with those interesting drinks.

I spotted a large pantry across from me, practically begging to be explored. Its door creaked open, revealing hidden treasures. It wasn't packed to the brim, but it held the promise of a tasty meal. As I reached out, my fingers brushed against the chilly shelves, revealing a collection of instant noodles and a small stash of dry pasta. The air felt mysterious and delicate, much like the comforting presence of the woman who found solace within these walls.

Excited by the discovery, I decided to turn ordinary ingredients into something extraordinary. I embarked on creating a simple meal, and as the aroma of pasta sauce filled the room, it brought a sense of comfort for me during these uncertain times. While the kitchen warmed up with the delicious cooking smells, I couldn't shake the feeling that a secretive dance between danger and desire was unfolding in this hidden place. It was as if both protector and prey were entangled in the complexities of the night, creating an enchanting atmosphere.

Inside the kitchen, the soft lights made everything feel warm and innocent. I was cooking dinner for two, and the pasta sauce was sizzling in the pan. The yummy smells mixed together, making the air smell like a tasty adventure.

I placed the food on the plates just right, remembering how to do it from my time in the military. The table was all set, and it was going to be a super comfy dinner. In that secret kitchen place, the meal felt like it was more important than just stopping my stomach from growling. And guess what? The security system was quietly buzzing, reminding me to stay alert, even when I was going to have dinner.

But, oh boy, I was all by myself in the kitchen and yet I couldn't resist taking a little taste of the sizzling pasta. The flavors exploded in my mouth, making a happy dance on my tongue. It was like a tiny break from all the serious feelings in the apartment that floated around like a quiet cloud. And, you know what else? The clock's rhythmic tick-tock in the background, was telling me that time passed by as I enjoyed the meal all on my own.

As time passed by, I started to realize that Amara might be fast asleep, not even catching a whiff of the delicious food. I carefully put away the extra food in the fridge, thinking about how difficult it was to balance between looking out for someone and the peaceful embrace of sleep, especially when you're tired.

I made a quiet decision in my mind, feeling like it was time for a change of clothes. I shrugged off my jacket, revealing my T-shirt. Walking into the living room, I found comfort on the soft sofa. The fancy fabric of the sofa felt nice, making me feel all snug, especially in those uncertain moments.

As I settled into the cushions, the tiredness from the day started to weigh on me. Sleep seemed to be calling my name, a friendly hideaway that embraced all my senses. My yawns matched the soft hum of the security system, like a silent friend watching over the night's tale unfold.

And then, I wondered if Amara was also drifting off into dreamland, missing out on the tasty smells and comfy vibes. "Hey, Amara, you comfy in dreamland?" I thought with a playful smile. The night had its own story, and we were both part of it, wrapped in the quiet magic of sleep and security.

∞

The moonlight spilled into the living room, casting a soft glow that turned it into a magical place where my dreams played out. I curled up on the cozy sofa adjusting myself as I finally found a spot that felt like a fortress of calm. But tonight, I was a different man; it felt like a secret world where my dreams painted pictures that I couldn't control.

As I lay there, thoughts floated in my mind like fireflies, buzzing softly in the quiet night. Memories from my time in the military, which was like being a crusader but with real-life battles, popped up like scenes in a movie. It was like my mind was a puzzle, and each piece was actually a piece of my past.

Closing my eyes, I let myself tumble into the world of sleep. But instead of fluffy clouds and rainbows, my dreams turned into a maze of memories. The kind that makes your heart race and your mind feel like a rollercoaster.

In the dream, faraway gunshots rang out, making my heart beat fast. It was like a strange song, a melody of danger that played in my head. Amid all the noise, a ghostly voice called my name in a hurry, like a secret message.

Suddenly, I jolted awake, surrounded by the darkness that felt so thick.

But my sleep felt all mixed up, like my brain was in a big fog. It took me a bit to figure things out. In my dreams, it was like a war zone, all crazy and loud. But then, whoosh! It changed into an apartment, smelling all sweet like Amara's place did. Even though I was chilling on a comfy sofa, getting rid of Amara's voice from my dreams was tough.

"Whoa, that was intense," I mumbled to myself, still feeling the echo of the dream. I blinked a few times, getting used to the darkness as my heart slowed down. It was just me and the quiet night, like partners in a dance.

The sofa was super soft, not like the hard ground I knew from the military. It held me like a gentle hug. Going from the wild dreams to Amara's real-life apartment was a bit confusing. Her voice kept ringing in my ears, making me shiver in the quiet night.

I felt stuck in the middle of two worlds—one where war memories stuck to me like glue, and the other where Amara's coolness was like a puzzle I couldn't solve.

The confusion hung around, making my thoughts all jumbled up like a song that didn't finish, messing with my mind.

There were marks, some you could see and others hiding away, telling the stories of battles inside me and outside. As the dream sounds faded, I started to get something weird. It was like the ghosts of war mixed up with the mystery of Amara being there, making this strange truth that I couldn't quite put my finger on.

In the dark living room, I wrestled with the leftovers of the night's spooky shadows. The room, once a place full of shadows and whispered memories, slowly turned back to its usual self. But the trembles of the dreams stuck around, like an unerasable mark on the night canvas, which was a mix of being open and hopeful for some good sleep.

I dreamt about a person, like a ghost from a battlefield, urgently calling my name, cutting through the quiet night. The real and unreal things mixed up so much that I woke up suddenly. Instead of the torn-up war land, it was Amara sitting next to me, her kind eyes showing the vulnerability left from my bad dreams.

"John," she said gently, her voice pulling me out of the dream like a rope. Going from the wild battle chaos to the calm apartment felt strange.

The clock ticking away measured time, like a guide showing the difference between the scary past and the current moment.

As I slowly came out of the dream's grip, I found

myself sitting up, trying to shake off the echoes still ringing in my mind. Luckily, Amara was right there next to me, a comforting presence in the middle of the dream mess. Her words reached me like a safety line, connecting me back to the real world I had momentarily lost.

"Hey there, sleepyhead," she said with a grin, handing me a glass of water. "You were having quite the adventure."

I took the glass, feeling grateful for her company. "Really? What happened?" I asked, still trying to piece together the fading fragments of my dream.

"Well," Amara began, settling in next to me, "I was just heading to the kitchen for a midnight sip when I stumbled upon the crazy show playing out in your dream world. Dragons, spaceships, and all sorts of wild things."

I chuckled, relieved to have someone to share the weirdness with. "I guess my dreams are turning into blockbuster movies lately."

"Yeah," Amara agreed with a playful smile. "I was half expecting popcorn to start popping in that brain of yours."

We both laughed, and suddenly, the dream seemed less intimidating with Amara by my side. Her words were like a safety net, connecting me back to reality. It was nice to have someone who could turn even the craziest dreams into a good story.

In that kind of scary moment, neither of us really needed to say anything else. We both knew we had some sad stuff in our hearts, and it was just hanging there in the air. After a bit, as the spooky dream feelings slowly went away, the apartment felt like it was holding its breath, waiting to see what was going to happen next.

∞

Amara sat there with me on the sofa, giving me this quiet, calming feeling. It was totally different from the crazy dreams I just had. It reminded me that even though we both had some tough times before, right now, we were dealing with things together. We had this special connection that didn't need words, something we understood without talking about it.

I kind of coughed a little to break the quietness in the room. I wanted to get rid of that tense feeling that was all over the place. When I looked around, it felt like the living room relaxed, letting go of the leftover dream vibes. The night kept going, and it felt better with both of us there.

Looking at Amara, I noticed that she had on a robe that barely covered anything underneath. I quickly turned my eyes away and focused on the soft lights from the city outside. London looked so cool at night, telling stories about a city that never sleeps.

I stood up, mumbled a quick sorry for messing up the vibe, and tried to keep things cool. Amara, this really nice and delicate woman, looked at me like she had something on her mind. The room got super quiet, and it felt like we both wanted to talk, but we didn't know where to start.

I was fidgeting a bit, and Amara finally broke the silence, "No worries, things happen. Are you okay?"

"Yeah, yeah, just feeling a bit sleepy," I chuckled, trying to ease the awkwardness.

She smiled, "Well, we've all been there. By the way, I have some spare clothes if you need them."

"Oh, thanks!" I replied, feeling relieved. "That's really nice of you. I'd appreciate it."

"No problem at all," she said, her kindness making me feel at ease. "I have something in my cupboard that'll fit you. Let me grab them for you."

After a bit, Amara went back to her bedroom, and the living room got all dark, and the shadows started moving around like they were having a little party. It was like they were happy about something, but I didn't know what. Amara's perfume was still in the air, making it feel like a magic song was playing quietly in the background. I didn't follow her directly into her bedroom because, you know, it was better not to invade each other's personal space.

A couple of minutes later, Amara came back with a bunch of clothes that looked like they've been through a lot of stuff. They seemed to have lots of stories to tell. I wondered whose memories were in these clothes. It was like they held secrets or something.

"Thanks, Amara," I said, breaking the silence. "These clothes have seen a lot, haven't they?"

She smiled knowingly, "Oh, they've been on quite a few journeys with me. Each lint and crease has a story."

∞

After saying good night to Amara, she went back to her room, and I was left all by myself on the sofa. I changed into comfy clothes, feeling the soft fabric against my skin as I sat down on the cushions. The room was really quiet, so I took out my phone and messaged The White Panther. But there was no reply, and it made me feel a bit worried.

It reminded me that finding out the stalker was

bothering Amara wasn't going to be easy.

The living room was kind of dark, with shadows all around, like it was watching a secret dance between me, the bodyguard, and Amara, the famous actress dealing with a creepy stalker. The night was full of suspense, and in the quiet parts of the room, a complicated story was starting to come together. It was a story about being in danger, keeping secrets, and the scary things we don't know about.

As I got comfortable on the cushy sofa, I felt a heavy responsibility on my shoulders. The clothes I had on, were a tad bit small, which clearly belonged to Amara. Looking at the borrowed sweatshirt, reminders of her presence, fueled my determination. We couldn't let the stalker continue. My mind became a chessboard, carefully considering every move and its consequences. Yet in the quiet, there was a promise hanging in the air – a promise to protect Amara from the scary things lurking in her world's shadows.

Staring out of the glass windows, I saw the city buzzing with life. My mind was spinning with thoughts about Mike, who shared an idea about catching the sneaky stalker. It felt like he planted a smart seed in my brain, and now I needed to take care of it. I imagined the plan happening like a careful operation done by a doctor.

Suddenly, my phone made a beep noise, and a

message from The White Panther popped up. It made me feel a little hopeful. Reading the words, a plan started forming in my head. "Still figuring it out, John," I thought, knowing that time was running out. I grabbed my phone and started typing back, getting ready to dive into the mysterious world of shadows and light.

My mind wandered to Amara, imagining her moving gracefully in her private bedroom, like a dancer on a stage. The air around me still smelled faintly of her perfume, creating a mysterious and enchanting atmosphere. Regardless of the thoughts in my head, Amara seemed delicate yet filled with the charm of a superstar in the making.

The mission ahead was clear – to uncover the hidden stalker in Amara's life. Mike's idea to use her as bait, a strategic move, made me think deeply. As her appointed bodyguard, my duty went beyond just protecting her. I had to play a double role – a silent protector caught up in the secret dance of our plan.

In my thoughts, a plan unfolded – a careful coordination balancing Amara's safety and the need to expose the enemy. The night, like a secret partner, hid the threads of our suspenseful story in its shadows.

I thought about the upcoming steps, ready to navigate the tricky path with precision. The city's nighttime rhythm matched the undercover beat of my mission. As I readied my mind to face the challenges ahead, a new determination sparked inside me – a promise to protect Amara from the intruding darkness, even if it meant dancing dangerously close to the edge.

Chapter Seven

The sky outside Amara's window was turning purple and gold as I woke up on her large sofa. It was super early, and everything was so quiet except for the faraway sounds of the city starting its day. I peeked at the clock on the wall, and yup, it was still really early, like the whole world was still half asleep.

Getting up from the sofa, my body felt all stiff from not having the best sleep. I let out a little groan as I stretched, trying to shake off that sleepy feeling. I tried doing some push-ups to get my body going, but my knee started hurting, so I stopped. I stood up and walked into the bathroom. The floor was cool against my bare feet as I splashed some water on my face, trying to wake up. It didn't feel like much, but it was my way of getting ready for the day.

As I was waking up, Amara came out of her room

wearing a cool green jumpsuit like dress. It really made her blue eyes pop. The apartment looked kind of dull, but she brought in this burst of color with her morning energy.

"Hey there, good morning!" Amara chirped, her voice all perky like an excited puppy ready to start the day.

I gave her a quick nod, keeping my words short. Mornings were never my strong suit, and I preferred letting actions do the talking. Sunbeams painted funny pictures on the walls, making it look like the room was wearing a sunshine coat.

"Sleep okay on that sofa?" Amara asked, her voice light and bouncy, like it had just bounced out of bed.

"Your sofa's an upgrade from my usual spot," I replied, hiding the fact that it wasn't exactly the comfiest. She laughed, but it wasn't music to my ears— it was more like a cat trying to sing. I definitely wasn't a morning person.

Amara laughed a little. "Sorry about that. It's not the fanciest place. I don't have a guest room."

"No worries," I replied with a yawn. "So, what's the plan for today?"

Amara shrugged, heading to the tiny kitchen. "Not

sure yet."

Ignoring my grumpy morning vibes, Amara suggested we venture out into the big wide world outside the apartment. Grocery shopping and breakfast were on the agenda, a welcome distraction from whatever gloom hung over us.

"Sounds good to me," I said, joining her in the kitchen. "I'm kinda hungry. So let's grab some breakfast first," my stomach growling like it was ready to start its own morning conversation.

∞

Early in the morning, when the city was starting to wake up, Amara and I set out. The sun was just beginning to paint the London streets with soft colors as we walked with a clear purpose. We weren't like everyone else - we stood out, but that was part of the plan.

Amara, with her hoodie on, covered up her shiny golden hair. Despite the disguise, she seemed to understand the city perfectly, almost as if she could feel it's heartbeat. Our steps made a rhythmic sound on the awakening streets as we moved forward into the chilly morning air.

What made our journey interesting was Amara's decision not to wear fancy disguises. It was like she wanted to show the world who she really was. At one point she even took off her hood, letting her face shine through without hiding. As she did, I saw a determined look on her face, a quiet strength that spoke volumes.

Wandering through the twisty streets, we found a breakfast café, and as we stepped inside, it felt so warm, especially when it was chilly outside. The delicious smell of a big breakfast filled the air, making me super hungry. I took Amara to a table in the corner, so I could watch everyone who walked in the café.

As we sat down, I said, "This place is nice, huh? What do you think?" She nodded, her eyes wide with curiosity.

"Yeah, it's warm in here," Amara replied, rubbing her gloved hands together.

We looked around, seeing people chatting and enjoying their food. The waitress came over, smiling, and asked, "What can I get you guys?"

After I gave her my breakfast order, I looked at Amara, thinking about how she was so slim. "You sure you don't want anything?" I asked, not quite sure. She just shrugged and said she wasn't hungry in the morning. I didn't get it – she was acting like she didn't care, but something in her eyes told a different story.

"I'm just not into breakfast," she said, looking

around the busy café. It was slightly weird – she acted tough, but her eyes showed there was more going on inside. They looked tired, like they had seen a lot, even though she didn't want to let on.

I tried to figure it out, "But don't you get hungry later if you skip breakfast?" She just shook her head, dismissing my concern. "Nah, it's this thing called intermittent fasting. It's like, skipping breakfast is supposed to make you healthier or something." I didn't get it, but I didn't want to bug her too much.

∞

Our table got a delivery of coffee, and Amara took small sips, looking around at everyone. The air was filled with the buzzing sounds of people chatting, like a mix of voices in a song that you can't quite make out.

"I noticed that you didn't have any dinner last night." I asked, just making regular talk.

She answered casually, saying she didn't really bother with dinner. This left me wondering if she truly didn't care about food or if there was some secret part of her life that made her uninterested in eating.

While the café was busy with people doing their morning routines, Amara's way of not eating and all the hidden stuff that came with it felt like a mystery. It was like a missing piece in a big picture that made up the whole story of who she really was.

I couldn't help but wonder what was really going on with Amara. She seemed tough on the outside, but there was something fragile underneath, something she wasn't saying. I decided not to press her too much, but I couldn't shake the feeling that there was more to her story than she let on.

In that busy café, the clinking of silverware and distant chatting made a nice mix of sounds. The yummy smell of breakfast mixed with the coffee brewing, making me anxious to eat. When my food finally came, I happily started eating, feeling super hungry.

My plate had bacon that sizzled, baked beans that were warm, and grilled tomatoes that tasted really good. All those smells and tastes made a picture in my mind, kind of like a delicious painting. It was so good that for a moment, I almost forgot about the fact that I was there as a bodyguard.

Amara, sat across from me, sipped her black coffee slowly. She looked at me in a way that felt strange, like she was thinking about something important. It was like her eyes were quietly checking me out. She's famous for being in movies, but right then, she looked just like a regular person in London, and that made everything more interesting. We didn't say anything, but it felt like we were talking in our own quiet way.

As I scooped up each bite from my plate, gobbling it down with a practiced speed that comes from military training, I couldn't help but feel Amara's eyes watching me. Eating turned into a little show, and Amara was right there, silently checking my plate. Her eyes spoke volumes about what she was thinking, even though she didn't say a word.

When I finished the last bite and put my fork down with a satisfying clink against the plate, I leaned back, feeling full. The waitress brought me a hot cup of tea, and she announced the arrival of the bill. I sipped on the warm cuppa, a brief interruption before we faced whatever challenges lay ahead at the grocery store.

But I hesitated for a moment before reaching for my wallet, a reflex ingrained in me from a long time ago. But Amara, with a friendly but firm tone, jumped in. "You're on bodyguard duty, John," she said, a playful glint in her eyes. "Think of it as part of making sure I stay safe."

I agreed with a little nod, feeling thankful inside. You see, I was dealing with money troubles, juggling part-time work and the high costs of city life. Amara's offer to cover my simple breakfast was like a small break from worrying about money.

As she paid the bill, Amara moved with a calm kind of grace, like she was used to a life of comfort and not being in the spotlight. The café, full of people coming and going, held the story of an unexpected friendship: me, the bodyguard doing my job; Amara, the famous person trying to get away from all the attention; and the quiet moments we shared, wrapping us in a safety net of unspoken feelings.

∞

When we left the cafe, a chilly breeze swirled around us, making us shiver. It felt like winter was grabbing hold of everything. Amara, trying to act tough, couldn't help but show a little shiver every now and then. Maybe it was because of the cold or perhaps the air felt kind of strange. She pulled her hood lower, covering her face from the glow from the morning sun.

I broke the quiet morning by asking, "So, what's the plan?"

Amara, with her eyes hiding in the hood's shadow, seemed a bit unsure for a moment. "Just going to the grocery store really quick. Nothing special. We just need to test how things go when I'm outside."

Her words sounded careful, like she was used to being really careful in her life. In that quiet time, it felt like the whole city was holding its breath, not realizing that two people—a famous actress looking for a safety and a man who didn't really want to be a bodyguard—were moving through its busy streets, wrapped in mystery.

We walked towards Tesco, this really big chain of supermarket store in the country. It had bright signs that kind of called us in, like it was saying, "Come inside!" The doors slid open, and we stepped into the grocery store. It was like a huge world of shopping, right in the middle of the busy city.

Inside, the supermarket, the space was massive, with lots and lots of aisles. Each aisle had tons of things to look at and pick from. The lights were bright, and it felt like we were in a busy store where everyone comes to get what they need for the day.

There were sounds all around – carts rolling on the floor and people talking far away. It was like a big, echoey room where everyone was busy doing their shopping. But Amara didn't mind all that. She just went ahead, knowing exactly where she wanted to go.

As we walked through the aisles, it was like a dance of people picking what they needed. Amara moved with confidence, like she had a plan. Each aisle was like a different song, with so many things to choose from – simple things and even some fancy ones.

We talked a bit while looking at the stuff. "Do you need anything?" Amara asked, checking out the options. "How about some veggies?" I suggested. We chatted about what we wanted to eat, and it felt like a little adventure in the supermarket.

As Amara checked off the items on her grocery list, I followed her around the store. It was like being in a big maze full of all kinds of stuff. The shelves were super tall, filled with different things, and the packages had bright colors that made the whole store look like a rainbow.

The air smelled like delicious fruits and veggies mixed with fragrances. It was kind of like a mix of dinner and laundry day. People were pushing their carts, and the cash registers made a cool buzzing sound in the distance.

I looked around carefully, trying to see everything. It was tricky because there were so many people, and they all looked busy. It felt like being a detective in a big crowd, where everyone is doing their thing, and you have to be careful.

As we walked through the store, Amara and I talked about what we needed to buy. She asked me to help find things, and we chatted about what snacks we should get. It was fun because I got to pick out my favorite treats.

And while we talked, I kept my eyes peeled, just like a bodyguard on duty. You never know what surprises might pop up in the grocery store!

While Amara was busy picking out things she needed, I was keeping an eye on everything around. It was kind of funny because she was choosing everyday things, and I was making sure everything was okay, like a secret agent. We were like opposites, doing different things but in the same place, Tesco.

All the while that Amara moved through the grocery store, everyone couldn't help but notice her. Even though she was just picking out regular stuff, there was something special about her. People sneakily looked at her, whispering if a famous person was shopping among them. It was like she had a magic pull that made everyone curious. But thankfully, nobody recognized her.

It felt like a special dance, a mix of different worlds colliding right there in the supermarket. Even though Amara was used to being a big star, she also wanted a normal life. It made the simple act of shopping for groceries more interesting.

As Amara moved through the aisles, smoothly pushing her cart and grabbing things she needed, the supermarket hummed with activity. It was as if Tesco was its own little world, not knowing about the famous movie star, shopping under its bright lights.

It was like a hidden adventure in the most ordinary

place.

We walked together to the checkout, our steps making a cool tapping sound on the floor. We were like a team, moving smoothly through the aisles filled with all sorts of things. I looked at Amara, and she was really focused, taking careful steps.

∞

The checkout was rather quiet, with only the sound of our movements and the beeping of the self-checkout machines. I liked the routine of grocery shopping because it made me feel safe, away from the paparazzi that would have followed Amara everywhere.

Time felt slow, like it was stretching out in the big Tesco store. Each beat of our hearts sounded like a drum in our ears. Amara finished paying at the self-checkout and not even wondering if something might be waiting for her outside those doors.

As we walked towards the exit, the sounds of people talking and carts rolling made a weird mix. And then, out of the corner of my eye, I saw a tall man, who had his face covered with a hoodie. He was like a shadow, blending in with the other busy shoppers. But it didn't feel right.

My instincts kicked in, telling me that something

was about to happen. I wanted to protect Amara. The person in the hood was getting closer, like they had a plan. Their face was hidden behind a mask, and they seemed like they were part of a secret show, playing their own game.

It happened so slow, like a dream where everything's weird. The guy's hand came out of his pocket, like he'd planned something bad. It felt like time stopped, each move hanging in the air. I jumped in front of Amara really quick, my instincts kicking in.

Bam! It hit me fast and hard. Me and the masked guy crashed together, and my chest hurt badly. The guy had a knife, and he wounded me.

But before I could react, he was like a ghost, slipping away in the parking lot maze.

I gasped for breath, holding my chest. The pain was like a big reminder of how risky being a bodyguard was. Amara stared at me, scared, holding onto the grocery bags like they were a lifeline.

"Are you okay?" she asked, her voice shaky.

"Yeah, just a little banged up," I said, trying to sound tough.

"Who was that guy?" she wondered, eyes wide with worry.

"No idea, but we better be careful," I warned. "This is getting serious."

People around us started whispering, making worried sounds as we stood there. It was like a wave of concern and curiosity spreading among the shoppers. The big store, Tesco, just kept on doing its usual stuff, not bothered by what was happening. It was like it had no idea about the little drama that had happened outside their doors.

But the whole encounter with the masked guy hadn't last long. It was a bit like a quiet warning from an unseen troublemaker. Afterwards, me and Amara were left there, but I was hurting both on the outside and inside. It showed how serious things could get when you're protecting a famous person with a stalker.

I could see how the normal, everyday stuff we took for granted got shaken up. It was like a thin cover had been ripped, showing the real struggle Amara was going through. Her safe place was feeling a bit shaky because of the danger always following her. And then I completely blacked out.

∞

As I started coming back to reality, everything seemed a bit fuzzy. The place smelled clean, like the stuff they use to keep things germ-free. I was lying on a stretcher that they set up in a sort of medical area.

The colors around me were all bland, just whites and grays, and there was this distant hum from the bright lights above.

Two paramedics hovered over me, their faces a mix of worry and professional calm. I could hear hurried footsteps and distant sirens, like the background music of a big emergency. It felt like chaos all around.

"John, are you okay?" Amara's voice quivered, full of concern. Her eyes, full of worry lines, searched for reassurance.

I tried to smile to calm her down, but my chest hurt. "Just a scratch, Amara. I've been through worse stuff." Even though I said that, my words didn't hide how serious it was, and Amara looked really scared.

The paramedics, realizing things were urgent, got to work quickly. They wore gloves and carefully checked my injury, moving through the mess of blood. As they worked, they talked quietly to each other, giving me some comfort that they knew what they were doing. It was like their words were a lifeline, keeping me connected to what was happening right then.

∞

The manager at Tesco stood back, trying to decide whether to help or worry about the store. He had called the police, his voice bouncing off the big walls of the supermarket as he tried to control the crowd. It was only a little while ago that people were buying groceries, unaware of the danger that lurked nearby.

While the paramedics took care of my scratches, I realized the problem was bigger than I thought. The small wound on my chest, which I thought was not a big deal, now seemed like a sign of weakness. I wasn't some superhero; I could get hurt, make mistakes, but the stalker following Amara affected more than just her peace.

"Are you okay?" asked the manager, looking concerned.

"Yeah, just a scratch," I replied, trying to downplay it.

"Should we call someone for you?" he asked, unsure of what to do.

"No, thanks. I'll be fine," I assured him, though doubt lingered.

The loud police sirens grew closer,—the people who made sure everything stays in order. They had to be called to handle the mess left behind by a failed surprise knife attack on me. The medics, finishing up their careful work, glanced at each other. Their looks showed how serious the situation was, but also how committed they were to their job.

I tried to tell the paramedics I was okay, but my words didn't really mean much. The paramedics kept on fixing me up, putting bandages on my chest like a sort of makeshift armor. I kept saying I was fine and could stand up, and they looked at me all serious, but I just nodded my head like I really meant it.

∞

When I finally stood up from the stretcher, Amara, who still looked worried, locked eyes with me. We didn't need to say anything out loud. We both knew there were hidden dangers all around us, things we don't always see right away.

"I think we're good to go," I told the paramedics, kind of ignoring their offers to help more. I couldn't forget about how the attacker's knife was drugged, which lead to my black out. It was a reminder that danger isn't always something you can see, especially in the shadows.

But, guess what? Just when we thought we were free to leave, the bright, colorful lights of a police car showed up out of nowhere. And who was behind the wheel? None other than my younger brother, Ronald.

"John?" Ronald's eyes got super big when he saw

me, like he couldn't believe what he was seeing. He looked really serious and asked, "What in the world happened here, brother?"

The paramedics, retreated back to the ambulance when they saw Ronald and decided to give us some space. They disappeared, leaving us in a kind of weird quietness. Amara, being the smart cookie she is, noticed something was up. She checked out tension between me and Ronald realizing that our grocery store adventure had turned into a big family drama, with secrets and connections all mixed up.

"Uh-oh, trouble in paradise," Amara whispered to me, and I couldn't help but smirk. Things were getting interesting.

I gave Ronald a quick nod, showing that I understood the serious stuff about him being both a police sergeant and my brother. "Lots to talk about. I'll tell you everything, but let's leave this crazy place first."

Ronald's serious face turned into a little smile as he signaled for us to come with him. The blinking lights from the police car made the street look strange as we climbed in. It felt like we were on a secret mission, trying to find out important things while keeping it all in the family.

As we sat in the car, I started explaining what had happened at Tesco, and Ronald listened, asking questions here and there. It was like we were in a detective movie, trying to solve a mystery together. The car rolled through the quiet streets, and I felt a mix of curiosity and a bit of excitement about what was going to happen next.

The police car cruised down the morning streets, making a gentle sound as it moved. Every now and then, a distant siren added a dash of excitement to the air. Inside the small space, there was a feeling of something important waiting to be said, hiding beneath the regular police radio talk.

As we drove through the twisty-turny streets on our way to the police station, Ronald, who was behind the wheel, looked at me through the rearview mirror. He broke the quietness with a question that hung in the air like a puzzle we needed to solve.

"Hey John, why did you decide to be a hero in the grocery store?" Ronald's eyes met mine in the mirror, as if asking about the secrets we were keeping.

I leaned back in the seat, smelling the faint mix of old leather and a clean, hospital-like smell. "It's a bit tricky, Ron. I'm working as a bodyguard for Amara here."

Ronald's eyebrows shot up in real surprise, and he turned his gaze to the mysterious woman sitting next to me. "Amara? Amara Delacroix?"

Amara, maybe sensing we needed to make things clear, gave a little smile. "Yep, that's me. And you are John's brother?"

Ronald laughed, sounding lighter. "Ronald Stewart, police guy, and turns out, your bodyguard's brother. I had no clue you were mixed up with this troublemaker."

A short quiet time filled the car as Amara tried to process this surprising news. Outside, the streets flashed by with bright headlights from passing cars, making quick shadows dance on her face.

"Hey, John," Ronald said, his voice sounding like a friendly warning from a big brother. "Can you tell me what's going on? What's up with this bodyguard stuff, and why does Amara Delacroix need one?"

I thought about it for a bit, trying to figure out how much to spill. "Okay, Ron, here's the short version. Someone's been following Amara. But then things got crazy, and that's why I stepped in."

Ronald nodded, looking serious. "Following? That's not good. We'll figure this out at the police station."

And as we got closer to the police station, the whole situation felt heavy. The mix between being a brother and being a bodyguard made everything more complicated. It was like I was stuck in a puzzle of danger, secrets, and the mysterious world of Amara Delacroix.

Chapter Eight

Inside that tiny room, it was really dark, that you can't even see who was in there. But a man sat there, all wrapped up in his big jacket, hiding in the shadows. You couldn't even see his face because of the hoodie. He looked like a mysterious figure, with only the faint light from the computer screen showing a bit of what was going on.

His fingers were busy tapping on the keyboard, like they were playing a secret song only he knew. The blue light from the computer screen felt kind of cold, making the scars on his face stand out even more. That made his face look weirdly pale, like a ghost.

He had this creepy smile on his face, like he was really happy about something strange. It was because of the weird jobs he had to do lately. His life was already full of strange stuff, but this client he worked for, was even more unusual. It was like a mystery that kept getting weirder and weirder.

One day, a secret message arrived in a shadowy way, like a little electronic whisper that only he could hear. It asked him to do something puzzling. Normally, he would expect to be asked to do his usual job—getting rid of people quick and clean. But this time, the task was different. He had to deliver bunches of roses, but he had to leave it inside the apartment. When he got there, to his surprise, the front door was even unlocked.

Several months after doing this strange job, his mysterious boss gave him an even weirder task. He had to write a message on the front door of a house far away on the outskirts of the city. As he thought about it, he wondered if it was just a scary message or part of a bigger plan.

Even though the jobs were odd, he kept doing them because the money was good. But what really got him curious was trying to figure out who this client was. As he thought about the new task that he had just gotten, the room felt like it was buzzing with excitement. Planning things carefully was something he was good at, and this job needed him to be extra careful to make sure everything worked out just right.

In that dark hideout, the man thought about the exciting dance he was about to join. Outside, the big city went on with its daily life, totally unaware of the secret moves happening in his hidden place. With each press of the keyboard, he went deeper into the hidden artwork, uncovering the connections that tied him to the mysterious puppet master.

But inside the quiet room, a spooky feeling hung in the air, like the calm before a storm. The man, marked by scars and covered in shadows, embraced the strange dance with a sort of wicked grace. He was all set to carry out a plan that would make a big impact beyond just now.

∞

The next morning, wearing a mask and hiding under a hoodie, he stood outside Tesco, thinking about the strange instructions he got. He needed to find a woman wearing a green dress. So, he watched the people going in and out of the store, like a sneaky hunter in a big city.

Suddenly, in the middle of all the regular people, a lady walked inside the store. She was wearing different shades of green. And guess what? She had a really tall friend with her. The man was supposed to be like a bodyguard.

But the man in the mask was careful, trying not to be noticed. He whispered to himself, "There she is, just like the client said, with a green outfit and her tall buddy. Time to see what they're up to."

The mysterious man wearing a mask sneaked into the store like a silent ghost, quietly moving through the aisles, keeping his distance. As the lady and her bodyguard finished picking up groceries, he lingered nearby, like a spooky shadow following them. When they stepped out into the fresh morning air, he adjusted his position, getting closer to them as if an invisible force was pulling him in.

With a careful plan in mind, he came face to face with her bodyguard. In just a quick and sly move, he followed the instructions he got. A knife, covered in just enough fentanyl, found its way into the tall man's chest, without him realizing. Everything seemed to slow down, like a moment frozen in time.

After the stalker had made his move, he knew that soon there was going to be chaos all around. Fueled by adrenaline, he dashed through the busy streets of London. The air felt tense, with a mix of urgency and danger. It wasn't a happy or exciting feeling, but more like a dark beginning to something even scarier. The client who asked him to do this had some dark plans, and it seemed like this was just the start of many more things to come.

As he walked through the tricky, twisty streets, the man knew the shadows hid secrets, and his client used them like a puppeteer pulling mean strings. The woman, now dealing with the sudden attack of her bodyguard, stood at the middle of a secret web—without knowing about what was coming her way.

The stalker, finishing his weird job, smoothly blended into the busy London crowd. His hood was low, and his mask hid his face as he walked with a purpose through the tricky streets. The city's sounds made it hard to hear his steps. He was really good at being invisible, thanks to years of learning to be a pro at hiding in plain sight.

London, a city bustling full of people, the man successfully blended among the busy crowds. Everyone around him seemed like a blur, their faces mixing together into a sea of strangers. The loud noises of the city acted like a shield, making it harder for anyone to notice him. He pretended not to care, acting like he was just a small part of the busy rhythm of the city.

In a world where cameras watched everything, he had become really good at avoiding being seen. Walking through the crowded streets, even the city's cameras, perched on buildings and lampposts, couldn't see him. His talent for blending in was like magic, making him a shadowy ghost in the eyes of the cameras—a living ghost moving quietly through the regular world.

During those quiet moments after he finished

his work, the man navigated mindlessly through the busy streets. He left the results of his actions to happen without anyone suspecting him. The city, unaware of the person hiding in its midst, kept going with its busy rhythm—a mix of life and hidden secrets, something he was really good at handling.

He kept moving through the busy streets, blending into the flow of people without leaving any clues behind. The city, with all its noise and constant movement, became his hiding place—a special spot where he could disappear like a shadow.

As he walked further into the city, the man thought about his strange job. He was a hitman for hire- but managed to stay hidden all these years, which was his specialty. No one was able to find him or figure out what he was doing. The idea of being caught and revealed scared him, so he made sure to stay a mystery. He even had his entire digital footprint erased, he was simply a man without a name.

Chapter Nine

The bright blood stain on my brother, John's shirt made me feel worried that the knife wound must have been deep. That morning when Amara Delacroix walked into the police station, it was like adding a surprising twist to the already confusing situation- an unknown assailant knifed John in broad daylight. I couldn't help but think about my brother, who usually doesn't say much, being caught up in this whole mix of celebrity drama where it's hard to tell what's real and what's just for show.

I guided John and Amara carefully into an interview room where the lights were gentle and not too bright. But being inside a police station was nothing like the cold and serious feeling you get at a hospital. There were big, comfy sofas that seemed to say, "Take a break and relax," even though the air in the room felt heavy with worry.

Amara Delacroix, the super famous actress who was trying to get away from an obsessed stalker who was bothering her, looked worried but determined. Her eyes were serious, like she had a strong spirit inside, maybe from dealing with her constant fame and always wanting a bit of privacy. The way their lives came together, with John, who used to be in the military but left because of his injuries, and Amara, the famous actress with a mystery stalker, felt like a surprise you'd find in a lottery ticket.

As they settled down on the sofas, I couldn't help but think about how strange and unreal everything was. My brother, John, who usually keeps his feelings inside and has been through tough times, now sat next to Amara, an actress known to millions but struggling with a problem that wouldn't go away. What were the odds of that happening?

"John, you okay?" I asked, trying to keep it calm. The paramedics had helped John's wound, but being his brother, I was worried.

"Yeah Ronald, it's just a scratch," John said, looking at the blood stain on his sweatshirt.

I looked at John and whispered, "Sit tight, John." My voice carried a mix of worry and familiarity, letting him know I was here to help.

Amara's eyes stayed on John, gratefulness shining

in them, "I never thought I'd be in this kind of spot. But thanks for helping."

I approached with the practiced calm of a seasoned sergeant, acknowledging the reserved greeting in John's eyes. The air was charged with unspoken gratitude, the unyielding bond between brothers tested in the crucible of adversity.

"No problem. We'll figure this out," I said, trying to sound confident and reassuring.

∞

As time passed, the room became a picture of strength—an injured and tough ex-military guy, a famous actress caught up in a story she didn't plan, and me, a police officer juggling duty and brotherhood.

In this close space, the details of their partnership unfolded—a connection formed not just by chance but by their shared determination to face an unknown enemy. But little did they realize, the story was only just starting, and the shadows outside the cozy room hid secrets waiting to be discovered.

"Let's take a break. Amara, do you need anything? Water, maybe?" I asked, trying to sound both professional and understanding.

She replied calmly, assuring me that she was

alright and could handle the unexpected situation.

I had specifically chosen a soft interview room, with sofas and not too bright lights. I wanted them to feel like they were in a safe place after all the crazy stuff that happened outside Tesco. But I insisted on getting them some water to drink and I went out. But that was only a ruse, I wanted an excuse to get out of that room.

∞

After I got two water bottles from the vending machine, I stopped by the busy security room. Walking inside, I found a bunch of police officers busy watching screens with lots of videos. There, officers were checking live camera feeds, like on those detectives shows on television shows. The screens showed different rooms where people were being asked things, and it looked like they were really busy. The security room was filled with the low voices of the officers and the soft light from the screens showing everything that was happening at the station. But to me, it always felt like something big was about to happen. I was always on the edge.

Watching the screens with John and Amara, I couldn't help but wonder. How did John get mixed up in all this drama with a famous actress, and what was their story? The air in the room felt strange, like we were in a movie where things were happening that we didn't expect. It was like a mystery unfolding in front of me.

The blinking videos from the security cameras made the room feel mysterious, casting moving shadows on my face as I tried to figure out the puzzle happening next door. John, who's always calm and serious, was in an intimate conversation with Amara, which seemed a bit strange to me since usually he was interested in men. Amara Delacroix, the famous actress full of secrets, was sitting next to him.

Finding out that John was Amara's bodyguard added another layer to the story, making my mind spin as I tried to understand this unusual partnership. Watching the scenes play out on the surveillance screens, I couldn't shake the feeling that there were still many secrets waiting to be uncovered. But right then, to me, she looked like she might be in some kind of trouble. What was she hiding?

As I looked around, I noticed how busy everyone was. The officers were all focused on their work, but you could feel the curiosity in the air. It was like a puzzle waiting to be solved.

Even though the officers inside the security room were busy, I couldn't keep this surprising news to myself. I wanted to show off that I was interviewing a famous actress. It was a big deal at our small police station to have a famous person like Amara Delacroix involved in my case.

"Hey, you won't believe who just walked in – Amara Delacroix!" I exclaimed out loud, a hint of surprise in my voice. The news was well received with audible gasps, and everyone in the room looked as amazed as I felt.

Constable Brown raised an eyebrow, "No way! Amara Delacroix, the actress?"

"Yeah, that's the one. She's here," I replied, watching their faces light up with curiosity.

My work buddies, who are really into celebrity stuff, started chatting about Amara's crazy life. They shared all sorts of details about her scandals, relationships, and mysterious disappearances. It was like they were talking about a super exciting movie! I listened, super interested and a little worried, realizing that my brother, John, was now part of this big celebrity drama.

Sergeant Thompson leaned in, "Did you hear about that scandal last year? Crazy stuff!"

While my colleagues went on and on about Amara Delacroix's late night partying adventures and quirks, I couldn't help but worry about John. Famous or not, she was now someone my brother was looking out for, and that made me feel a bit stressed. The responsibility of keeping her safe was now on my shoulders too.

Even though I was not really into all the fancy stuff and famous people, the stories that went around about Amara's life sounded suspicious to me. The officers around me, kept talking in hushed voices, and I tried to catch bits and pieces of Amara's life as they floated around the room. And yet the mystery about how she was connected to John and the strange things that brought them to our police station made me feel even more uneasy. It was like the story was getting more complicated, and I couldn't stop wondering how deep my brother had gotten into Amara Delacroix's world.

Back in the interview room, I gave John and Amara each a water bottle. The room felt a bit tense, like there was something important hanging in the air. The water bottles sat there on the table, not a sip taken, showing how they both didn't trust me fully.

John glanced at me, and I could tell he was worried, even though he tried not to show it. Amara, though looked worn out, seemed like she too was unsure of trusting the police. It was kind of strange seeing a tough ex-military guy and a famous actress caught up in this stalker case.

"Thanks for the water," John said, breaking the silence. Amara nodded in agreement.

"No problem," I replied. "We're here to figure this out together."

The questioning started again, and I asked John some regular things. He answered carefully, only giving the most important details about the attack. We didn't know why the person did it, but one thing was clear — they were after Amara. It was kind of scary to think that someone was following her. The investigation got more complicated with this new information.

In the room, even though it was quiet all three of us had a serious feeling. I kept asking John about what happened during the attack with the masked man. His military training showed in how careful and precise he was with his words. He really cared about Amara, and I could see that in the way he talked. But why did I feel like, something was missing?

Meanwhile, Amara looked like she was still scared from what happened. But even so, she showed a strong side, like she was used to facing tough situations. It was interesting to see the mix of John's military world and Amara's glamorous entertainment world coming together in this small room. It was unexpected but kind of cool.

I exchanged glances with my brother, realizing that the quiet guy had somehow found himself in the middle of a celebrity whirlwind.

The lines between regular life and the world of Amara Delacroix were getting blurrier, and I couldn't shake off the feeling that things were about to get even more complicated.

My questions just kept coming, like raindrops tapping on a window. I explained our investigation plan to John and Amara. The police team would look at camera footage from the store, there were other officers at scene who were talking to witnesses, and make a timeline of what happened. While we did our investigation, I told John and Amara that they had to stay away from the streets. They had to find a safe place to stay until we catch the man who knifed John. There was no doubt in my mind that he would try and attack again.

"John, Amara, it's important you stay hidden for now. We'll get to the bottom of this, but you need to be safe," I told them.

John nodded, his eyes serious. "We'll do whatever it takes. Just tell us if you catch the bastard."

"Yeah, we don't want any trouble." Amara added, "We'll be careful."

The seriousness of the problem had hit them, making it feel like a big, dark curtain hiding scary secrets. The air was tense as we moved carefully between staying safe and finding out more, each side feeling important than the other.

I patted John on the uninjured shoulder. "Good.

We'll get this sorted out. Just stick together and stay out of sight."

After talking with John and Amara, I told them I'd let them know if anything new happened. It was like we all understood that what lay ahead in the investigation was full of questions. The pieces of the puzzle were all over the place, and it was my job to put them together. I need to figure out who this masked man was, the one hunting Amara Delacroix.

But as they left, I could see the worry on their faces. The city outside seemed quieter than usual, as if it was holding its breath. The investigation had just begun, and I couldn't shake the feeling that there was more to this mystery than met the eye.

∞

Feeling the urgency, I quickly got on with my investigation, retracing the steps that brought me to the moment of the knife attack outside Tesco supermarket. The store manager, a tired-looking person, led me to the security room, where the hum of surveillance equipment filled the air like a distant melody.

"Can I check out the camera shots of the front entrance? It's really important, especially with what happened to Amara Delacroix and John," I said, stressing the seriousness of the situation.

The manager nodded, understanding the gravity of the matter. "Sure, follow me. I'll pull up the footage for you," they replied, leading me to a row of monitors.

As we approached the screens, I couldn't help but feel a sense of tension in the air. "Thanks for helping with this. I need to find out who did this and why," I explained, my words laced with determination.

The manager sighed, "It's a terrible thing that happened. This has shaken all of us up."

"Yeah, it's really shocking. But we'll get to the bottom of it. I just need to see the footage," I replied, trying to reassure both of us.

With a nod, the manager operated the controls, queuing up the video on the monitor. The front camera displayed the busy entrance of the supermarket. As the story unfolded on the screen, I saw the person wearing a mask coming towards John and Amara. It was like a weird and dangerous dance, the person moving on purpose and with a plan.

The knife suddenly shone in the dim light of the store, and I held my breath when I saw John getting stabbed.

As the events played out on the screen, I couldn't help but verbalize my shock. "Look at that! The person in the mask is moving so deliberately. It's like they had this whole plan."

The manager grimaced, "It's chilling to watch. I never thought something like this would happen here."

"Yeah, it's tough, but we'll piece it together. Did you notice anything unusual before the attack?" I inquired, hoping to gather more information.

The manager thought for a moment. "Well, there was a person hanging around near the entrance, but we didn't think much of it at the time."

"That could be our lead. Can you describe them?" I asked, eager to uncover any clues.

"They were wearing a dark hoodie. Looked like anyone else, really," the manager replied, recalling the details.

I nodded, determined to follow this lead. "Thanks for your help. We'll catch this person and bring them to justice," I assured, as we continued to scrutinize the footage for any additional hints.

But what caught my attention the most wasn't the person causing trouble—it was how Amara reacted, or, well, didn't react. There she stood, like a mysterious character in the middle of all the craziness, not showing any surprise or fear. Her face stayed calm, totally different from the wild scene happening around her.

It made me wonder. Did Amara know who the assailant was? Was there something else she knew that the rest of us didn't? Her mysteriousness got even more confusing, like a puzzle waiting to be solved. Now, my investigation wasn't just about John and Amara's safety; it was about uncovering the secrets of Amara Delacroix's life.

Knowing that, out there was more to her than what I could see, made me even more determined to get to the bottom of things. The line between being a protector and an investigator got blurry as I tried to figure out the hidden parts of Amara's life. Each new piece of information felt like a new color on a painting, making the whole picture even more interesting.

And so, my investigation was just getting started. As I walked out of Tesco with a bunch of new questions, the air felt charged with excitement. The mystery around Amara Delacroix wasn't just a regular gossip story about a famous actress. It felt like there was a whole different tale hiding behind the scenes. The mix of danger and curiosity had taken an unexpected twist, and I was determined to find the truth, no matter how tricky it might be.

Chapter Ten

Sitting inside Amara's apartment, the air felt heavy with worry as I waited anxiously for Amara to come back. Thoughts whirled in my mind, all tangled up with the recent events that had happened. All I knew was what Amara had texted me, "Sarah, meet us back at my place."

Thinking back to when Amara first hired me, I remember being a young and new assistant entering the exciting yet challenging world of a rising actress. Memories of our journey together flashed through my mind like a movie. Amara was always full of energy and had big dreams. Over the years, our friendship grew, but she kept her past life a secret, making it clear that there was a line between personal and professional life.

Now, faced with this new and unsettling situation, I felt like I was in unknown territory. Amara's constant stalking had pushed me to my limit, and I didn't know if I could handle the growing danger. I struggled with the decision to talk to Amara about wanting to quit, worried that my own lack of experience could put her safety at risk.

The door swung open, and in walked Amara, looking tired in every step she took. I couldn't hold back my concerns any longer, "Amara, we need to talk about what's been happening. I'm worried for your safety, and I don't know if I can handle it anymore."

I glanced at John, who had pain etched on his face but still had a determined look. It made me worried. John, took a seat on the sofa, still wincing from his pain. Seeing him like that made me even more concerned.

"Oh my god, Amara, what happened to John?" I asked, sounding worried.

Amara looked relieved and troubled at the same time. She said, "Sarah, someone tried to stab me with a knife, but John stepped in and saved me."

My eyes widened in shock, and I quickly put a hand on Amara's shoulder. "Oh, my goodness, Amara! We have to call the police. This is getting really bad."

Amara hesitated for a moment, and her eyes met John's. "They are already on it, but John doesn't think they'll help. He doesn't trust them."

John, leaning back on the sofa, winced again. "Yeah, they are useless, Sarah. Trust me."

"Excuse me, guys," Amara said suddenly, offering a small, uneasy smile. "I need a moment."

With that, Amara quickly headed back to her room. The door closed softly as Amara left, and we were left with the sounds of our own muffled thoughts.

∞

Feeling the weight of the serious situation, stuck between being loyal to Amara and facing the tough reality from John, I knew I had to do something. "We can't just stay here doing nothing. I'll call Mike. He'll know what to do."

As I pulled out my phone, I noticed John closing his eyes. The pain on his face hinted at struggles that went beyond what was happening right then. The room felt charged with a mix of fear, determination, and an approaching storm that seemed to wrap around us. My fingers impatiently tapped on the phone as I dialed Mike's number. His voice crackled through, blending with the noise of the busy pub.

"Hey, Mike. It's Sarah. We need you at Amara's. Something happened."

Mike's response, somewhat muffled, carried a hint of concern. "I'm in the middle of a shift. Can it wait?"

In the background, the sounds of the pub clashed with the seriousness of our situation. I let out a sigh, frustration hanging in the air. "No, it can't. We need you now, Mike. It's serious."

After a moment, he agreed, promising to rush over once he finished his shift. Ending the call, I turned to John, who looked like he was carrying the weight of the world on his shoulders. Leaned back on the sofa with his eyes closed, he seemed lost in a world of pain.

"John," I said softly, worry lining my voice, "how did you get hurt? Can you tell me what happened?"

He winced and shifted before meeting my gaze with tired eyes. "Somehow, the stalker knew where Amara would be this morning. I stepped in, but..."

A heavy silence hung in the air as the unspoken words weighed down on us. The danger felt real, and I needed answers not just for myself but to keep Amara safe.

"What do you mean by 'somehow'?" I asked gently. "Do you have any idea who might be doing this? Someone who wants to hurt Amara?"

John looked at me, pain mixing with

contemplation in his eyes. "I can't figure it out, Sarah. You've been with her for years. Can you think of anyone who might have a grudge?"

I sighed, thinking hard. "I don't know, John. I really have no idea, it could be one of her fans or anti-fans. Maybe we should talk to her, see if she has any idea who could be behind this."

As we spoke, the urgency of the situation pressed on us. John winced again, reminding us that time was of the essence. I took a deep breath, ready to face whatever challenges lay ahead to protect my friend.

∞

Settling into a cozy corner of the sofa, I shared some interesting stuff about Amara's older movies. You know, the ones where she played characters like the classic damsel in distress or the 'dumb blonde.' A lot of people out there, believe that's who she really is. It's kind of weird how make-believe can mess with reality.

John leaned in, curious to know more. "So what's Amara like in real life?" he asked.

I grinned, remembering Amara's smart and kind side. "She's super clever, one of the smartest people I know," I said. "But, you know, with all the recent chaos, I started thinking about changing jobs. Safety first, right?" I spilled the beans to John about my doubts and worries.

"Why stay if it's getting so scary?" John asked, looking worried.

I chuckled a bit. "Mike. He's the one who makes me feel strong about facing all this. If it wasn't for him, I would've left a while ago."

The room felt unsure, like something awkward was going on. Tension hung in the air, touching every part of it. While we waited for Mike to show up, I felt like the truth we needed was playing hide-and-seek, hiding in the mystery of Amara's past.

John winced, a small frown appearing on his face as a bit of pain zipped through him. Worried, I looked at him and asked, "Are you okay? Do you need something for the pain?"

He shook his head, but I could see a tight expression on his face. "Nah, I've had worse. This is nothing."

Even though he tried to act tough, the lines on his face showed he was hurting. Remembering Mike's stories about his military days with John opened up a chance for me to talk about things we hadn't before.

Summoning up some bravery, I decided to

explore that shared history. "Mike told me about your time in the military. He said you guys were like brothers."

John looked uncomfortable, but he stared at me, curious. "What else did he say about me?"

I took a moment to think before answering, "He told me that you and him were really close until you got hurt, and then you were honorably discharged from the military."

A huge sigh came out of him, as if it was carrying lots of memories. "Those were the best times ever. Being in the Military with Mike… it was everything."

His feelings showed through, and it made me understand more about his past. I smiled to let him know I understood, and it seemed like he was letting me see a bit more of who he really was, beyond his tough exterior.

I remembered those times when Mike and I really wanted John to come to our house for dinner. We asked him many times, but he always said he couldn't make it. I felt like maybe he didn't like us, but today, when we finally got to talk, I realized there was more to the story.

It turned out, John was going through some tough times, dealing with his own problems. It had nothing to do with not liking us.

As we chatted, we began to understand each other better. I made a silent decision that once all this was over, I would invite him to dinner again. I wanted to be friends with him and make our friendship strong without any secrets or stalkers lurking around.

∞

As time ticked by in a nervous wait, we couldn't sit still, all jittery and worried, just hoping to see Mike soon. The air felt heavy with all the nervous energy as we eagerly anticipated his arrival.

Finally, there he was, swinging the door open, carrying a bag of fish and chips. A wave of relief swept over me, like a cozy blanket on a chilly day.

"Mike!" I exclaimed, feeling a mix of joy and relief. He grinned, looking pleased with himself.

"I thought you guys might be hungry, so I grabbed us some fish and chips," he said casually, holding up the bag.

"Wow, you're the best!" I couldn't help but gush, and I planted a big, grateful kiss on his lips. He chuckled, clearly happy to see our worries melt away.

"That's why I love you," I whispered, my words

wrapped in a warm smile. Mike blushed a bit but was clearly pleased with the appreciation.

"Anything for you my love," he replied, as he walked towards the dining table, leaving me to enjoy the comforting aroma of the tasty treat Mike brought with him. The atmosphere shifted from tense to relaxed, thanks to a simple bag of fish and chips and my thoughtful fiancé.

I decided to check on Amara, my curiosity getting the better of me. It's been a few hours since she disappeared inside. So, I quietly approached her room and gently knocked on the door.

"Hey, Amara," I called softly. "Dinner's ready. Are you okay?"

There was a moment of silence before I heard a muffled response, "Yeah, I'll be out in a bit."

I hesitated, wanting to make sure she wasn't feeling alone or upset. "Mind if I join you for a moment?"

The door creaked open, and Amara sitting on the bed, gave me a small smile. Her room was dimly lit, and I could see a mix of emotions in her eyes.

Without saying anything else, I walked in and sat on the edge of her bed.

"Something on your mind?" I asked softly, trying to sound as casual as I could.

She sighed, looking down at her hands. "It's just a lot, you know? Sometimes, I feel like I can't keep up."

I nodded, understanding. "You don't have to face everything alone, Amara. We're here for you. Dinner's a good start, though."

A flicker of a smile crossed her face. "Really? What's for dinner?"

"Fish and chips, straight from the pub," I replied, trying to lift her spirits. "Come on, let's go grab a plate. It's always better to face challenges with a full stomach."

The four of us huddled together at the small kitchen table, and the delicious smell of crispy fish and tangy sauce floated around us. We all knew that something serious was going on, but no one said a word. The only sounds were forks clinking and drinks slurping.

Mike took a break from munching on his fish and turned to John with a concerned look. "Hey, John, how you doing, buddy?"

John flashed a big smile, almost like he was trying to convince himself. "Better than ever, Mike! Couldn't be better."

But as soon as John said those words, Mike's face went quiet, like he was thinking about something from the past. It felt like there was a story there, something hidden beneath the surface. The clatter of forks on plates slowed down, and a thoughtful silence settled over the table, as if the room itself was waiting for Mike to say something more.

But I knew that we were all thinking about the things that could go wrong, and even the delicious fish and chips couldn't make us forget it. Each bite felt heavy, like it carried the weight of something we didn't understand completely.

Mike looked at Amara and John, knowing that they needed to figure things out, quick. "We gotta make a plan," he said, breaking the quiet.

We all agreed with quick nods, and in that moment, we silently promised to face the danger together. We were like a team, deciding to stand up to whatever was hiding in the shadows and keep our lives as normal as we could.

Chapter Eleven

As the night wrapped up, Mike and Sarah said their goodbyes, leaving John and me in the calm aftermath of our laughter and the quiet shadows that hid the danger that I was in. The sound of the door closing echoed through the apartment, leaving a big silence behind. It felt heavy, like the worries we didn't talk about.

John, trying to hide how tired he was, stood up to get some water. But as he turned, his tiredness showed on his face, and it was clear he was exhausted. I felt a wave of concern inside me, like the feeling when the tide rises at the beach.

"Hey John, are you okay?" I asked, my voice showing how worried I felt.

He gave a weak nod, trying to reassure me, but I

couldn't ignore the tired look on his face. Something wasn't right. I rushed to his side, and that's when I saw a small blood stain forming on his white T-shirt, like something was wrong underneath. Panic set in as I realized he was bleeding out of the knife wound.

"Come on, follow me," I said, leading him to my room. To me, the space suddenly felt a bit tight, and there was this weird feeling in the air.

I motioned for him to sit on my armchair while I dashed to get the first aid kit from the bathroom.

Under the soft ceiling lights, shadows danced on John's face, making it look like he was at my secret hideout. It felt like we were sharing something important, even though we didn't say that to each other. Maybe it was because we both knew that the knife wound was deep and I wanted to help him out.

Taking off the old bandage from John's side, the injury looked worse than I thought. The room suddenly felt even smaller, and it got kind of quiet, like when you're waiting for a big storm.

My hands moved quickly but carefully, wiping away the blood as I tried to figure out what to do.

"You okay?" I asked, trying to break the quiet.

John winced a bit but nodded. "Yeah, just hurts a

little."

"You really should get stitches," I said, looking closely at the cut. "The paramedics could have taken you to the hospital."

John, trying to act tough even though it clearly hurt, just shrugged, saying, "Nah, it's just a little scratch."

"But it looks deep," I argued, worried. "What if it gets infected?"

He winced a bit but kept his cool. "I'll be fine. I don't need to go to the hospital for this."

I sighed, realizing he wasn't going to change his mind easily. "Okay, at least let me clean it up and put a bandage on it. We don't want it to get worse."

As I reached for the first aid kit, John finally gave in and raised his other arm and pulled up his T-shirt, "Alright, alright. Do your thing, doctor."

I chuckled, "I'm no doctor, just trying to keep you from turning into a mummy with all those bandages."

He laughed too, wincing again as I gently cleaned the wound. "Ouch, easy there, Doc."

"Sorry, tough guy," I teased, sticking a large

bandage on the cut. "There, good as new."

"Thanks, Amara," John grinned, a hint of gratitude in his eyes. "Guess I should listen to you next time."

I nodded, feeling relieved that he let me take care of his knife injury. "It's better to be safe, you know?"

"Yeah, yeah, I got it," he admitted, realizing maybe toughing it out wasn't always the best idea.

My eyes wandered over the strong lines of John's chest, marked with scars that spoke of battles and triumphs. My fingers lightly traced those marks, prompting John to pull away, emphasizing the professional boundaries he firmly upheld.

"I don't cross personal lines with clients," he asserted as he pulled down his T-shirt, his voice carrying the weight of unwavering principles.

In an attempt to ease the tension, I reached for his face, hoping for a crack in his stoic behavior. However, my efforts were met with a firm refusal. "Amara, I'm not interested in you like that," he stated firmly, casting a shadow over my fleeting hopes.

Undiscouraged, I persisted, "John, we've been through a lot together. Can't we just be real for a moment?"

He sighed, the lines on his forehead deepening. "It's not about that. It's about keeping a clear line between personal and professional. It's for both our sakes."

Feeling the need to shift the focus, I suggested, "Alright then, no hard feelings. You should go grab your things from your apartment, and we can figure out our next move."

As he left, he added, "And don't open the door for anyone until I'm back. Safety first."

The night hung heavy with unspoken truths, and the fragile balance between fear and the comfort of shared danger. I couldn't help but wonder about the stories behind each scar and the battles John had faced.

∞

After John left, everything got really quiet, and I couldn't stop thinking about him. The room felt kind of lonely and chilly, like something was missing. I tossed and turned in my bed, trying to get some rest, but it was hard because my mind was still spinning from all the stuff that happened today.

John was really a serious guy and didn't show much emotion, which both interested and bothered me. I kept thinking about how strong he was and how safe I felt when he was with me. It was like a big contrast to the scary time we had with the crazy masked man. I got a little shiver down my back just thinking about those moments where John protected me from danger.

Feeling trapped by the thoughts in my head, I quickly grabbed my phone. My fingers moved fast, tapping on the screen to send a message to Sarah. She responded, telling me that she and Mike made it home safely. That made me feel a bit better. Afterwards, I put my phone away, and the light from the screen slowly disappeared in the dark room.

I let out a sigh, feeling a bit more at ease now that I knew they were safe. I sat back, thinking about how important it is to stay connected with friends, especially when worries creep up. My bedroom was quiet, and the soft glow of the nightlights outside, peeked through the curtains. I felt how nice it was, to have a friend like Sarah, who could offer comfort even from a distance.

But sleep just wouldn't come, slipping away like the tricky strands of my thoughts that danced around John. His voice lingered in the quiet, and his actions were like drawings etched in my mind. In the dark of the night, I wrestled with a strong liking, not sure where the line between work and personal feelings was.

The night felt super long, like a big painting filled with uncertainty and a special connection that didn't follow the usual rules. But soon, I found myself dozing off.

Suddenly, I woke up, leaving behind the scary echoes of my nightmare to the weird quiet of my living room. Going from a nightmare where I saw my father again, to real life was quick and confusing. The dim night lights made strange shapes on the walls, making everything feel a bit unreal.

When I sat up, the quiet around me seemed to stretch out and twist, as if it was whispering secrets that I couldn't understand. But my bedroom felt safe, but also a bit strange, and the air was heavy with a feeling that I couldn't figure out. I listened hard, trying to figure out where that weird feeling in my not-so-good sleep came from. Was I imagining things again?

But in the quiet darkness, a faint noise caught my attention, barely noticeable but enough to make me uneasy. It was a soft creak, a gentle rustle, a presence that seemed to tiptoe at the edge of my awareness. My heart started beating faster, matching the growing feeling of unease that surrounded me.

I slid out of bed, moving quietly towards the living room. The chilly floor sent a shiver through my bare feet. I could feel the apartment's creaks and groans becoming eerie whispers.

I reached the doorway, hesitating before taking another step.

The living room had a soft glow from the city lights outside, seeping through the curtains. Everything looked normal, but a strange feeling lingered—an intangible sense that something had entered my safe space.

A sudden whoosh of wind shook the windows, making the nighttime sounds frightening. I tried really hard to figure out what was real and what my mind was making up. But everything felt strange, and I had to be super careful with my senses. For me, the night, which was usually so calm, turned into a picture of not knowing what's was actually going on. Shadows were dancing around like they were playing a weird dance that I couldn't understand.

I started wondering if I was going a bit crazy, still feeling the scary bits of my bad dream. Standing there, a shadowy shape popped up, flickering in and out of the dark. I got really scared and took a big breath, stuck between my leftover nightmare and the weird real stuff happening in front of me. I ran back inside my bedroom, and locked the door behind him. I was running on an autopilot mode as I found myself grabbing my phone from the nightstand.

My shaky fingers struggled with the buttons on my phone as I called the emergency number. With every second, my heart raced like a speedy rabbit. Even though my apartment was supposed to be safe, the feeling of the intruder's visit stayed with me, like a ghost in my thoughts. The person on the phone became my link to safety, a bit like a fragile rope in a scary climb.

As I told them about what was happening, my eyes kept darting towards the bedroom door. I half-expected it to give in to the unseen power that followed me. Fear was all around, like a heavy fog that wanted to take away my ability to think. While the person on the phone asked me to stay online, with a promise that things would get better.

I leaned against the door, trying hard to block out whatever was on the other side. The seconds felt super long, like they never wanted to end. I strained my ears, hoping to hear any sound that meant the intruder was leaving. Was it a person who was not thinking right, a ghost from my past, or something even scarier? These questions made me more and more worried, turning the room into a battlefield between feeling weak and standing strong.

But out of nowhere, I felt like something was pushing me away from the door. I screamed, and the walls made my scream bounce around. Panic took over as I tried to understand what was happening. The shadows in the room twisted into a confusing mess, and I couldn't figure out what was real anymore.

In that really scary moment, everything got all mixed up, like when you're in a super weird dream. It felt like the room was twirling around, and I got pulled somewhere I didn't understand. I yelled for help, but nobody answered, and it was like the whole world turned super dark and spooky.

While I was getting pulled away, it felt like I was falling into a place that didn't make any sense at all. I tried to hold on to what I knew, but it was like everything was disappearing. I felt really scared, and it seemed like my past and real life were all jumbled up together.

It was so strange; I felt like I was slipping away, going down into a super deep hole that didn't make sense at all. I tried to stay awake, struggling against the force that was pulling me, but he was stronger than me. The line between what's real and what's just in my head got even more blurry, like I was stuck in a really confusing dance with something I couldn't see.

And then, suddenly, everything turned completely black. It was like falling asleep really fast, and I couldn't see anything. My bedroom, where all this strange stuff happened, disappeared, and I was left with a lot of questions but no answers.

The dark feeling wrapped around me, and I couldn't figure out what had just happened. It was like a mad song playing in my mind, making everything feel mysterious.

In that quick fall into darkness, I didn't know what was real anymore. My life was just hanging there, waiting to see what would happen next.

Chapter Twelve

Walking away from Amara's apartment felt like escaping from yet another woman who tried to seduce me and failed. The air outside carried the heaviness of the night, and the street lamps flickered with a faint glow, just enough to show the way. My heart, which had raced to protect Amara, started to calm down. Instead, a persistent ache in my chest lingered, a reminder of the danger I was facing.

As I moved through the poorly lit streets, the distant sounds of the city whispered around me, creating a strange background to my urgent task. The city's pulse seemed to match the beat of my limping steps. Each one brought a dull pain from my injured chest.

Stepping into the local pharmacy, I gently pushed the glass door, and a little bell chimed happily to announce my arrival. The coldness from outside disappeared instantly. The place smelled super clean, like the doctor's office, and all the shelves were neatly stacked.

As I walked towards the section where they kept stuff to help with pain, the lights above me buzzed softly. They were bright and made everything look clean and official. There were lots of pill bottles and boxes all neatly lined up, waiting to help people feel better.

I carefully looked at the labels on each bottle, hoping to find something strong that would make my pain go away, even if just for a little while. While I was doing this, I could hear people talking around me. Some were customers like me, and others were chatting with the person behind the counter, who I guessed was the pharmacist.

It was like a lively tune of regular life, completely different from the scary and dangerous things I had just experienced. The people in the pharmacy were talking about everyday things, like what medicine to get or how they were feeling. It felt weird to be in a place where everything seemed so normal, especially after what I had been through.

Approaching the counter, I saw the pharmacist, a nice lady with friendly eyes. She greeted me with a kind smile, as she glanced at the tiny blood stain on my T-shirt, "Did you have a long night?" Her voice sounded like a gentle song in the clean, white store.

"Yeah, something like that," I said, giving her a small smile back. I decided not to share all the details of what happened tonight. Some stories are better kept as secrets.

Finishing the transaction, I got a little plastic bag with the relief I needed, in my hand. Stepping back outside into the night, the city surrounded me with its busy streets. But painkillers in my bag felt like a weak shield against the tough job I had just done.

I took one pill from the box and swallowed it dry, feeling rather lazy to get a drink to wash it down. As I walked to my apartment, I couldn't help but wonder about the many questions and worries. Inside me, it felt like a storm of uncertainty. Even though the painkillers helped a bit, I couldn't shake the feeling that the night wasn't really over.

∞

After a really long and tiring walk, I finally got back home. It felt so good to be in my own space, like when you find a prize after a big adventure. The soft light from the street outside came through my curtains, making everything look calm and safe.

I quickly changed out of my tired clothes, wanting

to forget about all the craziness from earlier. My chest began to hurt, reminding me of the scary stuff Amara and I went through. Even though I had taken one pill a few minutes ago, it didn't seem to be working. So, I took two more of the pain killer pills and washed them down with water, hoping they would work.

As I settled into my favorite chair, I couldn't help but think about everything that happened. I wished I could forget it all, but the echoes of that wild day lingered in my mind. Just then, my phone buzzed with a message from Amara. I hesitated before opening her text message, half expecting her to bring up our awkward encounter earlier.

"Hey, are you okay?" she asked.

"Yeah, just tired," I replied immediately. "That was a crazy day, huh?"

Amara agreed, saying, "Totally! I can't believe we made it through. Thanks for having my back."

"No problem," I said. "We make a great team."

Feeling a little better after chatting with Amara, I thought it was time to catch some much needed sleep. I carefully settled onto my small bed, and it felt like a soft cuddle as the mattress took the shape of my tired body. But, you know, I still couldn't forget how serious things had gotten. The messages from The White

Panther kept popping up on my phone, asking me to jump back into the mystery. It was like a big red flag that said the night was far from finished.

So, I sent a message back, setting up a call. Soon, my phone buzzed, and it was like a secret conversation was starting. The White Panther's robotic voice came through, making the air feel mysterious, like we were in the middle of some big secret. She told me she found where the Amara Delacroix's stalker was hiding.

The way she shared the location of the stalker was super-efficient, like a secret agent. I thanked her quickly, leaving no time for long elaborate explanations. We were in a race against time, and I had to do something before the stalker's grip around Amara got even tighter.

I hung up the phone, feeling the weight of the important mission ahead. Looking out of my window, the city seemed quiet, not knowing about the secret stalker living in its shadows. Armed with new information, I promised myself I'd keep Amara safe from the shadows trying to take her.

∞

I got ready for the dangerous journey into the stalker's hideout. My military-grade knife, sharp and strong, rested against my leg, hidden inside my old leather boots. A cold, tough bulletproof vest wrapped around me like a protective shield, reminding me that danger was close.

In my dimly lit apartment, I reached for the small locked box under my bed. It felt like a special moment as I opened it, revealing my sleek handgun. The shiny metal showed my quiet promise to defend and confront the shadows if I had to.

Taking careful steps, the painkillers running through my blood, made the constant ache in my chest feel a bit numb. In the dim light, the mix of pain and the danger outside my door strangely calmed me. The adrenaline in my veins brought a strong determination, a decision to face the dangers around Amara with bravery.

Standing at the doorway of my apartment, the city outside shared its secrets with the night breeze. It felt like the city was whispering stories to the wind. There was a feeling of excitement in the air, like something risky was about to happen. It was like a secret dance was happening in the shadows, and I was a part of it.

Quietly shutting the door behind me, the silence wrapped around me like an air filled blanket. I felt like I was stepping into the unknown, like a hidden adventure was waiting for me. The city, unaware of the exciting journey happening right under its nose, slept peacefully. It didn't know about the secret struggle that was about to take place within its streets.

As I walked down the dimly lit streets, the glow of streetlights created pools of light on the pavement. I could hear the soft sounds of the cold night – the distant hum of cars, the rustle of leaves, and the occasional giggle of someone passing by. It was a world of mystery and quiet excitement.

It was really late at night, when I got lucky to grab a taxi in London. The taxi zoomed through the city, kind of like blood flowing through veins, following the city's roads with a bumpy rhythm. The city made a humming sound with cars far away, like a beat that changed from what I knew to something new. When I got closer to the address where The White Panther told me about, everything around me changed. It went from bright, busy streets to a darker, the part of the city where things weren't so good.

The taxi driver stopped on the edge of a neighborhood. He said he wouldn't go any farther because he was scared of the gangs. I thanked him and paid the fare. As I stepped out, I couldn't help but notice how different it was from where I started.

"Are you sure this is the right place?" I asked, looking around at the graffiti-covered walls.

"Yeah, mate. You're on your own from here," the driver replied with a casual nod.

I took a deep breath, feeling a mix of excitement

and nervousness. "Alright, thanks. Take care," I said, closing the taxi door behind me.

∞

Strolling down the poorly lit pathways, I looked around and saw what was left behind by people who lived on the edge. Old buildings, like dreams that had lost their colors, showed signs of being forgotten. The alleys, messy and untidy, hid the secrets of hushed talks, where whispers took the place of open chats, and people exchanged things they needed quietly.

At a distance, the glow from neon signs twinkled weakly, like little stars giving light every now and then. This dim light touched the faces of those walking in this lonely place. This world was like a hidden one, a place not many visited - a world where tough times shaped the faces of the people who lived there. You could see their wrinkles, each one telling a story of battles fought in the shadows.

I overheard two people talking near a crumbling wall. One said, "Life here isn't easy, is it?" The other nodded, "Nope, but we manage somehow." They spoke quietly, like they didn't want anyone else to hear. It made me realize that even in this hidden world, people found ways to survive and help each other.

Approaching the apartment building, part of the address given by The White Panther, I felt a heavy tension hanging in the air, as if there were secrets waiting to burst forth. Far-off footsteps echoed in the narrow passageways, creating a sort of song of uncertainty as I ventured into the center of this mysterious place.

The building itself looked like a keeper of hidden stories, its outside revealing nothing about the mysteries concealed within. Each step I took seemed to hold the weight of something about to happen, knowing that inside those walls, the dangerous stalker was hatching plans. The city's ongoing struggles formed a confusing melody around me, and every step I took echoed the rhythm of a meeting that was just around the corner, where it was hard to tell who was the hunter and who was the hunted in the darkness of the night.

I walked up the stairs and went to the first floor. As I moved closer to my target, I pulled out the gun from my holster. But when I reached the stalker's apartment, the front door was left open.

∞

Inside the dimly lit and messy apartment, I carefully looked around the room. My eyes moved over the chaos like a detective solving a puzzle. Fear seemed to be the conductor of this disorder, orchestrating a symphony of desperation that played out in flipped furniture and belongings scattered all over.

As I took in the scene, I couldn't help but wonder what kind of secrets were hidden in this forsaken enclave. I knew that finding the truth would require unraveling the clues scattered in the wreckage around me.

Amid all the chaos, something shiny grabbed my attention—a tiny camera sitting on the corner of the ceiling, its eye fixed on the leftover mess from the stalker's hiding spot. A chill ran down my back, making me feel like something heavy was on my shoulders. Someone had been watching, quietly peeking from the shadows.

As I stared at the little device, the room felt like it was closing in on me. I knew there was an invisible enemy spying on me, making the air tight and tense. It was like a game between two hunters, where every move was thought out, and every detail was noticed. The stalker expected me, and now the roles were flipped, with a creepy smile on his face.

Breaking the silence, I bravely spoke into the quiet room, challenging the hidden enemy. "I will find you," I said, my words slicing through the heavy air. There was no confusion; the chase had turned into a determined game, and I was set on uncovering the person pulling the strings.

With a quick move, I grabbed the camera, pulling it down with a satisfying snap. The wires hung loose, like the threads coming undone from the stalker's control. It was like saying, "No more hiding in the shadows!"

The apartment, once a place full of secrets, echoed with the loud sound of the camera hitting the floor. At that moment, it was just me, surrounded by the mess of a messed-up situation. The stalker had gotten away, but all that was left were bits of his bad intentions.

But, there was something in the air—a promise to myself. The chase got more serious, the game more exciting. As I threw the broken camera to the floor, I felt determined. The game wasn't finished; the stalker had just gone deeper into the maze, and I was going after him.

"I'll get you," I whispered to myself, ready to keep going, "if that's the last thing I ever do."

Chapter Thirteen

The street lamp's soft orangey glow peeked through our curtains, making the room feel like a fairytale. Next to me, Sarah, my fiancé, was sound asleep. She breathed in and out, like a soothing song, making the night peaceful. Her hands, warm and comforting, hugged me close, and she rested her head on my shoulders.

I lay there in the quiet, looking at the shadows on the ceiling. The bedroom, so calm and quiet, was like a safe place—a break from the shadows that sometimes creeped into my thoughts. Sarah definitely gets it, helping me to feel connected to the present.

In the hushed room, I whispered, "Hey, Sarah, you awake?" She mumbled a little and snuggled even closer. I smiled, feeling happy and safe.

In those quiet moments, my thoughts drifted back to times before, filled with tough battles and good friends. The army days left marks on my soul, but it was Sarah, always by my side, her presence made me feel better.

Looking at her sleeping peacefully, I couldn't help but appreciate the calm she brought into my world. Sarah, with her strong spirit and understanding ways, was like a bright light showing me the way through the darkest thoughts in my head. Her love was like a safe place, where the loud sounds of guns were replaced by the gentle rhythm of her breathing.

But as I lay there, I felt desperation building up inside me. Grateful for the warmth Sarah's love gave me, but still wishing for the peaceful sleep that sometimes stayed just out of reach. The heaviness of my old memories stuck around, like a quiet ghost that sometimes woke up in the middle of the night. Some were like marks on my heart and mind, while others hid deep within me, invisible to the eye. Sarah, my best friend and partner, had been there with me through all of it, understanding me without ever blaming me for my shortcomings.

Letting out a soft sigh, I gently moved a strand of hair away from Sarah's face. She looked so calm and peaceful as she slept. The room was so quiet, and it felt like our connection spoke for itself. Right there with her, I found comfort—a break from the constant reminders of a past that stayed in the shadows. I closed my eyes, ready to fall asleep, feeling grateful for this peaceful moment.

But a memory popped into my mind like a bright picture, taking me back to the time when we were all just starting out at military training. It happened on a regular day, with the air full of the stench of following rules and the excitement doing our part for the country. We heard the buzz that a bunch of new guys would be joining our group, bringing in some new energy.

When the new recruits walked in, this guy stepped forward, looking all sure of himself, leading them through the fresh morning breeze. That guy was John Stewart, and little did I know, he was going to be a big part of my story. The tough sergeants, doing their evaluations, had their eyes on John as he guided the newbies through all the exercises. It was like he was painting a picture of skill with every move they made.

The sparring session kicked off—a sort of dance where soldiers prove their courage. Destiny paired me with John, who had the reputation of being an experienced fighter. His eyes showed determination, but as we clashed, I glimpsed a hint of vulnerability in his every move.

Despite John's initial skill, I spotted openings, took advantage of weaknesses, and used maneuvers that made him stumble for a moment. Dust settled on his uniform as he got back up, determined. With a friendly vibe, he reached out his hand.

"Hey, I'm John. Cool moves, buddy!" His voice was full of excitement, creating a bond beyond just competition. I shook his hand, feeling a strong grip that conveyed understanding. "I'm Mike," I told him.

At that instant, a spark seemed to leap between our hands, hinting at a connection that would grow into a friendship tougher than military drills. Little did I know, this meeting would be the start of a friendship enduring the challenges of battle, uniting us like brothers in the forge of shared trials.

I thought about the time when the desert wind, shared stories with us, and we learned about the true meaning of friendship under the scorching sun. All the while, John's journey up the ranks happened super-fast. It showed how much he cared and how good he was at what he did. I was his right-hand person, kind of like his sidekick. It was a big deal, but nothing compared to how great John was at leading.

One of those days, we were deployed out in the desert, and the sun was almost burning us alive. We had a talk about our next move.

"Hey, John, what do you think we should do next?" I asked, trying to figure out our strategy.

John looked thoughtful, squinting his eyes against the bright sunlight. "Well, we need to stick together and be smart. The desert can be tricky, but we've got each other's backs."

I nodded, feeling reassured by his words. "You're right, John. We make a great team."

John grinned, patting me on the back. "Absolutely! Teamwork makes everything easier."

As we continued our journey, memories of the past flashed through my mind. I remembered the times when John and I faced challenges together, and he always knew just what to do. Even though I was his second in command, I felt proud to be by his side.

∞

The desert winds whispered around us, carrying the secrets of our adventures. And under the blazing sun, our feelings grew stronger, making our friendship shine like a shining light in the vast desert.

As we marched across the sandy ground, the crunching of our boots echoed in the air. Our team felt like a close-knit group, understanding without words that each one's life depended on the person next to them.

Leading us was John, a mix of authority and

humility that made everyone look up to him.

Our mission took us deeper inside the hot desert, where we were up against tricky opponents who blended into the surroundings like shadows. The sun beat down on us, making the air thick with tension, and mirages on the sand, played tricks on our eyes. In this tough terrain, John's smart planning was like an oasis of hope for us.

"Watch out for those sneaky insurgents," John warned as we walked. "Stay close and keep an eye on each other. We're a team, and we've got each other's backs."

We trudged on, the desert stretching out endlessly. "I wish we had something to cool us down," I sighed.

"Yeah, I know," replied John with a grin. "But you know what? I always save the desert from my meal kit for you."

"Really?" I asked, surprised.

"Absolutely," John chuckled. "We might be in a tough spot, but we can still share a bit of sweetness, right?"

And with that, the desert seemed a bit more bearable, knowing we had each other's company, even in the scorching heat.

I remembered a time when the squad, huddled up inside the command tent, were discussing tactical plans on how to move forward. John, our leader, had a serious look on his face, but he was determined. We weren't just soldiers; we were like a family, working together on a mission that needed everything we had.

At another times, when the night sky sparkled with stars over the desert, we found comfort in each other's company. John and I would take a break from the military talk to sit quietly. He'd tell me about his life, the things he hoped to do in the future, and I'd listen, understanding the dreams and worries of someone I admired.

In those nights, the faraway sounds of gunfire couldn't drown out the bond we were building. John, the leader who carried the heavy responsibility for all of us, and me, his loyal friend, stood strong together. Little did we know that the challenges of the desert were just the beginning. The real tests of our friendship were waiting for us, challenges that would push us to our limits in ways we never imagined.

∞

And it happened on a day that I'll never forget, the memory of which haunted my dreams like a vivid picture. It was just another stroll in that quiet desert city, where everything usually felt calm and sleepy. But out of nowhere, a sudden burst of gunfire broke the peaceful quietness.

The air was filled with loud bangs from guns, people shouting in panic, and the smell of smoke making my nose scrunch up. It was like the whole world turned into chaos. Soldiers were running around, desperately trying to find somewhere safe to hide. The streets, once so peaceful, were now chaotic.

In the middle of all this craziness, John, our squad commander, shouted loud and clear. His voice cut through the confusion like a superhero trying to save the day. "Find cover, everyone! Stick together!" he commanded, and it was like a lifeline in the middle of the ambush.

I looked around, and the other soldiers and I quickly huddled together, following John's lead. The noise was deafening, but John's words helped us focus. He told us what to do, and it felt like we were part of a team, even in the middle of all that scary stuff happening around us.

Huddled behind some rocks for safety, the ground shook beneath us. Boom! An explosion echoed through the air, making everything feel like slow motion. I turned around and couldn't believe my eyes. A grenade was flying toward us!

"Look out!" John shouted, grabbing my arm and pulling me away. I stumbled and fell to the ground just as the grenade exploded. The noise was deafening, and I covered my ears.

Confused and wobbly, I stood up in the midst of the smoky mess and scattered bits of things. The loud sounds of fighting filled my ears, but I saw John through the haze. He looked really hurt, barely awake, blood everywhere, his knee was badly banged up. All I could think about was getting to him as fast as I could.

My head was all fuzzy, and my ears were still ringing. I ran toward John, yelling his name as loud as I could over all the noise. It felt like the most important thing in the world to get to him. When I finally reached him, he looked at me with pain in his eyes.

"John, can you hear me?" I asked, feeling the weight of the moment.

Tears welled up in John's eyes, and he struggled to keep them open. I felt a rush of willpower— I had to help him, and fast.

"Hey, cover for me, guys!" I shouted to the other soldiers, my voice cutting through all the noise. They got it, and immediately started firing at the enemy, giving us a chance. With all my strength, I dragged John towards a crumbling building, where it was a bit safer.

The other soldiers joined us, seeking refuge from the relentless enemy gunfire.

It was scary and intense, but it was also a moment that showed how much we cared for each other. I held John close, feeling the weight of his injuries. The heart-thumping sound of gunfire surrounded us, changing the once-quiet desert neighborhood into a chaotic battleground. In that moment, the bonds we had formed in the tough times of war became even stronger.

But soon, the loud bangs of the guns slowly faded away, and there I was, holding onto John. He looked like he was on the edge of death, and my face was all dusty and messed up from crying. I begged him to keep breathing, to not let go, even though death was trying to take him away. The moment felt really heavy, like something was squeezing my heart.

"Come on, John, please don't leave!" I said, my voice all shaky and worried. I held him tight, hoping that just touching him would make him stay. With every hard breath he took, I realized how serious it was.

I kept talking to him, "You can't go, John. We need you here. Stay with me, buddy." I felt so scared, like everything was falling apart.

Suddenly, a far-off sound reached us, like the buzzing of busy bees.

We perked up, and a tiny bit of hope sparkled in the dark. The cavalry, our heroes, had come! They showed up through the mist, looking like protectors sent to rescue the hurt ones.

The new arrivals checked out what was going on. Then, out of the sky, a big rescue helicopter came down. Its spinning blades made a rhythmic noise, chopping through the air. The rush of the moment got even more intense. They carefully put John onto a stretcher, making sure he was safe. His injuries looked really serious against the war scene.

"Hang in there, Commander! Help is here," shouted one of the rescuers.

"Thanks a bunch! We thought we were done for," replied another soldier, relieved.

The medic onboard quickly got to work, checking John's injuries. The other soldiers started talking about how the reinforcements had just made it in time.

"Good thing we held our ground until they showed up," said one soldier.

"Yeah, it was tough, but we did it together," added another.

Amid the swirling dust stirred up by the helicopter landing, I couldn't help but feel a mix of sadness and determination. My hands, shaky and marked by John's blood, stretched out to gently touch his shoulder while the medics got him ready to go.

"Stay strong, buddy. We're gonna take you out of here," I said softly, making a promise and a wish all at once.

While the medevac team skillfully worked to help John, a fellow soldier, who made through tough times, put a hand on my shoulder. Without saying anything, he gave me a comforting nod. We both stood there, watching as the medics lifted John, knowing that the road ahead was uncertain, and the possibility of losing him loomed.

The thud of the helicopter blades got louder, covering up the other sounds from the battlefield. With John inside of it, the helicopter rose into the air, heading toward the waiting airplane that would carry him to the hospital.

I kept looking until the helicopter's shape disappeared far away, like a tiny light that's slowly fading in the middle of the broken land where the war happened. After the dust went away, a weird feeling stayed with me, like an empty space inside. I was standing in the middle of where the battle was, feeling how fragile life is and how scary war can be.

∞

Even after everything had calmed down, the

memories from that scary day stayed in my head. They wouldn't go away, even when it was dark and quiet. There I was, lying next to Sarah, and her sleepy breathing made a soft sound in the room. But, even with that comfortable sound, I couldn't shake off this heavy feeling that something wasn't right.

The memory of holding John close, his tired and hurt body, kept playing over and over in my head. The noise of guns and the faraway sound of a rescue helicopter mixed with it, making everything seem like a blurry dream. But in the middle of all that chaos, a strange truth was hard to accept.

Soldiers, when they fight together, become really close, almost like family. But when I thought about John's face, I couldn't shake off this weird feeling. It felt like there was something more than just being friends, something like a special kind of feeling.

A big struggle was happening inside me, and you could almost hear my thoughts in the quiet room. Sarah, who was snuggled up next to me, moved a bit in her sleep, not knowing what was happening in my head. Without thinking, I pulled her in closer, trying to find comfort in the warmth of her being there.

"I can't," I said quietly to myself. It was like I was trying to stop my strong feelings towards John, from messing up my life. Sarah, let out a happy sigh in her sleep, trusting that our future together was solid.

At that moment, I was trying to figure out why love is a big, complicated thing. The love I had for John, built on us going through tough times together, showed how strong human connections could be. But, at the same time, the love I had for Sarah tied me to a different closeness—one filled with promises of a future made up of dreams we shared and secrets we whispered.

The mix of these feelings, like a storm getting ready far away, left me feeling unwell. As each second passed, the line between being brothers-in-arms and being intimate, got blurry, and I had to find my way through the tricky waters of my own heart.

The night wrapped around me and Sarah like a cozy blanket, making everything hushed and peaceful. I felt a mix of feelings inside me - a bit like when you're happy and sad at the same time. It was like a puzzle of war stories and love stories all jumbled up in my head.

But I just couldn't fall asleep. As if I was playing a game of hide-and-seek with the sandman. The room, now all dark and mysterious, was like a big coloring book waiting for memories and wishes to be drawn on its pages. Sarah slept soundly next to me, snoring a little, lost her own dream world. She didn't know about the storm inside me, like a swirl of wind and rain in my heart.

In the quietness, I thought about the battles I

fought, not with swords and shields, but with my own feelings. But this time, it was different. The fight was about things that mattered a lot to me, and the end game was like a secret scar hidden deep in my heart.

As exhaustion fell over me, I tried to close my eyes and let sleep take over. I imagined talking to Sarah about all the things buzzing in my head. "Hey, have you ever felt like your heart is a little confused, like it's playing a game it can't win?" I wanted to ask her, and maybe we would share our thoughts until the quiet room became a space filled with our conversations.

But the sandman kept hiding, and my thoughts kept spinning like a merry-go-round. The night was a difficult time, a little mysterious and full of secrets. Even though I longed for sleep to take me away, I also wanted to stay in that moment, trying to figure out the puzzle of my own heart.

∞

In the magical land of dreams, where reality mixes with imagination, I found myself standing in a dreamy world painted with shades of deep, midnight blue.

A soft breeze whispered secrets, carrying the weight of unsaid words. As I turned around, I saw John standing there. His silhouette glowed in the moonlight that seemed to appear from nowhere.

John's eyes, usually serious and guarded, now showed a softer side, reflecting the unknown parts of my own heart. In this dream world, where everything was different from the real world, a hidden truth connected us.

"I never told you," John spoke in a gentle way, his words flowing through the quiet like a magical discovery. Stepping closer, he brought a comforting warmth that went beyond the dream itself. "Mike, there's something I need to tell you."

I looked at him, curious and a bit anxious. "What is it, John? Tell me."

He hesitated for a moment, then opened up, "I've always wanted to say that I loved you. You mean the world to me." The dreamland seemed to shimmer with the honesty of his words, and I felt a special bond forming between us.

In the quiet land of dreams, our words flowed like a gentle river, telling a story of hidden feelings and wishes left unexplored. With each spoken word, the weight of unsaid things lifted, and a shared story unfolded—a story of friendship, brotherhood, and a love that went beyond mere friendship.

As John spoke, the invisible walls that held us back

seemed to vanish, and I got pulled into the magic of his revelation.

It was like a dance, moving between the echoes of what's real and the boundless freedom of dreams, a dance that hinted at exciting possibilities just beyond our awareness.

"Wow," I said, my eyes wide with amazement. "I never knew all this was hidden in our dreams."

He smiled warmly, "Dreams have a way of showing us things we might not see when we're awake."

"Tell me more!" I urged, excited to uncover the secrets of our dream world.

And so, he continued, unraveling the threads of our shared history with each sentence. The more he spoke, the more I felt connected to him, like pieces of a puzzle falling into place. We talked about the adventures we had, the times we stood by each other, and the deep bond that tied us together.

As the dream unfolded, I couldn't help but wonder about the amazing things dreams could reveal.

It was like an unexpected journey through the unexplored corners of our minds, where emotions and memories danced freely.

"I never thought dreams could be so powerful," I said, caught up in the enchantment of it all.

"Sometimes, the most important things are hidden in the places we least expect," he replied, his eyes reflecting the wisdom of our dream-filled adventure.

In the dreamy world, John and I got closer, our breaths mixing as we moved nearer to each other.

The dream made everything feel strange, and the intimate feelings got even stronger. It was like the line between being awake and dreaming didn't really matter.

But, in the middle of all the dreamy happiness, a bit of real life stuck around. Sarah, who was sleeping next to me, had no clue about the secret meeting happening in my dreams. While the dream did its magic, I was caught in a mix of feelings. I couldn't decide if I should stick with the comfy feeling of Sarah's hugs or explore the new feelings John's words brought up. The dream, like a special place for wishes, showed a picture of my emotions. I felt like I was hanging between what I knew and what I hadn't figured out yet.

But I knew that I had to figure out my own feelings.

It was like sailing through the ups and downs of

my heart, stuck between the memories of before and the new things waiting for me when I woke up.

∞

The loud ring of Sarah's phone woke us up, making our peaceful sleep disappear in an instant. Feeling confused and still sleepy, I opened my eyes to the sound of Sarah's urgent voice as she picked up the call.

"Oh no, I'm on my way," she said with wide eyes, a mix of surprise and worry on her face. Suddenly, I was wide awake, sensing the seriousness of the situation, a tight feeling growing in my stomach.

"Sar-ah, what's happening?" I mumbled, still half-asleep. She turned to me, her eyes filled with both fear and determination.

"Amara was attacked in her apartment last night," she said, the words hanging heavy in the air. I felt a shock go through me, freezing me for a moment. Amara, our friend, had been hurt by someone.

Without waiting, a burst of energy surged through me as I got out of bed. Sarah, already half-dressed, told me to hurry. The need to act quickly pushed away the sleepiness, and I found myself getting ready in a rush.

As we hurried along, I asked Sarah, "What

happened to Amara? Is she okay?" Sarah filled me in, her words tense with worry and urgency. We both knew we had to move fast to help our friend.

I quickly put on my clothes, feeling the cold reality sink in. As I tied my shoelaces and put on my watch, my mind raced, thinking about the possible dangers hiding in the shadows.

Sarah, looking anxious but determined, waited by the door for me. Worry lines marked her face, showing how serious the situation was. Without saying anything, we left our safe home, going out into a world where danger was lurking, ready to disrupt the delicate balance we worked so hard to keep.

"Stay close," Sarah said, her voice steady but carrying a hint of concern.

I nodded, feeling the weight of the situation on my shoulders. We walked together, the air tense with uncertainty. The streets, bustling with taxis during other times, now seemed empty, as if holding its breath.

The chilly London air made us shiver as we walked quickly towards Amara's apartment. Our breaths turned into white clouds in front of us, like little ghosts in the early morning. The city was still dark, hiding secrets that whispered about things that could be scary and tricky.

As we walked through the quiet streets, I couldn't stop thinking about what was going to happen. Going to Amara's apartment felt like a big adventure but also kind of scary. The only sounds were faraway noises from the city waking up. It was so quiet that you could feel something heavy and kind of scary in the air, like a big invisible hand holding onto us. Our steps were loud in the quiet, like they were saying, "Hurry, something important is waiting."

We prepared ourselves for whatever we were going to find at Amara's place. It felt like we were going to discover the truth that would break all the things we knew. The truth that would untangle us and take us to a place full of danger where anything could happen. We were getting closer to a big moment where we would have to face the stalker who caused all the trouble and messed up the peace we wanted to keep.

Chapter Fourteen

Just as we turned the corner, a taxi appeared, all empty and ready for us. It was almost the crack of dawn and the city lights mixed together, creating long streaks of colors as our cab zipped through the twisting streets. The air felt super chilly, even though the layers of clothes we had on. Next to me, Sarah held onto my gloved hands tight, her face showing that same worry that was also swirling in my head.

"Mike," she said in a quiet voice. "Do you think Amara's hurt? I can't stop thinking that the worse is yet to come."

I gave her a smile to try and make things better, squeezing her hands with my gloved fingers. "John's with her right now. He knows what to do, Sarah. Amara will be fine."

Our taxi smoothly moved through the maze of buildings until we got to Amara's place, a spot we knew well. When the cab stopped, Sarah and I got out, bundled up in warm coats to shield us from the cold. Walking into the chilly air, we could feel the urgency hanging between us, like a secret we hadn't spoken yet. As we approached the entrance, the sound of our footsteps echoed in the stillness of the night.

"Mike, do you think Amara's gonna be okay?" she whispered to me, her breath visible in the frosty air.

"Yeah, I hope so," I replied, glancing around nervously.

As we stepped into the lobby, the warmth wrapped around us like a snug blanket, a total opposite to the chilly outside. The security guard, who we often saw during our visits, gave us a quick nod. His eyes held a mix of familiarity and curiosity, like he wanted to ask about the day's happenings without saying a word.

Waiting by the elevator, Sarah's hand squeezed mine a bit tighter. "Mike, should we have gone to the police?"

Thinking about it, I felt the heaviness of the situation. "Sarah, we can't just rely on the police. John's got a plan. Let's trust him for now. He knows what he's doing."

The elevator pinged, and the doors slid open, revealing a shiny interior. We hopped in, surrounded by the soft hum of its ascent. Sarah looked at me, concern in her eyes. "I just hope everything will be okay. It's all so strange."

I nodded, understanding her worry. "John's got our backs. We just need to stick together, and everything will work out, you'll see."

As the elevator reached our floor, the doors opened, and we stepped out into the hallway. The air felt a bit tense, but I knew we were in this together. The apartment door was just ahead, and with a determined look, we walked towards it, ready for whatever awaited us inside.

Approaching Amara's apartment, a hush fell over the hallway, and Sarah pulled out the key she gave her. The door creaked open, revealing a dimly lit inside. It was really quiet, except for some faraway sounds of the city.

"Amara?" I called, my words hanging in the air. The apartment looked the same, but there was something quiet and weird about it.

In the living room, where soft lights made everything seem familiar, Amara and John were sitting on the sofa. Sarah hurried over to Amara, her face all worried.

"Amara, are you okay?" Sarah's voice wobbled a bit, her eyes checking Amara's face for any trouble.

Amara, staring off into the distance, nodded. "I'm okay, Sarah. I just... I can't remember much. John found me passed out."

As soon as I walked in and closed the door behind me, John got up from the sofa as if to greet me. His tired eyes looked right at me when I moved towards him.

"Hey Mike, so when I came in, Amara was unconscious on the floor. She can't recall a thing, but she's pretty sure someone was in the house," John shared, speaking in a hushed and serious way.

I checked out the apartment, looking around carefully to see if anything seemed out of place. Everything, though, looked the same, like nothing had happened earlier. I turned to Amara, who seemed a bit scared but still strong.

"Amara, did you see anything strange before you fainted?" I asked, my voice calm but worried.

She shook her head, looking confused. "Nope, not really. It's all kinda fuzzy. But I'm sure someone was here. I just have this feeling, you know?"

A thick quiet filled the room, only interrupted by

the distant sounds of the city. I looked at John, a question on my mind. "Did you check the security cameras? What about the building security?"

John hesitated, glancing at Sarah before speaking. "I wanted to wait for you guys to arrive before I did that. Safety first, you know?"

Understanding his caution, I agreed, "Okay, let's look at the security footage together. Maybe we can see who was here."

I turned to Sarah, wanting to make sure she was comfortable. "Are you okay staying here alone with Amara? We won't be gone for long."

Sarah, looking concerned but determined, reassured me, "I'll stay with her, Mike. Just find out who did this."

Grateful for her support, I followed John out of the apartment. Uncertainty weighed on us as we entered the hallway. It, usually a passage, now held a disconcerting truth – danger could hide within the walls of Amara's safe place.

In the hallway, I asked John, "What do you think we'll find on the security footage?"

"I'm not sure, but it's worth checking. We might catch a clue about who was here," John replied.

As the elevator went down, the lights above us flickered, making shadows jump and dance on the walls. It felt like we were entering a place where surprises were waiting for us at every turn.

John shared something important about finding where Amara's stalker lived. I turned to him, my face showing a mix of surprise and worry. "You figured out where this person lives? How did you do that?"

Looking at me, John seemed strongminded but also a bit tired. "Contacts, Mike. You know how it goes."

I nodded, remembering how John always knew people who could help him. But I felt a bit frustrated. "John, you can't just go in by yourself. What if it's a trap? You should have called the police or told me so we could go together."

John smirked, a familiar and kind of charming look that I hadn't seen in a while. It made my heart skip a beat. "Old habits, Mike."

I shook my head, a bit annoyed but also happy to see him like this. "No excuses. Next time, call me. We're a team."

John gave a playful salute, like he was still in the army. "Got it, Captain. Your orders will be followed, promise."

A giggle slipped out from my mouth, like a little burst of laughter trying to escape the serious air around us.

∞

We were standing in the lobby of the building after the elevator doors opened, all set to uncover the secrets that were waiting for us. The security guard, a tired-looking man with weary eyes, gave us a puzzled look when John told him about what happened at Amara Delacroix's apartment.

"No way," he exclaimed, sounding unsure. "We've got really good security. Nobody can just stroll in without noticing."

John raised an eyebrow, looking serious. "Well, somebody did, my friend. We need to get to the bottom of this mystery."

The security guard scratched his head, still not convinced. "I've been here since last night, and I haven't seen anything unusual."

I nodded, understanding the skepticism. "We appreciate your help. Maybe we can take a look at the security footage together?"

John's face stayed serious, his eyes locked on the security guard. "Let's see what happened last night.

Show us everything."

The security guard, looking a bit scared by the seriousness of the request, took a moment before agreeing. "Okay, come with me."

As we walked through the dark hallways, you could feel the quiet tension in the air. Every step we took seemed to echo the unease that surrounded us.

The door to the security room opened with a squeak, revealing a space filled with screens showing different parts of the building. The security guard struggled with the controls, worry written all over his face.

"Look here," he said, pointing to two screens— one showing the front lobby and the other focused on Amara's floor.

John leaned in, carefully studying the footage for anything unusual. "Let's start from last night, around midnight."

The security guard quickly tapped some buttons, and the screens buzzed to life. The lobby, hushed with occasional residents passing by, had no idea about what was about to happen inside Amara's apartment. John stared intently as the footage sped up, focusing on the screen that displayed Amara's floor. Then, out of the blue, something caught his eye.

A quick, subtle movement, like a shadow dancing in the moonlight. John squinted at the screen, his face tensing. "Pause that."

The security guard did as he was told, freezing the frame just as a mysterious figure appeared outside Amara's door. The room seemed to hold its breath, and the quiet was heavy with the unknown.

"What time is this?" John's words broke the silence.

The security guard stumbled over his words, "Around 3 in the morning."

John nodded, deep in thought. "Did anyone else enter or leave the building around that time?"

The guard scratched his head, "I'm not sure. I can check the other cameras, but it might take a while."

"Take your time," John said, his eyes fixed on the frozen image. The tension in the room was palpable as they waited for more clues to unravel the mystery.

My brain raced, trying to piece everything together. The break-in, Amara being knocked out—it all pointed to this mysterious visitor. John kept staring at the frozen frame, and the room got super quiet. I could see him thinking hard, trying to figure out what was going on.

"That...that guy looks a lot like the one who attacked me at Tesco," John said. His voice had a mix of surprise and anger. The connection between the two things was so clear, like a terrifying story unfolding right in front of us.

I was just as surprised as John. "So, you're saying the person who went after you is also mixed up with what happened to Amara?" It was a lot to take in, and my stomach felt all twisty.

John nodded seriously. "Yeah, it seems that way."

I urged him, "Hey, John, we can't handle all of this by ourselves. We really need to get the police involved. This is way more serious than anything we've dealt with before."

John hesitated for a bit, and you could see the seriousness on his face. After a moment, he said, "Okay, fine. I'll call Ronald. He's the only one I trust, and he'll know what to do in situations like this."

I felt a big sense of relief. "Thanks, John. We can't keep going like this alone. Amara's safety is in danger."

John reached for his phone, dialing his brother's number. While he did that, I thought about all the crazy stuff that had happened since last night.

Things were more intense now, scarier.

But in the middle of it all, our friendship felt super strong. That was the only silver lining.

John spoke quietly on the phone, explaining how urgent things were and connecting the dots between what was happening. While he talked, you could feel a tense feeling in the air, like we were standing on the edge of something really unknown and dangerous.

When the call ended, John looked at me with a determined face. "Ronald's on it. He's going to investigate. Even if we don't totally trust the legal system, Mike, I'm choosing to trust my brother."

And as the weight of involving law enforcement settled in, I couldn't stop thinking about what kind of tough situations and surprising discoveries were ahead of us. It wasn't just about helping Amara anymore; it was about all of us stuck in this tricky web of secrets and lies.

Chapter Fifteen

Back in Amara's apartment, the air felt tense, like when a storm was about to arrive. Mike and I exchanged glances, silently understanding that something important was going to happen.

Sarah, looking worried, suggested, "Maybe we should rent a house or a hotel room to make sure Amara stays safe."

Amara, with a mix of emotions in her eyes, took a moment before saying, "I know a place where I can lay low for a while."

Mike leaned in, his concern etched on his face, "What do you mean, Amara? Is there really a safer place? Where is it?"

There was a quiet moment, like when you hold

your breath. Before Amara could respond, I spoke up, talking quietly, "Maybe you shouldn't say it out loud."

All eyes turned to me, staring me down, as if I had said something wrong. The room suddenly felt like it could hear everything, and I couldn't afford to let our secrets slip out. Amara, her eyes carrying a hint of fear, nodded in agreement. She then turned to Sarah, a trusted friend who had always been there for her.

"Sarah," Amara spoke with urgency, "I need your help packing. We have to move fast."

Sarah, sensing the seriousness in Amara's voice, immediately responded, "Of course, Amara. What's going on? Where are you leaving to, in such a hurry?"

I glanced at both of them, realizing that time was ticking away. "We can't talk here. The walls might have ears. Amara, grab what you need. Essentials only."

As Amara and Sarah went inside Amara's bedroom, Mike stepped forward, his face showing that he had lots of questions. "What are you thinking, John?"

"I don't trust anybody," I admitted, my voice low as it can get, "especially not Sarah."

Mike got really frustrated. "Come on, you're seeing things that aren't there. Sarah's always been there for Amara."

I shook my head, a yucky feeling in my mouth. "Trust is like a luxury we can't afford right now. There's definitely more to all this than we understand."

As we talked, the air felt heavy with tension, like a balloon ready to pop. I could see Mike's eyebrows scrunching together, and I could almost taste the worry in the room. I felt a bit anxious but also curious about what would happen next. I knew very well that I was playing with fire, but I wasn't afraid to get a little burnt.

Mike's eyes blazed like a fiery storm, full of anger and a strong loyalty to his fiancé Sarah, that showed on his face. "You can't push everyone away, John. You just can't," he said firmly.

His words hit me hard, like a truth that stings but needs to be faced. But I couldn't ignore the growing sense that danger hid in the shadows, pretending to be friends by hiding in plain sight. The line between who's with us and who's against us got blurry, making sure that the path ahead was full of surprises, just not the good kind.

But Mike was really upset, and I could tell he was angry. He looked right at me, and it seemed like his frustration was as strong as fire. "Sarah's my fiancée, John. You can't throw accusations about her to my face."

I stared back at him and let out a big sigh. The truth felt heavy, like a heavy weight on my chest. "Mike, Sarah was the only other person who always knew where Amara was. She even has the key to this apartment. She literally knows everything about Amara."

Shaking his head, Mike spoke with a lot of force, "You're crazy, man. Sarah would never—"

"Mike," I said, cutting him off. My voice was steady. "Think about it. She's the common denominator in all of this. The one person with access to everything."

Mike crossed his arms, looking really stubborn. "I don't believe it. Sarah loves Amara, too. She wouldn't do anything like that."

"But Mike," I insisted, "we need to consider everything."

Mike looked away, clearly frustrated. "This is ridiculous. I can't believe you're accusing Sarah."

I could see how upset Mike was, but I couldn't ignore the facts. "But we can't ignore the possibility that Sarah might know more than she's saying."

Mike's face tightened, like a storm brewing in his eyes. "This is crazy. You're saying things about the woman I love without any proof."

I looked at him, my words carrying a heavy weight. "I get it, Mike. But think about it—why didn't you come to see me at the hospital all those years ago?"

His defensiveness flared up, wounded pride in his eyes. "What do you mean? I got hurt too in the blast, in case you forgot."

A bitter chuckle escaped my lips, holding unspoken truths. "Day after day, I lay in that hospital bed, fighting for my life. But somewhere deep inside, I hoped you'd come."

Mike's eyes widened, realization hitting him. "What are you suggesting?"

"Where were you, Mike?" My question hung in the air, a ghost of unspoken words between us. "When I needed you the most, where were you?"

A heavy silence filled the room, more profound than any we'd experienced. The truth, like a shadow, lingered in the spaces between our breaths. Our friendship fractured, and a growing sense of dread filled the air.

As our shattered trust lay scattered, the road ahead became uncertain, a landscape defined by secrets waiting to surface and alliances threatening to crumble.

Mike looked like he was about to share something, but before he could, Amara's bedroom door quietly creaked open. She stepped out, carrying her bag over her shoulder, her face showing a mix of vulnerability.

I hurried to help her with the bag, reminding us that our safety was hanging by the thinnest of threads. "Don't bring your phone, Amara. They might be able to track you."

She looked at me, with uncertainty in her eyes, and handed her phone to Sarah, who was standing beside her. Sarah said with real worry, "Be careful, Amara. Call me if you need anything."

Amara just nodded, and we walked out into the hallway, leaving behind the worries that her apartment was no longer safe for her. The door clicked shut, and all of a sudden, I felt that we were now in a world full uncertainty.

∞

As Amara and I strolled down the quiet hallway, Amara's trust in me and the suspicions about Sarah hung heavily in the air. A shiver ran down my back, and the painful knife injury in my chest served as a reminder about the numerous unanswered questions that persisted.

"Why did Mike leave me that day?" I often

pondered this, trying to make sense of it all. He just disappeared, leaving me to navigate my long recovery alone. It wasn't until fate, in its mysterious way, reunited us after he left the army. We found ourselves in a busy veterans' support group in London. The moment our eyes met, a profound silence enveloped us, louder than any words we could have spoken.

Mike had constructed a new life for himself as a bartender at a local pub, his eyes filled with laughter, a facade of normalcy hiding the scars we both carried. But as I looked back at Amara's apartment building, an eerie feeling lingered – it was as if I were still standing in that desolate desert, with time slipping through my fingers like sand, desperately seeking answers amidst the betrayal and shadows that haunted the landscape.

Amara waved for a taxi, and in a matter of seconds, one pulled up next to us. She looked at me, her eyes filled with all sorts of feelings, and told the driver, "To the train station, please."

I held the door open for her, and it made a squeaky sound, like it didn't want us to leave. We sat in the taxi, and it felt like a bubble of nervousness was all around us. The buildings and streets outside the window went by really fast, like they were watching our story unfold without making any noise.

While we zipped through the twisty-turny streets,

I peeked at Amara. I had so many questions in my head. Where were we headed? What was her big plan? But I didn't ask because I thought talking about it right then might not be a good idea. Plus, I wasn't sure if I was ready to hear about where we were going. There was a good chance that I might change my mind.

The air in the car felt heavy with words we hadn't spoken. I looked out of the window, watching the city lights twinkle like a bunch of colorful stars. My mind was like a jigsaw puzzle, pieces scattered everywhere with memories, regrets, and a strange feeling that wouldn't go away.

We sat in silence, not saying what needed to be said. I thought back to when I talked to Mike, arguing with him about the suspicions floating in my head like shadows. But the truth, it seemed, was a tricky thing. I was still trying to understand that the man I secretly loved might be hiding secrets.

The taxi kept rolling on, each street sign passing by marked another moment in this seemingly never-ending journey. Inside the cab, I couldn't help but wonder if where we were going would bring answers or just more questions. It felt like we were in a hidden bubble, and I questioned if the destination held the key to unlock the secrets woven into the fabric of our pasts.

As we approached the train station, I braced myself for what was coming. It felt like a storm was waiting for us in the place Amara had chosen to seek refuge. I took a deep breath, ready for the secrets to unfold and reveal themselves in the chapters of our shared history.

The taxi grumbled to a stop at the train station, letting out a tired sigh as it finished its trip. Amara and I stepped out into the bustling London train station. It was buzzing with people walking fast and the far-off sounds of announcements about departing trains.

∞

Amara, wearing big sunglasses that covered most of her face, moved smoothly to the ticket counter. She looked like a cat, slinking up to the counter with a quiet kind of grace. The big shades hid her eyes, but even if they didn't, the person behind the counter barely noticed her. They were lost in the usual routine, not paying much attention to us. It felt like a little win, a moment when we became invisible to curious looks.

A gentle tap on my shoulder made me turn towards her, and I joined her as she got our tickets. She pushed her sunglasses down and looked at me, saying, "We have some time before the train arrives. How about we find a nice, quiet place to sit?"

I agreed with a nod, feeling a bit nervous about being in open spaces. "Sure, let's stick to the station.

It's safer that way."

As we walked through the bustling station, the noise of chattering travelers and rushing footsteps surrounded us. We found a cozy corner with cushioned seats, away from the crowd. She sat down and smiled, "This looks perfect. Now we can relax."

I sat next to her, feeling the relief of being in a more secluded spot. "Yeah, it's much better here. So, what should we do to kill time?"

She chuckled, "Well, we could play a game or just chat. What do you feel like doing?"

I thought for a moment, "How about we take a look around?"

As we walked through the crowded concourse, a strange feeling came over me. Everything around us felt different, and yet I couldn't shake off the worry that something might still go wrong. The busy atmosphere and the thought of possible trouble made me feel heavy inside. Amara must have noticed and she looked at me with a worried expression on her face.

"You okay?" she asked, speaking softly.

"Yeah, I'm fine," I replied, trying to sound confident. But underneath, I was feeling a bit uneasy. I looked at the people passing by, all going about their normal lives, unaware of the other things happening around them.

The station was alive with the energy of people rushing around and the sound of announcements in the distance. Amara, the one leading us on this uncertain journey, kept a close eye on everything. At that moment, I realized how our lives were like a delicate balance between staying hidden and being exposed.

In the shadows near the station, we stood, our anticipation building. The minutes seemed to stretch endlessly, each tick of the clock echoing like a drumbeat in the symphony of uncertainty. The quiet before what felt like an approaching storm surrounded us, a fragile moment suspended in the dance of time. While we waited, I couldn't shake the eerie feeling that the journey ahead held secrets waiting to be revealed.

Feeling the tension in the air, Amara tried to lighten the mood with a suggestion. "How about we do a bit of shopping while we wait? It's a good way to pass the time."

Her idea lingered between us, a brief distraction from the heavy silence that had settled over our shared adventure.

I managed a small smile, thankful for the attempt to bring some normalcy into our secretive mission.

"Sure, sounds like a plan."

As we strolled towards the nearby shops, the soft glow of the morning light spilled onto the pavement. Amara nudged me, pointing to a display of colorful candies in the window. "Look at those! Should we grab some snacks for the journey?"

I nodded, feeling a sense of relief as we immersed ourselves in the bright and cheerful atmosphere of the train station. The chatter of people around us, the rustling of shopping bags, and the smell of freshly baked bread created a comforting backdrop. We moved through the aisles, picking up a few treats, and for a moment, the weight of uncertainty lifted. The station's shadows seemed to fade, if only temporarily, as we embraced the ordinary joy of shopping in the midst of our extraordinary journey.

∞

As we wandered through the station's shopping area, other colorful stores caught our attention. They had all sorts of things, from cool trinkets to awesome clothes. Amara, looking really determined, led me into a clothing shop. Inside, it felt so different from the busy station – it was all calm with soft lights and the artificial smell of new clothes.

Amara got busy picking out clothes, running her fingers over them like she was finding comfort in their softness. She looked at me with a playful smile, holding a bunch of stuff. "I thought you could use some new clothes. You didn't pack anything, right?"

I shook my head, feeling really thankful. "Nope, didn't get a chance."

Amara kept on picking out clothes, all focused. She gave me a bunch of them, saying I should change into the new outfit she picked. I hesitated for a bit, checking out the quiet shop. Then, with a little nod, I agreed and went into the dressing area.

Putting on the new clothes, I heard the fabric making a soft sound, like a gentle whisper in the midst of all the craziness around us. It was a simple moment, showing how life can be uncomplicated even when everything else feels chaotic.

When I stepped out wearing the new clothes, it felt like a quiet way of saying that life is always changing.

"Hey, what do you think?" I asked Amara, twirling around a little to show off the outfit.

Looking up from sorting some supplies, she said, "Wow, you look great! It's amazing what a change of clothes can do, huh?"

Grinning, thankful for the distraction, I replied,

"Yeah, it's like a small escape from all the tough stuff."

Nodding thoughtfully, Amara said, "Sometimes, it's the little things that keep us going."

∞

Exiting the store with our bags, we felt a bit lighter, like we were carrying the secret of our adventure with less weight. The happiness from our quick shopping still floated around us, reminding us that even in tough times, we could find moments of normal life. We walked back into the busy station, my new clothes giving me a sort of protection.

Our arms were filled with bags from our unplanned shopping trip, swinging as we strolled through the station. The smell of fresh coffee and the sound of people chatting filled the air. Amara, with her strong determination, guided us to a small store selling sandwich, that was tucked away in a quiet corner.

"Let's grab a quick bite," Amara suggested, and I agreed, looking around for a comfortable spot to sit.

We found a spot at a weathered table, surrounded by the comforting scent of warm bread and tasty fillings. The train station's gentle hum played in the background as we prepared to enjoy our simple meal. Amara, with a friendly grin, unwrapped the sandwiches, offering a moment of calm in the middle of our challenging journey.

My new clothes clung snugly to me, a reminder of the brief break we took to shop for necessities. Amara's eyes sparkled with kindness, showing her strong spirit that went beyond the surface.

I couldn't help but smile, something rare in the midst of our complicated situation. Amara noticed and looked at me with a lingering gaze. "Feeling better?" she asked, her voice like a soft tune.

I nodded, feeling a sense of gratitude growing inside me. "Yeah, thanks to you."

The sandwiches were like a pause button from the hectic events around us. As we enjoyed each bite, an unspoken understanding settled between us—a shared recognition that, even in the midst of chaos, simple moments and connections could still be found.

Between bites of my sandwich, I mustered the courage to bring up something we hadn't talked about before. "I think I might have misunderstood you at the start," I admitted, staring down at the table.

Amara glanced over, her eyes curious. "Really? How?"

I paused, the words lingering for a moment before finally making their way out. "Maybe I shouldn't be so quick to push people away. Maybe I've been too fast to think of others as enemies when they could actually be allies."

A gentle smile appeared on Amara's face, showing that she understood even without saying a word. "I get it," she said, those two simple words carrying the weight of our shared struggles and the promise of a possible friendship.

The busy train station, filled with its own stories, witnessed our quiet conversation. In that moment, as the sun started to set and the station's lights flickered on, I sensed a small change in our journey. The unknown elements were still there, but in the newfound glow of our understanding, the shadows seemed less scary.

∞

Hours later, as our train's departure time got closer, Amara got up from our makeshift meal with a clear purpose in mind. She had a few bags in her hands from our shopping adventure, swinging gently as she led the way through the maze-like hallways of the train station. I followed, paying close attention, my watchful eyes checking for any possible problems. You see, I was playing the role of the not-so-excited bodyguard in this interesting story.

Following Amara, I looked up at the display above

us, flashing different destinations. London to Glasgow—it blinked in big letters. I was surprised, like a sudden plot twist in a spy movie. Glasgow wasn't where I thought Amara would want to go. But then again, I did tell her to keep everything hush-hush, warning her not to spill any details to anyone.

It hit me that Amara really trusted me. Glasgow, with its twisty streets and hidden spots, now set the scene for our story. The sound of footsteps in the distance and announcements echoed around us as we got near the platform. But Amara didn't let the noise bother her. She kept her eyes fixed on the path ahead, determined and focused against the busy station background.

"Come on, we don't want to miss our train!" Amara said, her voice filled with excitement.

"I'm right behind you," I replied, my eyes still scanning the area.

When we reached the platform, Amara checked her watch. "We've got a few minutes."

As we stepped inside the train, my eyes quickly checked out the inside of the carriage. I couldn't help it; it's just something I always do.

The train's engine hummed in anticipation of the journey, and the passengers chatted softly as they settled into their seats. It felt like a cozy bubble of activity, a special place moving through the night and holding the weight of secrets.

Amara took the lead as we made our way to our own special sleeper compartment, a hidden nook that let us have a little privacy from everyone else around us. The little space was all decked out in calm colors and had soft lights, making it feel extra snug compared to the busy train. With a mischievous grin, Amara said, "I figured we could have some time just to ourselves during the trip."

Even though the room was small, it felt like a special place—a safe spot where we could let go of any hidden worries, at least for a little while.

As we stepped inside the train compartment, a gentle hum surrounded us, like a soft lullaby that made everything feel cozy. Amara, with mischievous glints in her eyes, pointed towards the bunk beds in the small space. "Look here, I've got the top bunk all to myself. Thought you might enjoy some extra legroom, being all... strong and stuff."

I couldn't help but let out a laugh, a real one this time, breaking the seriousness of our secret journey. "Strong, huh? I'll take that as a nice thing to say."

With a graceful move, Amara climbed up to the upper bunk, leaving me to settle into the one below.

The train's rhythmic swaying created a calming background as I organized our things in the snug space, thinking about how we were always on the go, never staying in one place for too long.

"So, what's the plan once we get there?" I asked, trying to keep the conversation going. Amara peered down from her bunk, her eyes still full of mischief. "Oh, just wait and see. It's going to be an adventure, that's for sure."

"So, Glasgow it is," I said to Amara, a little amazed. "Any reason you chose this place?"

Amara grinned, "Well, it's got its charm, plus, I thought it would be the last place anyone would think to look for us."

I chuckled, realizing that Amara had thought this through. The train rumbled on, carrying us and our secrets toward Glasgow, a city ready to hold our story in its twists and turns.

∞

From our small beds, a silent understanding passed between Amara and me, like a secret language only we knew. It was as if our tiny sleeping space turned into a magical canvas, where trust and openness painted beautiful pictures, connecting us in the story of the night.

As the train zoomed through the dark night, Amara's voice broke the rhythmic sounds around us. "John, are you feeling okay down there?"

I smiled and nodded, a comforting feeling wrapping around me. It wasn't just because of the thin bed but also because of the understanding we had. In our small sleeping area, the journey turned into a collection of special moments and the excitement of secrets waiting to be uncovered.

"Good," Amara said, her eyes reflecting a kind warmth. "I'm glad you thought of this idea, staying somewhere no one can find me."

I agreed, feeling lucky to share the train ride with someone nice like her. Our words were like brushstrokes on the canvas of the night, creating a picture of friendship and discovery. The train's rhythmic hum joined in, turning our nighttime travel into a melody of connection and companionship. The train zoomed ahead, cutting through the darkness like a flashlight, holding our secrets and the special ties of trust that connected us in the dance of the night.

Chapter Sixteen

Exiting Amara's apartment building, the chilly air clung to my coat. The echoes of our talk still whispered in the London breeze. Amara and John had taken off, leaving us wondering where they'd gone. John emphasized the need for caution, mentioning Amara's stalker might be listening.

Sarah and I exchanged a warm goodbye. "Mike, take care, okay?" she said, giving me a tight hug.

"I will," I replied, holding her close. "Text me when you're home, please."

"Absolutely," she said, smiling. "And promise you'll be cautious too. We don't know what we're dealing with."

"I promise," I assured her. "We'll figure this out

together."

As she stepped away, a brief but meaningful kiss sealed our parting. "See you soon," she whispered before disappearing into the glowing warmth of a passing taxi. I watched until the yellow taillights vanished around a corner, feeling worried about the turn of events.

I walked down the quiet streets, with a feeling of uncertainty bubbled up inside me, even though I looked somewhat calm on the outside. John's mysterious words kept playing in my head, making the peaceful air feel a bit unnerving.

"Why didn't you come to see me at the hospital all those years ago?" His words repeated themselves in my ears.

I couldn't help but wonder, why did he wait for me at the hospital? My steps got faster, not because it was super cold, but because I really wanted to figure out the mystery John had thrown my way.

Thoughts of the past completely took over my mind, reminding me how life can change in just one moment. As I walked alone through the quiet morning, a feeling of fear weighed on me, and memories of a time when John's life was at risk lingered in the air. The memory of helicopters cutting through the night sky rushed into my thoughts. It was the day in the desert when John got lifted by a helicopter, all broken and out cold, and taken to the hospital. I can still see the chaos, the lights flashing, and the distant sirens' hum as I, too, got brought into the medical tent on the field. My injuries were bad, but nothing compared to what happened to John.

As I got my wounds tended to, my mind went back to the time when I thought I might lose John. The picture of him lying so still on that stretcher, looking so weak, it stayed with me like a ghost that often visited me in my dreams. The deep pain of seeing someone you love so close to life and death changed something inside me forever.

I didn't go see John in the hospital, not because I didn't care, but because I needed to protect myself. I couldn't handle the idea of going through that moment all over again. Just thinking about seeing John in a hospital bed, all weak and human, made me feel like the strong walls I built around myself were about to fall apart from that heartbreaking pain.

∞

The pub stood tall up ahead, its familiar shape outlined against the sky that was just starting to light up with the morning sun. I put the key in the door and turned it, and the door swung open. I turned on the lights, but even their warm glow couldn't completely chase away the cold feeling inside me.

Behind the counter, I moved around like a well-oiled machine, doing my usual tasks. Bottles made a little clinking sound, and the coffee machine let out a hiss, breaking the quietness of the place. The fridges softly hummed, and the taps had a rhythmic drip, creating a kind of quiet music. But even with all these sounds, John's words echoed in the room.

"I don't trust anybody, especially not Sarah."

His words hung in the air, like a mist that just wouldn't go away. It made me feel uneasy, like there were tiny claws scratching at the edges of my mind. Trust is like a delicate thing, and the weight of John's suspicion kept bothering me.

As I tackled each task, my thoughts kept wandering back to the mystery that surrounded John Stewart. He used to be my close friend, like a brother, but now he was covered in layers of secrets. The hospital, the helicopters, and the scars on his body were constant reminders of our shared past, but we struggled to talk about it.

∞

In the back office, sitting in front of the computer, I couldn't help but replay John's words over and over in my mind. Sarah, who was always there for me, was now stuck in the middle of his doubts. John's lack of trust cast a shadow over my work, and every tap of the keyboard echoed the silent gap between us.

The truth was bitter, Sarah knew where exactly Amara was. The weight of that responsibility burdened her, and in a way, it burdened me too. It felt like a gentle dance, trying to balance the secrets we held and the need to keep Amara safe from the lurking shadows.

As I waded through the sea of numbers and papers on my desk, my thoughts danced between trust and trickery. John's caution echoed in my mind, a faint breeze hinting at the chance of being let down.

The cozy pub, lit up with gentle lights, shared stories from days gone by as I made my way through the well-known spaces. The air conditioner softly hummed, as if it held hidden whispers, and the smell of old wood and spilled drinks brought back memories as I took my place behind the bar.

As I started my job for the night, my thoughts went back to how it all started – the very first time our paths crossed. It was a busy evening at the pub, full of laughter and the sound of clinking glasses. Among the crowd, a new face caught my attention, and that's when Sarah stepped into my life like a quiet storm.

She sat on a barstool, a solitary figure in the lively chaos around us. Her gentle beauty made me look twice; the kind of charm that unfolds slowly, making you want to explore more. I went up to her, like I always did, wanting to know the ways of my new customers, like the back of my hand.

I asked, "What can I get you?" Our eyes met briefly, creating a small connection.

She replied with a simple "anything you recommend," and the words hung in the air. I liked the challenge. There's something special about those who trust me to make their drink – it always warms my heart.

After thinking for a moment, I handed her a tall glass of cold beer. Her eyes lit up with surprise, and she asked how I knew she liked it. I chuckled, a loud and happy sound that echoed in the busy room.

"I'm just good at this," I said, smiling. "I know what people like to drink."

Her laughter joined the background noise, creating a happy tune that signaled the beginning of a friendship. Little did I realize, in that simple moment, I had started an adventure that would connect our lives in unexpected ways.

"So, what brought you here?" I inquired.

She took a sip, savoring the taste, and then replied,

"I love discovering new spots, and this place seemed inviting. Plus, I've heard they have the best bartender in town."

I couldn't help but blush at the compliment. "Well, you heard right," I joked, "And now that you're here, it just got even better."

Our conversation flowed effortlessly as the night continued. We chatted about favorite books, shared travel stories, and found common interests. The pub's lively atmosphere provided the perfect backdrop for our newfound connection.

The pub, a place where so many tales have unfolded, kept the magic of when we first met. Even though the glasses might look different now and the people here have changed, the memory of how it all started stays with me, like the familiar tune of a favorite song. As I enjoy the beat of the night, the special moments from our past wrap the pub in an intimate feeling.

∞

In the days that came next, me and Sarah got all caught up in a fun guessing game at the pub. We were like dance partners in this silly game, trying to figure out what people wanted to drink, without actually knowing them. Sarah, with a playful sparkle in her eyes, challenged me to see the wishes hidden behind everyone's faces.

As I looked around at all the different people, Sarah quietly watched and grinned. There was this guy in a fancy suit over in the corner – looked like a big-shot businessman. But guess what? He ditched all the fancy stuff and just went for a simple pint of lager. I nudged Sarah and whispered, "Bet he's tired of all those meetings, huh?"

Sarah giggled, "You got that right! Sometimes, all you need is a quiet pint."

Then, we turned our attention to the rowdy gang of friends, making a lot of noise and having a blast. I couldn't help but overhear their laughter. I leaned in to Sarah and said, "Mojitos, huh? Who would've thought?"

Sarah chuckled, "People surprise you, don't they? You never know what someone might enjoy behind all that noise."

We continued our guessing game, weaving in and out of conversations and laughter. It was like we had our own secret language, understanding the unspoken stories of the people around us.

The pub turned into our playground of mysteries, with each sip and each laugh revealing a little more about the folks sharing the space with us.

But when I looked back at Sarah, a mischievous spark twinkled in her eyes. "Mike, what would you pick, if you could order anything, without trying to show off?" she asked.

I thought about it, the thumping sound of the pub creating a lively beat for our quiet talk. "I'd choose a tall glass of you," I said, a sly smile on my face.

Her laughter was like music, blending with the chatter around us. It felt like a special moment, a secret we shared in the midst of the pub's usual evening buzz.

From that day on, Sarah was a regular at the bar. Our talks, once filled with guessing games, turned into shared secrets and a kind of silent understanding. Every time she was about to come, I couldn't help but feel really excited.

I liked calling her "Sarah." It sounded nice and simple, just like our growing friendship. When she walked into the pub, it was like the whole place noticed, like there was a strong connection between us.

As the nights went by, Sarah and I became buddies in this special place, making our stories a part of the pub's history. Among the laughter, the sound of glasses clinking, and all the lively talking, being with Sarah made me feel really good. She became my supportive girlfriend, who showed me there was more to people than just what you see—my fiancé who, without me realizing it, became the center of the unfolding mysteries in our connected lives.

∞

Amidst the rhythmic ebb and flow of patrons, I found myself immersed in a web of my thoughts. The pub, once a bastion of simplicity and shared laughter, now harbored the weight of unspoken revelations. As I wiped down the counters, the echoes of our early days ricocheted through my mind.

Sarah, perched on her familiar barstool, had once confided in me about the disdain she felt for her boss. The lines etched across her forehead betrayed the frustration that festered beneath her composed exterior. In those candid moments, she bared the vulnerabilities that lurked behind her work ethic.

"Why don't you quit?" I had asked, a question woven with the threads of genuine concern.

Her response, delivered with a hint of resignation, had lingered like a shadow in the corners of my memory. "But it's good pay."

She sighed and, looking around to ensure no one was eavesdropping, leaned in to share a secret.

"You know," she whispered, "if I had a choice, I'd get fired. Imagine the freedom! I'd use the severance pay to travel the world, see places I've only dreamed of."

I chuckled, the idea of an adventurous escape tickling my imagination. "That sounds like a wild plan."

Now, standing at that same bar, a quiet hush wrapped around me, almost choking me. I couldn't help but wonder if she just didn't like her job for a little bit or if it was a big problem bothering her all the time. Was her dislike for her boss deeper than she showed? And, really important, were there things John tried to warn me about that were true?

As I looked around at the familiar spots in the pub, questions started spinning in my head like a whirlwind. John's words made me feel like something wasn't quite right, pushing me to uncover the mysteries and figure out what was really going on.

I couldn't help but wonder why Sarah kept working at a job she didn't like. Maybe it wasn't just about getting paid. There was something more, like a secret feeling hiding underneath. It made the pub feel a bit weird, like a note in a song that didn't quite fit.

I sighed and kept doing my job. Glasses clinked, and people talked quietly, making a strange sound in the background. I tried to figure out what was going on, like a mystery I wanted to solve. The truth seemed like a hidden dancer, popping in and out of sight, giving me little hints but not showing itself completely.

As the night went on, the pub got quieter, as if everyone was holding their breath. It felt like the warning John had given about Sarah, could have some truth to it. The possibility hung in the air, like a delicate spiderweb waiting to be uncovered. In that special moment, where secrets felt like they were being whispered all around, I prepared myself for whatever was going to shake up our connected stories.

Chapter Seventeen

The train click-clacked along the tracks, making a comforting sound that filled our sleeper compartment. It was like a song that kept me awake, and the small space we were in was safe enough, but also a bit lonely because of the dim lights.

I lay on the top bunk, and the thin mattress was not very comfy. The train's gentle rocking made me pay attention more, and since I couldn't fall asleep, I looked down at John, who lay on the bunk below.

"Can't sleep?" I asked, talking quietly so we wouldn't disturb the quietness of our compartment.

John, staring at the cabin ceiling, nodded a bit. "Not used to trains," he admitted, his voice sounding a bit strained. It was like he was sharing something he wasn't used to talking about.

I shifted my weight, leaning down a bit from where I was lying to see his face better. "It might feel strange at first," I said, and we both understood the feeling. "Trains have a way of making it hard to sleep."

He looked at me, and we both knew we shared a special connection because of the night train. "So, Glasgow, huh?" he asked, breaking the quiet. "Is that where you're from?"

I nodded, thinking about my hometown, a place with memories that were both happy and sad. "It's not a place I go back to willingly. London is way different—it's a bit crazy, but I can handle it better."

He listened carefully as I spoke, quietly taking in the stories I chose to tell. "You left something behind in Glasgow, didn't you?" he asked kindly, inviting me to share parts of my history that I usually kept hidden.

I grinned sadly. "Maybe I was going towards something, or maybe I was leaving something behind. Either way, I don't really want to go back to Glasgow."

The train kept moving smoothly, its rhythmic sound filling the air with a comforting background noise. In the quiet moments between our words, I couldn't help but wonder if our journey to Glasgow would reveal more than just memories. Maybe it would bring back echoes of my pain, that had been forgotten for a long time, or uncover secrets that had slipped through my fingers.

The city of Glasgow floated in the air, like a quiet mystery waiting to be discovered, but I kept its secrets safe, like a delicate treasure. "Did you live there when you were a kid?" John asked, breaking the quiet and making me face my old memories.

"Yep," I sighed, not wanting to go into my stories that stayed in the narrow paths of the city. "I'd rather not talk about it."

John gave me a little nod, showing that we understood each other without saying a word. He changed the subject smoothly, like a captain steering a ship away from rough waters. "So tell me more about Sarah?" he wondered, genuinely interested. "How long has she been working with you?"

Hearing Sarah's name brought a smile to my face. "A lot of years, more than I can really count," I said, feeling thankful. "She's the one I trust the most."

The train's rhythmic hum matched the flow of our talk, a constant beat underneath our words. In that small space, you could feel the invisible connection between Sarah, John, and me.

It was like a special bond, made strong by keeping secrets and sharing the load together.

Curiosity sparked in John's eyes, and he couldn't help but ask about the recent chaos in our lives. "What about the person who broke in?" he inquired cautiously, "Do you really think someone could have a spare key to your apartment?"

I looked at him, uncertainty showing on my face. "I honestly don't know," I admitted, feeling the weight of suspicion on my shoulders. "But the only person who had a spare key, other than me is Sarah."

John leaned forward, his brows furrowed. "Are you sure Sarah can be trusted?"

I sighed, grappling with the doubt creeping in. "I've known her for years. We've been through thick and thin. I can't imagine her betraying me."

He nodded thoughtfully. "But how do you explain the strange occurrences in your life, then?"

I shrugged, feeling the need to defend my friend. "Maybe it's just coincidence. I don't want to believe Sarah would do something like that."

A contemplative silence settled between us, and John broke it with a sigh. "Look, I get it. Trust is crucial. But we need to consider all possibilities. Maybe we can find some evidence to ease your worries."

As we discussed the situation further, I found

myself torn between loyalty to Sarah and the unsettling feeling that someone might still be watching. But the conversation with John lingered in my mind, and I couldn't shake off the nagging doubts about Sarah.

John looked at me, his eyes steady, silently showing he trusted me. "The only way to prove I'm wrong," he said, "is this secret trip. Sarah doesn't know where we're going, so we'll find out as time goes on."

The train compartment felt tense, like there were things we weren't telling each other. As the train moved ahead, I couldn't shake the feeling that each mile brought us closer to uncovering the secrets of my past and testing the trust between us. The journey wasn't finished, and I got ready for what we would find in Glasgow and the twists in our connected stories.

The train wheels went click-clack, making a rhythmic sound in the quiet sleeper compartment. John's eyes told a story, just like mine. We were both strangers on this train journey, connected by chance, going somewhere we didn't completely get.

I felt a heavy feeling in my chest, thinking about Glasgow. It used to be my safe place, but now, it felt like a bad decision. How could a city that once kept me trapped, now make me feel it's the only safe option left for me? The irony played with the shadows on the walls of our compartment as we lay in the half-dark room.

As the train zoomed through the dark night, memories of my younger self rushed in. Back then, I thought escaping to the city was the answer. London, my first pick, was like an unexpected helper in the ongoing story of my life. But I couldn't quite understand how my past was connected with what was happening now.

The train's gentle shakes matched the rhythm of my jumbled thoughts. Coming back to Glasgow felt like making a deal with fate, a decision that traveled through time, molding the mystery we were now caught up in.

Resting in the quiet compartment, I felt a mix of strange feelings. I kind of wished I never left home, thinking maybe things wouldn't be so dangerous if I stayed. But in my mind, I thought that if I stayed, all the weird stuff happening with my stalker wouldn't have happened. That was far from the truth, because I know what would have happened if I stayed in Glasgow. There was a good chance that I would kill myself or be killed.

∞

The cityscape outside seemed kind of worrisome but also sort of comforting. It made me feel both peaceful and uneasy. But the secrets of my past were like a mysterious song, pulling me closer as the train chugged along.

Amid the thoughts of things I shouldn't have done and the unsure moments, I felt something deep down. The girl who once wanted to run away was now facing her past. In the quiet train compartment, a strong feeling lit up inside me—a sign that big things were about to happen in my childhood town, full of echoes and shadows.

The train, zoomed through the dark night, like a slow metal snake, softly telling us it was almost time to stop. My mind wiggled between dreams and being awake, thinking about Glasgow and the dangerous present, I found myself in. The rhythmic sound of the tracks made me feel all fuzzy, and I started to doze off.

A soft touch woke me up from my dreamy nap. John, standing by my bed, was like a watchful friend getting me ready for what's coming. His eyes were tired from the long trip, but they also had a comforting glow. He whispered, "Amara, we're almost there."

I rubbed my eyes to clear away the sleepiness, and I could see the excitement on John's face. Getting out of my top bunk was a bit tricky, and I felt a bit sleepy still, like I didn't want to leave.

John put his strong arms around me to help me balance as I stepped down. His touch felt protective and close, making me feel all tingly inside. I smiled secretly, like we had a special understanding without saying anything. I knew that our journey together was becoming more than just something we had to do.

As he gently let me down on the floor, I held on to his arms without even thinking. It was a bit surprising how close we were for a moment, like a warm feeling that hung between us. I looked away, pretending to be a little shy, as if my eyes could give away the things I was feeling for him.

The train slowed down, acting like a big, well-behaved animal following our wishes. Glasgow, a city full of stories and hidden tales, was right outside our compartment. I peeked at John, and his eyes showed he was excited than I was. This journey, like a dangerous adventure, brought us to the edge of finding out something important. Is Sarah behind it all?

But in our tiny sleeper compartment, I held tight to the connection I formed with my bodyguard, knowing that Glasgow was not only a place from my past but also where the next part of our story was waiting to unfold.

The train took its last deep breath and stopped, making a sound like a big metal sigh that meant our journey had finished. Our compartment, once full of secrets and late night conversations, opened its doors, letting us step out into the chilly morning in Glasgow. The city was there, covered in a soft mist that hid its mysteries, ready for us to discover.

As we stepped off the train, the cool breeze greeted us, feeling like an old friend. Glasgow, bathed in the soft hues of dawn, showed itself as a city full of surprises. People's breath hung in the chilly air, making us shiver a bit.

∞

Navigating through the bustling train station, John and I were surrounded by a sea of faces lost in their own stories. The cold found its way through the seams of my coat, reminding me that Glasgow's embrace wasn't always warm. In the hush before the city woke up, I waved down a taxi, its black color standing out against the muted morning tones.

"Hey, we're heading to 23 Maple Street," I said to the taxi driver, giving John a reassuring glance that the ride would be quick.

"Sure thing lassie, hop in!" replied the friendly driver.

John's eyes flickered with a touch of anxiety as he peered out of the taxi window at the unfamiliar sights.

"Are we almost there?" he asked, his voice a bit shaky.

"Yeah, don't worry, it's just a short ride," I

reassured him, trying to ease his nerves.

As the taxi rolled through the waking city, John glanced around with wide eyes. "Glasgow looks different than I imagined," he remarked.

"It's a city of surprises," I replied with a smile. "Wait till you see it fully awake."

The taxi rolled along, and as I peeked out the window, I saw a city filled with gray buildings, bumpy streets, and hidden stories tucked away in its tricky alleys. We drove through the streets that were just starting to wake up, but a weird feeling settled in my chest, making me feel kind of uneasy. I wondered, what was I dragging John into?

The city was like a giant puzzle of memories and mysteries, and each turn of the taxi made me feel like something scary from my past was about to jump out.

John, sitting next to me, seemed to feel the same way. His eyes were glued to the outside, looking at the changing scenes. I tried to distract myself by looking at the city, but I couldn't help gripping the seat's edge a bit tight. Glasgow, where I grew up, was now unfolding before us.

It was like a mix of memories and puzzles, and with every block we passed, it felt like my past was creeping up on us.

Finally, the taxi stopped, and I paid the driver. We found ourselves stepping out, in front of the house where I grew up, and it felt like we were standing at the entrance of a big mystery. The journey had led us right to the door of something unknown. In the quiet of the early morning in Glasgow, it felt like the whole city was holding its breath, waiting for the secrets hidden between the familiar streets to come out.

My childhood home, felt like a treasure chest full of memories worn down by time and being a bit forgotten. The outside of the house used to be full of bright colors, but now, the paint was peeling off, telling stories of a time long ago. The windows, once full of life, now looked empty, like they've seen a lot of years go by and the quiet decay that comes with it.

We walked on the bumpy path leading to the front door, the stones making noise as we stepped on them. The front door, like an old guard protecting a place of forgotten sounds, opened slowly, just like how I felt inside. When we went in, the air smelled heavy with all the years that had passed, like a mix of old memories and things left behind.

The living room, where I used to laugh and play, looked frozen in time. Specks of dust were floating around in the faint sunlight, making it feel like a dream. The furniture, covered in old sheets, showed the marks of time - scratches from when I used to play around and the weight of secrets I hid in that house.

As I walked through the dark halls, memories popped up in my mind every time the floorboards squeaked beneath me. The rooms, which used to be full of life, now felt empty. On the wall hung an old family picture- me, my dad and my mom. Everyone in it looked happy, but you could tell things weren't perfect.

The kitchen, once a spot where delicious aromas filled the air, now only smelled like no one had been there for ages. Spiderwebs hung in the corners like silent ghosts, and the tap made a sad drip-drop sound, making everything feel lonely.

I climbed the stairs, noticing the walls in the hallway. They were like a history book telling the story of a family of three- that used to live here. Little pencil marks showed how tall I grew, until when my mother passed away. The bedrooms, once full of dreams and secrets, now stood quiet, like they were keeping some old stories to themselves.

The house where I spent my childhood was kind of like an empty treasure chest, holding memories that slip away like sand. The walls, even though they looked a bit worn, hid secrets underneath. In the quiet, I felt like there were ghosts around—soft laughs, sounds of arguments, and a gentle hum of a mother's love that used to fill every corner of these rooms.

In the middle of the quiet, empty house, a

strong feeling of wanting filled me up. Even though the house looked old and left alone, it held bits of a story that really wanted to be shared. Inside the quiet halls of where I grew up, I got ready for the answers to questions that have been hanging around for way too long.

The air inside felt still, like it was holding onto memories. It wrapped around me like a heavy blanket as we stood in the silent halls of my childhood home. I looked at John, and his eyes showed that he felt the seriousness of the moment too.

"We should clean up a bit," I said quietly, knowing there was work to be done.

John looked around the rooms, noticing the cobwebs that stuck to the corners like forgotten dreams. His nod said a lot without words—an understanding that we needed to clear not just the physical cobwebs but also the ones tied to our feelings.

Taking on the task of clearing away the layers of neglect felt like making a promise to face the ghosts that lived in these walls. The broom, a useful tool and a symbol at the same time, became more than just something to clean with; it turned into a magic wand to whisk away not only the dust but also the whispers of the past clinging to every corner.

As we walked moved into the forgotten spaces,

the sound of the broom going back and forth created a sort of song in the quiet house. The dust seemed to get a little upset, twirling around in the sunlight like tiny bits of memories. Even though the rooms were still a bit tired, they started to shake off the feeling of being left behind.

With every sweep, it felt like the weight of the past was lifting off my shoulders. Cleaning became a special kind of ritual, like giving a gift to the house that had seen good times and sad ones too. John, my quiet bodyguard on this adventure, tackled the job with a calm determination. His presence felt like a strong anchor in the midst of the dust and memories.

As we worked hard, the sunlight poured in through the open windows, making the place look alive and warm. The air, once kind of smelly from being ignored, started to smell fresh again, like a promise of new beginnings.

Cleaning the house, both with our hands and in a way that makes it feel good inside, became like a special routine. It was like we were on a journey to bring the house back to life and also put together the pieces of its history that got scattered. In the quiet changes, I could feel a little comfort, like the house saying it's okay to fix things up and leave the old feelings behind.

With my bodyguard, John by my side, we started fixing up a home that had been through a lot over the years. The sounds of us cleaning mixed with the creaks of the floor, showing how strong the house and our hearts were.

Chapter Eighteen

The late night in London hugged my tired body as I stepped into my apartment, a small place I rent with the salary I make as a police sergeant. The light from street lamps peeked through the curtains, making my old furniture look a bit shiny in my quiet space where I lived alone.

Working the graveyard shift had left its mark on my face, creating shadows under my eyes that tell stories like the whispers in the corners and alleys of London. All around me, the city was like a big, sleepy orchestra, singing a quiet song to a world that doesn't know about the hidden shadows.

For a long time, I've been pursuing this big dream of becoming an inspector. It's like trying to catch a tricky ghost that's always slipping away from my grasp. Tonight feels different, though. It's like my dream is right there, almost like it's tied to this stalker case I've been working on non-stop. The key to my promotion? An actress named Amara Delacroix. Her name is famous, whispered about, and shines like a bright star.

I take off my wrinkled police uniform, feeling super tired. This case has become my secret obsession. It's like a big puzzle, but the pieces just won't fit together.

Even though I'm in the middle of this storm, the rest of the world doesn't have a clue. They think their favorite actress Amara Delacroix was just taking a break, disappearing from everyone's social media feed, like a ghost.

I stood inside my bedroom, looking at my crime board with pictures, times, and places all mixed up like a puzzle. It was the puzzle of Amara's secret stalker, someone we couldn't see but who was always following her. My stomach felt funny, like a twisty knot, telling me that solving this case would help me get the promotion that I wanted.

I sank into my old armchair, and the morning light outside peeked through my curtains, making everything a bit brighter. The light shined on the hidden stories happening in the quiet parts of my crime board. While everyone else in London went on with their lives, I held onto Amara Delacroix's secret, a story that was going to unfold when the sun finally came up.

My phone buzzed on the side-table, snapping me out of my quiet thinking time. It was a text from Vanessa, my on-again-off-again girl. She knows me really well, and she's always got some drama going on.

"Hey Ronald, want to do something fun?"

I grabbed my phone, and its soft glow lit up her message. The idea of hanging out with Vanessa crossed my mind, making the heaviness of the previous night disappear. Our friendship is a mix of excitement and arguments, but she's my go-to person when things get tough.

"Sure, can't say no to your fun. Let's meet at our spot in an hour?"

She replied super-fast, adding a bunch of emojis to show how pumped she was. "Awesome! Can't wait, Ron. I'm in desperate need for some juicy gossip."

Our special place, a quiet cafe tucked away from busy eyes, called out to us like a secret hideout for friends wrapped in mysteries. I really wanted to spend some quality time with Vanessa, a break from the crime that always followed me around.

The gentle buzz of the cafe surrounded us like a secret meeting place. Vanessa, with her flowing curls and a mischievous sparkle in her eyes, smoothly sat down across from me. The smell of fresh coffee mixed with the stories we shared.

"Ronny, spill the beans," she smiled, the excitement for juicy news showing in the curve of her lips.

I leaned in, speaking in a quiet, secretive tone. "Amara Delacroix, the actress taking a break? Turns out, it's just a cover-up. She's got a mad stalker, and the media hasn't caught wind of it yet."

Vanessa's eyes widened, the thrill of a big story filling the air. "No way! This is huge. Why haven't I heard about it?"

"That's the tricky part." I lowered my voice again. "The whole thing is under wraps. If I can solve it, I might get promoted to inspector."

She leaned back, her eyes fixed on my face. "You've found a real landmine, Ronald."

Our conversation flowed, bouncing back and forth like a playful game of catch. Vanessa, with her sharp wit, added humor to the mix. "Ronny, imagine you're like a detective from those movies. What's your next move?"

I chuckled, enjoying the banter. "Well, first, I'm thinking undercover. Maybe pose as a waiter at the fancy restaurant she frequents. Get closer without raising suspicions."

Vanessa raised an eyebrow, a smirk playing on her lips. "Smooth, Ronny. Like James Bond with a coffee pot."

We both laughed, the air filled with the warmth of shared secrets. As we chatted, I couldn't help but notice how Vanessa looked—confident and stylish. Her outfit, a mix of casual and chic, highlighted her curves in all the right ways. The sunlight streaming through the cafe window caught the subtle sparkle of her earrings, adding an extra touch of allure.

And so, our conversation continued, as Vanessa's laughter echoed through the cafe, turning our secret meeting into a haven of joy.

As the evening unfolded, our giggles mixed with the soft whispers of secrets, and the cozy cafe turned into a special place for two hearts caught up in a dance of love, danger, and hidden stories. The city, busy with its own business, had no idea about our secret talks. It held its breath, not knowing about the mysterious plans being woven in the dimly lit corners—stories that were about to become public, all in the search for truth.

∞

The night hugged the city in a gentle embrace while Vanessa and I strolled through the dimly lit streets. It was like a maze of secrets, just like our own little world. The cool breeze passed through the narrow alleys, carrying with it the soft laughter of the city's night creatures.

Vanessa's apartment, a cozy place she shared with three friends, was a mix of different styles and colorful personalities. The door made a creaky sound as it opened, revealing a place filled with shared secrets and the joy of whispered conversations. We tiptoed through the living room where a TV played quietly, and laughter came from the shared space.

We continued our stealthy walk through the apartment, the night casting its magical spell. The sweet smell of vanilla candles lingered in the air, tempting us toward Vanessa's bedroom, our secret sanctuary.

"Whew, that was close," Vanessa whispered as we entered her room.

I chuckled, "Yeah, your roommates can't find out about your dirty little secret. Me."

As we closed the door behind us, the noise of the world outside faded, leaving us in Vanessa's enchanting room. Fairy lights adorned the walls, creating a warm atmosphere that embraced us like an intimate hideaway.

Vanessa winked, "Sorry, baby, you're my top-secret mission tonight. No one can know about us."

As I removed my jacket and took a seat on her bed, I couldn't help but ask, "So what's going to happen to me tonight, secret agent Vanessa?"

She grinned, "We solve the mystery of how sexy you are. You in?"

I nodded, "Fuck yeah! Get over here."

She strutted over, her hips swaying in a hypnotic rhythm. With every step, her body became more enticing. The curves of her breasts and ass were accentuated by the tight clothes she wore. As she moved, her dark hair danced around her, framing her face and highlighting her deep brown eyes.

She lowered herself on my lap, her body pressed against mine, and the warmth of her skin made me feel alive. She smelled like vanilla and a hint of jasmine, her signature scent.

She leaned in, her lips grazing mine. "Ready to be my dirty boy?"

I nodded, not able to speak, the moment so surreal. Every time I had sex with her, it was different.

"Good. Now let's get these clothes off," she said, her voice dripping with seduction as she unbuttoned my shirt.

Her fingers brushed against my bare chest, sending chills down my spine. She helped me take off my shirt, her touch like a whisper on my skin. The cool air of her room was a welcome relief to the heat that was rising within me.

"Mm... now let's get these fuckin' pants off," she murmured, her hands teasingly unzipping my jeans.

Her body was close to mine, and the tension between us was electric. The feeling of her breasts against my bare chest was exhilarating.

"Vanessa," I breathed, unable to contain myself any longer.

"Hush," she shushed me. "Now, tell me everything about this stalker."

I chuckled, feeling the excitement in the air. "Okay, listen. Amara Delacroix's stalker is like a ghost. No social media trace, nothing."

Vanessa bit her lip, a mix of thrill and concern in her eyes. "Oh Ron, this could be you big break or downfall."

"Vanessa, I need evidence," I said, in between kissing her. "But this guy is good. He's covered his tracks well."

Vanessa nodded, as she began to undress herself. "Well you dig deeper. Do what you're fuckin' good at."

I looked at her beautiful body, the curves of her hips and the soft swell of her breasts, and couldn't help but reach out and touch her. My fingers trailed along her smooth body, eliciting a moan from her lips.

"Ron, when you solve this case, promise me I'll be the first to know," Vanessa urged, her eyes earnest.

"I promise, Vanessa," I assured, kissing her soft lips and sealing our pact. She smiled and then pushed me on the bed.

It wasn't long before she took the lead and lowered her naked self on to me. That was what I wanted, and she knew exactly how to move her hips. She was riding me hard and fast, her body writhing on top of mine. I was entranced by her, her dark hair flowing around her face, her full lips parted as she gasped for air.

As we moved together, the world around us melted away. All that mattered was this moment, this feeling of being joined as one. We were lost in our own secret world, the night sky the only witness to our passionate encounter.

Vanessa's soft moans grew louder as she came, her body shuddering as she rode the waves of her orgasm. I could feel her muscles contracting around me, sending me over the edge as well.

"That was fucking hot," I murmured, holding her tight as we came down from our high.

She chuckled, "I know. I'm so fucking wet."

I pulled her closer, breathing in her intoxicating scent. The room was filled with the sounds of our heavy breaths, and the night felt endless.

Chapter Nineteen

The clock on the wall was making its loud noise, tick-tock, tick-tock, and it felt like it was getting louder as time passed. I was by myself in the not-so-bright room, sitting with my laptop that lit up the space like a secret mission headquarters. I really wanted to figure things out.

The air felt kind of hot, and it was like the room itself knew that I was getting more and more worried. Outside, the streetlights made really long shadows that played on the walls like they were dancing. It made the regular night in the neighborhood seem a bit strange. I felt something heavy in the air, like an anxious feeling, and it matched the heavy feeling in my chest.

Mike was supposed to be home from work already, but the house stayed silent, making my concerns even bigger. Questions swirled in my head, twisting my thoughts into a maze of worry. What if something went wrong? What if they were in danger? I couldn't shake the feeling of unease.

I sat at my laptop, clicking through folders and files, desperately searching for any clue about where Amara could be. It felt like a puzzle, and each piece of information was a potential answer to the mystery of her sudden disappearance. The worry gnawed at me, like a doubt that just wouldn't go away.

The last time I saw Amara at her apartment, something strange happened. She said a mysterious goodbye, before she left to go on a secret trip with John, her bodyguard. They disappeared without leaving a single clue. A weird feeling made my stomach feel funny. I had no way of contacting her, and I had no idea if they were safe. I nervously tapped my phone, sending a message to John.

"Hey John, it's Sarah. Where are you guys? We're getting worried. Please, just tell us you're okay."

As time went on, my worry grew. It felt like a scary mix of fear and uncertainty about what was going on.

The oven in the kitchen hummed in the background, as if it was teasing me for not being able to solve the mystery of where Amara and John went. The air felt heavy with suspense, just like the curious thoughts bouncing around in my head.

In the kitchen, where only the delicious smell of roasting chicken fills the air, I'm holding on to a special hope. It's like I'm trying to solve a riddle and bring Amara and John back from the darkness that's trying to swallow them up.

The front door made a squeaky sound, and I felt so much better when it opened. Mike came in, and I could see he was tired from a long day of work. His face showed all the hard work he'd done. It was like he brought calm into our home after a day full of worries.

"Hey," he said in a comforting way, his voice making me feel better. He walked into the room, and it seemed like he was leaving all the tough stuff outside.

∞

There was dinner on the table – just simple roasted chicken, but it smelled so good. The delightful smell floated in the air, making everything feel better. We sat down, and the quietness of our home surrounded us. Candles were lit, casting a soft light like little guards protecting us from the dark worries of the day.

The clatter of forks and knives echoed in the quiet room as Mike sliced into the juicy chicken. His eyes, usually warm and full of life, now hinted at a deeper thoughtfulness. Watching him, I could sense a heaviness in his heart, a weight he carried without saying a word.

"You seemed quieter today," I mentioned, my words carefully feeling the air between us.

Mike looked at me, a small hint of vulnerability in his eyes. "Just got a lot on my mind, Sarah. Work's been... tough."

I nodded, understanding the challenges that came with his job. His mental load often lingered long after he left the bar. In the morning, I'd see a tired version of the man I fell in love with. Our eyes met, and in that moment, we shared unspoken feelings—recognition, understanding, and a silent promise to face the complexities of the night together.

The taste of the roasted chicken, a labor of love and distraction, lingered on our tongues. Yet, beneath the facade of culinary delights, an unopened can of questions and worries wove itself into the space of our shared silence.

The warm candlelight wrapped around the table, making feel like a comfortable spot where secrets can be told. So, I gently put my fork down, and the emptiness seemed louder in the quiet room.

It's as if the sound carried the heaviness of the things we haven't talked about yet. "Mike," I said softly, my voice making a small sound in the quiet room, "do you think Amara and John are okay? I tried texting John, but he hasn't replied. I'm just worried—"

Mike looked up from his mashed potatoes, meeting my eyes with a careful gaze. "Sarah, it's been a long day. Work's been—"

He stopped talking, like a shield of tiredness and thinking too much built up between us. I looked at him, the lines on his face showing stories of battles fought beyond our safe place. Underneath, worry and frustration stirred, trying to break through the wall of toughness he put up.

"I know, Mike," I whispered, my voice sounding serious. "I just can't shake this feeling, you know? Something's not right."

He nodded, silently saying he understood my worries. But tiredness in his eyes showed he had his own struggle, not just with work, but with thoughts too.

"Just let them be, Sarah," he comforted, his words sounding real. "Amara needs this, to be away from her stalker. And John is there to protect her."

I agreed with a nod, feeling the worry ball up in my stomach. Even though Mike tried to make me feel better, the unsure shadows stayed in my mind. Unanswered questions danced in the candlelight, just out of my grasp.

After a moment, Mike sighed and put down his fork. "You know, John and Amara are tough. They can handle themselves. And they've got each other's backs."

I fidgeted with my napkin, twisting it in my hands. "I guess you're right, but what if something happened? What if they need help?"

Mike reached across the table, giving my hand a reassuring squeeze. "Sarah, we've got to trust them. They're strong, and they'll reach out if they need anything. We can't let worry eat us up."

I nodded, appreciating his attempt to ease my fears. Still, the minutes ticked by like slow heartbeats, each one adding weight to the uncertainty in the room.

Finally, breaking the silence, Mike said, "Let's just finish our dinner. Maybe after a good night's sleep, things will look better in the morning."

I managed a small smile, grateful for his comforting words.

We continued eating, but the shadows of worry lingered, casting a quiet spell over our evening. Dinner went on with the soft sounds of forks and knives gently tapping against plates, and hushed talking floating around like whispers. It felt like there were things we wanted to say but couldn't, hanging in the air like a storm about to happen. After we finished eating, I took away the dishes, and they made a clinking noise, kind of like an odd song playing along with the worries we weren't saying out loud.

As the evening went by, we both felt a bit better in the quiet. It was like a break from all the things bothering us that we didn't talk about. But if you listened closely, there were still quiet questions buzzing beneath the calm, hiding in the spaces between our shared quiet moments.

The clock on the wall ticks, making its steady sound, telling us that time is passing. Mike pushes his chair back with a tired sigh. The dinner plates are gone, but the smell of roasted chicken still floated around, and there are questions in the air, like awkward ghosts.

"I'm going to bed early tonight," Mike says, his voice quiet, like a secret hanging in the room. It disappears into the air, like a mystery that we don't understand.

I look at Mike, noticing the tired lines on his face. "Are you alright?" I ask, concerned.

He doesn't respond, just stares into the distance, lost in his thoughts. The silence stretches between us, like a big question mark in the room. I try again, "Mike, what's going on?"

He blinks, as if waking up from a dream. "I'll be fine. I just need some sleep," he finally says, his words heavy with something he's not sharing.

My eyes widened with surprise, and for a moment, the worry in my eyes took a break. It wasn't what he said that made me jump a little; it was what he didn't do – his usual bedtime routine that left me standing in the quiet dining room, feeling a bit puzzled.

He came closer, and instead of our usual goodnight tradition, he quickly kissed my cheek. Normally, it would be a sweet and familiar thing, but this time, it felt different, like a change in the routine that made everything feel weird.

His lips stayed on my cheek a bit longer than they usually did before he pulled back. It left me feeling a bit uneasy. I stared at him, trying to figure out what was going on underneath that calm surface of his face.

"Goodnight, Sarah," he whispered, his words barely audible in the quiet of the night.

"Goodnight," I replied, the word hanging in the air between us like a question that nobody asked out loud.

After Mike went inside the bedroom, I stayed sitting at the dining table. The lamp gave off a soft light, making long shadows that matched the confusion in my mind. I could tell that something had changed— a small shift in how we usually do things together.

Lots of questions filled my head, all wanting answers. It felt like Mike had his own worries, hidden behind his tired look and unsaid troubles.

I let out a big sigh, looking around the room. The shadows from the lamp were like playful tricks, dancing on the edges of what I could see. The night kept its secrets, and as I thought about why Mike left, a feeling of something bad coming settled over me, like a big dark blanket.

In the quiet that followed, while the night kept its mysteries outside the windows, I started thinking about the things we both worried about. The uncertain shadows of the night seemed to become a part of our worries, making everything that were once familiar feel strange.

Chapter Twenty

When I opened the creaky door, time seemed to stand still in Amara's childhood bedroom. It was like an abandoned place that nobody had visited for a long, long time. Dusty and quiet, the room told stories of Amara's years of growing-up.

As my feet tiptoed over the threshold, memories started to wake up, whispering tales in the still air. The sunlight played peek-a-boo through curtains that had seen better days, painting soft pictures on the pale walls. The wallpaper looked like it had a bunch of old secrets, echoes from Amara's younger days.

I was curious about the secrecies hidden in this room, wondering what kind of stories were tucked away in the chipped paint and worn-out wooden floor. My hand gently brushed the dusty top of a vintage dressing table. It held treasures from the past - little things and makeup that seemed to have taken a long nap. The smell of dusty powder hung in the air as I picked up a framed photo.

In the picture, a younger Amara smiled like a ray of sunshine, her innocence shining through. I could almost feel the room holding onto her memories, like a blast from the past.

The creaky wooden floor complained softly as I tiptoed through the room, my curiosity leading the way. A tired teddy bear slumped in the corner, quietly holding onto the secrets of many years. On the messy desk, an old diary waited, its pages telling stories of dreams never shared and secrets never whispered.

The room was so quiet, like it was holding onto stories from a long time ago. I wondered what hidden tales were kept in Amara's past, covered by the dusty memories of days gone by. I wanted to solve the puzzle of the girl who used to think of this room as her special place.

Carefully, I wiped away the dusty layers, revealing bits and pieces of a life filled with bravery and quiet rebellion. The room itself seemed to remember the sound of Amara's laughter and the shadows of her tears, telling a story that unfolded like a woven quilt.

As I cleaned up the room, it felt like I was watching a dance between her soft side and her strong side. The air held a mix of feelings, like a song that was both happy and sad. It was as if the room held secrets from Amara's life that were waiting to be told. Even though I tried to understand Amara better, it seemed like I was only beginning to discover the first parts of a story that was as detailed as the tiny specks of dust floating in the sunlight.

As I struggled with these thoughts, Amara appeared at the doorway. She looked strong and a bit fragile at the same time. Her eyes were like secret-filled pools, and she gave me a small, unsure smile.

"John, should we get some things for the house? We'll be staying here for a bit," Amara suggested, breaking the heavy silence.

"Yeah, that's a good idea," I replied, grateful for the distraction.

As we walked into the quaint town, the narrow streets whispered tales of their own. Amara glanced around, her eyes curious. "I wonder if there's a local store nearby. I can't seem to remember if they had one back in the day."

I nodded, "Most likely, there will be at least one in every town."

We strolled through the icy cobblestone streets of the small town, it felt like the stones themselves were telling stories from a long time ago. Amara had her sweater's hoodie pulled down low, looking cautious, like she didn't want anyone to notice her. The town, though, just kept going about its day like we weren't even there.

∞

We walked into the local market to pick up things we needed. Amara's eyes were moving quickly, like she was trying to be sneaky, the opposite of how she was back in London. I felt this strong need to protect her, and I promised myself to keep her safe from curious eyes.

While we were browsing the shelves, I whispered to Amara, "Are you doing okay?"

She nodded, but I could see a hint of worry in her eyes. "Just didn't think I'd be back here, you know?"

I understood. "Yeah, it's kind of unexpected. But we'll get what we need and get out of here soon."

In a matter of minutes, we left the shop, and the cool air outside welcomed us. "I honestly never thought that I'd ever come back here," Amara said quietly, her words carried away by the wind.

"Yeah, I get that," I replied, surprised to find myself in Amara's childhood town. "But it's good that you chose Glasgow to hide out. No one will find you here."

Our steps matched each other, like we both understood something without saying it out loud. The town, with its history and quiet secrets, seemed to wrap its charm around us.

As we continued walking, Amara broke the silence. "Do you ever think about, how life could have been different? Had you made different choices?"

I nodded, "Yeah, sometimes. But what's important is that we're here now, together. You're not alone, Amara."

She smiled, tugged her hoodie down, like a quiet wish for the town not to notice her back. Shadows stuck to her eyes, and I couldn't help but think about the secrets written on her face.

Right then, I felt that the small town was slowly turning into a safe place—a setting for the gentle dance of two souls tangled in a complicated story. As we strolled, I couldn't shake the feeling that the town, with its old streets and worn-out fronts, held the answer to figuring out Amara's past.

And as the sun went down, it painted the town with its final warmness, when we headed back to Amara's house. The air smelled like old memories mixed with a touch of unsure feelings, pulling us into a place where past moments linger.

"I'll make us some dinner," I said, trying to bring a sense of regularity to the quiet atmosphere. Amara just nodded, showing her thanks without saying a word.

∞

Once I was inside the dimly lit kitchen, I checked out our small stash of food—cans neatly stacked on the shelves, almost like a treasure trove for survival champs. The old fridge, now sat silent, making the possibility of storing any fresh produce, feel like a far-off dream.

As I looked at our options, it hit me—we were making our evening meal out of canned wonders and the basics of staying alive. But here in the calm kitchen, something special was happening—we were both working together to make a little home out of the bits and pieces of the past.

Amara quietly watched me, her eyes like a mystery as they followed every move I made. A small, almost invisible smile played on her lips, telling me without words that our pantry, with its options, didn't matter much.

What really held us tight was the strong bond of

strength we shared.

Amara observed my cooking silently for a moment, then curiosity lit up her eyes like stars in the night sky.

"How did you learn to cook like this?" she asked, her voice carrying a gentle wonder.

I grinned, flipping a spatula in the air before catching it skillfully. "Well, it's a skill soldiers pick up out there in the field," I explained. "You know, making meals out of dehydrated stuff and whatever you can find."

Her eyebrows lifted, impressed. "So a soldier and a chef, huh? That's pretty cool."

I chuckled, memories flooding back. "Yeah, it's not as glamorous as it sounds. I remember always saving my dessert for my buddy, Mike. Those were some rough times we had, where we were deployed together."

Amara's eyes softened, understanding the weight of those memories. "Sounds tough, but you're doing great now. And who would've thought canned veggies could become a feast?"

I shrugged, a touch of pride in my voice. "Adaptation, my dear. Sometimes you just make the best out of what you have."

As I cooked, the sound of canned veggies hitting the hot pan filled the air. It was like a simple concert, singing the story of dinners made up on the spot and the secret connection we shared. The metallic smell of the cans mixed with the herby fragrance, creating a special smell that painted a picture of how we adapted and stuck together to survive.

∞

I set our simple dinner on the kitchen table, and when I looked at Amara, I saw something in her eyes. It was like she was thinking about how our meal, which wasn't fancy, was connected to all the feelings we had. I didn't want to let her know that I too felt the same.

As we started eating, it was like we were having a secret conversation with our food. The flavors mixed together, and even though it wasn't that tasty, it felt like we were enjoying a warm meal. The old stuff that bothered us seemed to go away, at least for a little while. We enjoyed the food, and it was more than just filling our stomachs – it was like we were feeding this new connection we were building in that little kitchen.

There, the past and the present came together, kind of like a dance between making it through tough times and having hope for what lay ahead.

The last glows of our simple dinner flickered away, leaving behind the bits and pieces of our humble feast. Amara, shaped like a shadow in the dim light, vanished into the corners of the house. The floor squeaked under her steps, a kind of ghostly sound that announced her return, carrying the weight of some newfound knowledge.

She held an old bottle in her hands—a thing from a time long ago, its edges worn by the years. The amber liquid inside hinted at a history of enjoying life and escaping from it.

The air, heavy with the smell of old wood and the hushed whispers of forgotten stories, seemed to stop breathing as Amara stepped into the soft glow of the fire-lit living room. She gave me the bottle with a shy smile, like an invitation into the shadows of her own stormy past.

I said my thanks, turning down the offer with a friendly grin. "I don't drink on the job."

Her eyes, like pools filled with stories and openness, locked onto mine. "Well, in that case, more for me." Her words carried a kind of forced happiness, a thin cover hiding the depths of her loneliness.

As I arranged the firewood, feeling the cold night creeping into my bones, Amara started dancing with her own struggles. The fire crackled, and her heart's steady beat mixed in, making a quiet song of being alone yet together.

She lifted the old bottle to her lips with determination, each sip seeming to make her past troubles disappear into the flickering fire. Her vulnerability softened, replaced by the brave light that the drink brought.

I stood on the side, watching in awe as Amara took control of her own story with every gulp. It was like she was saying, "I'm in charge here."

The fire made the night warmer, with secrets hiding in the corners, just like the flickering light. Amara sipped on her drink, and it seemed like the warm liquid was doing some magic on her. Her eyes showed a hint of vulnerability, like a secret dance between being strong and a little scared.

As she sat down next to me, the old sofa cradled our shared space, and she talked with a sort of wobbly honesty that only comes out when you've had a bit too much to drink. "Hey, John, something's not right. I can feel it. Something's bothering you."

Her words hung in the air, like a strong echo that bounced around the quiet room.

Amara, with her tipsy wisdom, seemed to uncover the hidden parts of my serious face, like she was unraveling a mystery.

I looked at her, and it was like seeing a reflection of all the complicated stuff we both go through. "It's nothing, Amara. Just some old memories hanging around."

Her laughter mixed with the crackling sound of the fire, like a delicate song. "Well, whatever it is, we can be there for each other. That's what friends do, right?" Her words, filled with a sincere tipsiness, promised that we'd stick together in the quiet times that make up our lives.

Feeling the connection between us, Amara leaned closer, her words a soft murmur in the quiet night. The room, filled with shadows and the dancing fire, seemed to hold its breath, waiting for something special to happen.

Her kiss felt like a mix of warmth and gentleness, sparking a quiet rebellion against the shadows hiding in the corners of our shared history. In that stolen moment, it was as if the whole world outside disappeared, and the feelings we held in the room became like an unspoken promise.

We both knew that, in the tangled stories of our lives, we could find comfort in the shared feelings of this moment. I don't push away; instead, I let myself forget about Mike and the thoughts that keep bothering me.

As the flames danced in front of us, our mutual needs came together in a kiss that went beyond the complicated stories of our pasts. The room, quietly watching the meeting of two similar hearts, kept its secrets safe. It only revealed small pieces of the bond that grew in the stillness of the night—a bond that said no to the ghosts of the past and called us toward a tomorrow built on the delicate beauty of intimate feelings.

Chapter Twenty One

The harsh light at the police station gave the place a frightening feel. It was an office room where I felt like all eyes were watching me closely. Vanessa, my muse in this crazy situation, was somewhere out there, was reporting on the celebrity news. I sat there, the clock ticking loudly, matching the fast beats of my thoughts.

People around me were talking in quiet voices, and keyboards were clicking in the distance, setting the scene for the upcoming questioning. Soon, the news burst out like a big storm – Vanessa's special skills shining through as the news talked about the famous actress, Amara Delacroix. Now, everyone knew about her stalker story, filled with secrets and excitement.

Days later, I sat inside the main office, and the

Chief Superintendent you know, the big boss, was giving me this serious look. "So, Sergeant Stewart, what's going on with the Amara Delacroix stalking case? The media is covering about it a lot, and my superiors are not happy."

Two inspectors were standing next to him, and they looked like they had poker faces or something. Their faces didn't show what they were thinking. I felt like their judgment was harsh on me, like a super heavy thing that could break the thin strings I was holding onto.

"Working on it, Chief," I said, my voice not shaky, but inside, it felt like a big storm was happening. "I'm really close to figuring it all out, though. Super close."

The Chief stared right at me, wanting me to promise something. "We really need to figure things out quickly. This case is a big deal, and we can't make any mistakes. What's your plan, sergeant?"

The room felt super tense, like a balloon filled with too much air. Every word I said seemed super important because it was. I could feel the inspectors watching me closely, checking every little thing I did. If I messed up, the whole case would be gone from my hands, just like that.

Right there in that room, I felt like I had a big job on my shoulders. Vanessa's magic had started everything, and now it was my turn to figure out the mystery of Amara Delacroix and the stalker hiding in the shadows. It was like playing a game, and the stakes were super high.

As I talked about what we should do next, it was like doing a tricky dance. I knew I had to be really careful because one wrong step, and everything could fall apart. The room was so quiet, and you could feel how serious it all was. It was like the air was full of the same nervous feeling you get when something really important was about to happen.

The Chief looked at me for a moment, thinking hard. It felt like he was deciding something important. "Sergeant Stewart, you will stay on the case as an assist only. Detective Inspector Smith here is gonna be the one leading the way. We gotta get this sorted out, and we gotta do it right."

Detective Inspector Smith, a man who had seen a lot in his years of being a detective, stood there strong and serious. His eyes, hidden behind a lot of experience, told stories of all the times he had worked on different cases. You could see lines on his face, like little roads telling stories of all the hard work he had done. His hair, turning a bit grey, showed that he had been through a lot – battles won, good moments enjoyed, and tough times faced.

As the chief talked, a chilly breeze swept into the

room, carrying a feeling that something wasn't quite right—I could tell I was being left out. I looked at Inspector Smith, and for a quick moment, we both silently agreed on what was happening. I could sense he wasn't too thrilled about teaming up with me, a detective who's not from his usual crew.

The chief's not-so-hidden attempt to push me away hurt a bit, but I didn't let that bother me too much. I had worked hard to get here, working into this case, and I wasn't about to let it slip away. I tightened my determination like a superhero gearing up for a mission.

I turned to Inspector Smith and stuck out my hand. "It's an honor to be working with you, sir. I've heard about your remarkable track record."

Inspector Smith gave a kind of nod that said, "Yeah, yeah. We get each other." The room got more tense as the silent rules of our partnership settled, like dust after a big commotion, a sort of agreement made because we had to.

As the chief finished talking, a heavy feeling settled on me. It was like I had a big responsibility on my shoulders. The room felt tense, like something important was still hanging in the air. I told myself that I wouldn't take no for an answer. Things were different now, the plan had changed, but my goal was still the same—to find out the truth hidden in the shadows and catch the stalker who was causing trouble.

∞

Walking out from chief's office, I could feel my heart beating faster with each step. I was determined. Even though I might not be in the spotlight, I wasn't giving up. The game with the shadows was just starting, and I wanted to be the one leading it. I knew it wouldn't be easy, dealing with tricky partnerships and the favoritism, but I was ready for it.

Together with Inspector Smith, I walked down the corridor, and you could feel that something was a bit off. The air felt tense, like when you know something's not quite right but no one's saying it out loud. His eyes were sharp, like he could notice every little thing. Then, he looked right at me and asked, "Who is Amara Delacroix?"

I felt a tiny bit annoyed, like when someone you don't really know asks you a bunch of stupid questions. I thought, "Why do I have to work with this old-fashioned detective?" But instead of showing it, I just smiled and said, "Sure thing, sir. I'll bring you up to speed on the case. Just follow me, please."

Guiding him into an empty office, I quietly closed the door, blocking out the buzz of the police station. The room was all white, like a quiet cocoon where you could share secrets without anyone hearing.

"Amara Delacroix," I whispered, my voice soft, "is an actress who's famous for doing controversial roles. But there's this stalker who won't leave her alone. He sneaks around, follows her and leaves scary messages. It's like he knows everything about her."

Inspector Smith looked at me really seriously, trying to figure out what I wasn't saying. "This person," I told him, "seems to me, he is really mad at Amara. We've been trying really hard to figure out who he is and why he's after her."

I grabbed my phone to show him something important, sliding my fingers across the screen to find the message John sent me a few days ago. It said, "For Your Eyes Only." I looked at Inspector Smith, who was staring at my screen with excitement in his eyes.

I opened the message, and a blurry video started playing. Shadows in Amara's apartment building moved like dancers in a strange show, showing us a part of her life she didn't know was being watched. Inspector Smith squinted, getting really close to the screen to study every part carefully.

"That's the flat where Amara Delacroix lives," I whispered, my voice soft. "The stalker knows everything about her, always one step ahead."

Inspector Smith stared at the video of the masked stalker walking though the corridor, and a thoughtful quiet settled between us.

"Let's figure out who this is. Talk to everyone in her building. Someone there might know something," Inspector Smith said, breaking the silence. "This is our big break, Ronald. The person following her is closer than we think."

I agreed with a nod, thinking about what I needed to do. The screen showed the shadows dancing around Amara Delacroix's life, and I was determined to understand what was going on.

∞

The office room felt like it was filled with the importance of our job. Working with Inspector Smith, even though I wasn't sure at first, now felt like we were a real team. We had a chance to solve the mystery around Amara, and the shadows were telling their secrets. I was all set to listen and understand the spooky music echoing through the dance of being watched.

Finally, he said, "Ronald, I need you to look into every bit of her life. This stalker, from what you've said, is most definitely someone from her past. We gotta find the missing link. Let's be one step ahead in this game."

The instructions were crystal clear, and I was thankful. Working with Inspector Smith, the old guy, could really help. His years of knowing the ropes had sharpened his gut feeling, going beyond just regular detective work. He thinks like a bad guy because he's spent years figuring out how they tick.

Inspector Smith spoke, breaking the quiet tension. "Look, kid, we're in this together, whether we like it or not. Let's make the best of it."

I nodded, appreciating the honesty. "Absolutely, sir. We can solve this case together."

As we gathered around a table with scattered case files, Inspector Smith leaned in and muttered, "Don't take it personally. I'm not used to having a partner, especially one who's as young as you."

I grinned, trying to ease the tension. "No worries, Inspector. We'll make a great team." Throughout the investigation, our conversations shifted from cautious to collaborative.

We shared ideas, debated theories, and slowly, the unspoken awkwardness transformed into a mutual understanding. The chilly breeze that swept into the room earlier seemed to be replaced by a warmer, cooperative atmosphere.

As we closed in on the solution, Inspector Smith

clapped me on the shoulder. "You're not so bad, kid. Maybe partners aren't such a bad thing after all."

I smiled, grateful for the acknowledgment. "Likewise, Inspector. Teamwork does make the dream work, they say."

As we explored Amara Delacroix's life, I started to really like how Inspector Smith and I worked together. There we were, one detective with lots of experience and a young sergeant who was really determined. We were ready to figure out this tricky game where each move could bring us closer to finding out the truth.

The man stalking Amara didn't realize he was being setting up a kind of shadowy dance. Inspector Smith, with his wise experience, joined us like an important player. Now, we had a new partner in this never-ending dance of chasing clues and discovering the truth.

Chapter Twenty Two

In that big, quiet house, the memory of that special night stayed with me like a sweet smell. John's kisses were like a promise of things we hadn't discovered yet. But when the sun came up, John acted like he was hiding something, and it made me wonder if our stolen moment was real.

The old house had creaky floors and secrets whispered in its walls. It watched as John and I played a game of avoiding each other and yet being drawn together. Every morning, we cleaned a different part of the house, sweeping away dust from forgotten things. I liked the soothing sound of the broom, even though it couldn't get rid of the silent tension in the air.

In the afternoons, the backyard was filled with the rhythm of John's axe. The loud chops echoed, slicing through the quiet air. I stayed back a bit, observing from afar as he worked hard. His strong back muscles moved like rubber bands with every swing. Stacks of logs grew, showing off the result of his hard work. I couldn't help but be amazed by the power he had, battling against the chilly air that slipped through the gaps.

When the evenings rolled in, I sat by my bedroom window, keeping my eyes on his figure outlined by the fading daylight. These shadows mirrored the unsure feelings swirling in my heart. I felt a strong determination bubbling up inside me. The back-and-forth game of liking John and avoiding him had gotten really strong, and I decided it was time to do something about it.

I started dreaming about a new kind of warmth—one that was way better than the cold feeling in my old house. It was like the line between really wanting something and being excited about it was getting fuzzy. Something like a magic pull made me go closer to a feeling I couldn't put into words. The bed, which used to be all chilly, now seemed like it could be cozy for two, like an invitation you feel without anyone saying a word.

As I blew out the only candle in the room, it got dark really quick. I was hoping for a night where we could get close, like the walls between us disappeared. I wanted our wishes to shine bright and show us the way to a secret friendship. It felt kind of rebellious, but

I liked the idea of being close to John without anyone else knowing.

Living in that big, lonely house got kind of boring. Every day started feeling the same, just us and some quick glances from afar. When the food in the kitchen ran out, me and John went to town early in the morning. Our footsteps were like soft whispers against the still streets.

The little town, a soft whisper of a place, greeted us with warm memories. The market was like a familiar place with heaps of fresh fruits and funny-smelling spices, a perfect escape from boring canned food. People in the town chatted happily, and their curious eyes made shadows on the secret we kept hidden in my quiet house.

As we moved through the aisles, our baskets filled with all sorts of goodies, a cool idea hit me. It was like the taste of freedom stuck on my tongue, way better than the blandness of canned stuff. This feeling was much like the secret bond growing between John and me, a shared wish to break free from our self-imposed hiding.

In the middle of the busy market, surrounded by colorful fruit stalls and people chatting away, I had a cool idea. "Hey John," I whispered, making it sound like a secret, "what if we ditch the boring canned stuff for something way more awesome?"

He looked at me with a little curiosity in his eyes, asking, "Awesome?"

I smiled and let the idea hang in the air like a cool secret. "Steaks," I said with excitement. "A big, delicious feast. We'll cook them outside, on a fire. What do you think?"

A tiny grin appeared on his face, like we both shared a secret plan. The thought of cooking juicy steaks over an open fire promised a break from the usual routine, a real adventure into a world of tasty treats.

As the cashier counted up what we bought, a feeling of excitement settled between us. The smell of delicious meat and the idea of flames flickering in the night sky seemed like they could warm up the cold space that had wrapped itself around our hidden world.

∞

On our way back home, the silence made our special connection even more intense. The town, a short break from our mysterious bond, turned into a setting where something unsaid was unfolding—a story of secret times, wishes we both had, and a hidden closeness that bubbled just beneath everything.

The evening spread out like a big, colorful blanket of exciting moments. The smell of delicious steaks being cooked mixed with the snap and pop of the fire outside. Shadows wiggled and jiggled on the old walls of the hidden house, hiding the cool things we were up to. John, the expert fire-handler, took care of the flames like an expert.

Up in the sky, the stars twinkled as if they were giving a quiet thumbs-up, watching our secret party unfold. It was like we were the hosts of a super-special, undercover feast.

The old camping chairs made a creaky sound as we sat down near the fire. The warmth from the flames wrapped around us, making the air feel secret and snug. The sizzle of the steaks on the makeshift grill matched the excitement bubbling between us. Tonight was more than just a break from boring routines; it was something special.

John looked at me, his eyes filled with curiosity. "Hey, Amara," he said, his voice a quiet hum in the nighttime air, "tell me about when you were a kid."

The flames made his eyes sparkle, and it was like a light shining on the mystery that was John. I took a moment, memories from my past weaving around my words. "My mom passed away from a heart attack when I was very young. So it was just me and my dad," I said at last, the crackling fire making my stories feel safe. "He was strict, always telling me what to do. So, I rebelled a lot."

A smile filled with memories played on my lips, remembering the times I stood up against his rules. In the warm light of the fire, John burst into laughter, a shared understanding echoing between us. "I get it," he said, his face softening with a sense of friendship. "When I was growing up, rebellion was like my middle name."

The flames flickered as John leaned back, looking up at the star-studded sky. "You know," he mused, "sometimes breaking the rules is the only way to feel alive."

I nodded, the fire's glow turning our conversation into a secret pact. "Yeah, it's like shouting to the world, 'I'm here, and I'm not just following the crowd.'"

He chuckled, the warmth of the fire reflecting in his eyes. "Exactly! It's about finding your own path, even if it's a bit bumpy."

We sat there for a while, the crackling fire and the soft murmur of the night creating a cocoon of camaraderie. Then, with a mischievous grin, John pointed to the sky. "See that constellation over there?" he asked.

I followed his finger, spotting a group of stars forming a shape. "Yeah, what about it?"

"That's Orion," he said, his eyes gleaming. "My

father used to tell me stories about it when I was a kid. It's like a reminder that even in the vastness of the universe, we each have our own story."

As the night went on, we all started sharing stories about our lives. The campfire felt like a safe place, drawing us in with its warmth. John's tales about his adventures in the military and his battles with his own struggles made him seem like a mysterious puzzle, each story adding a new piece to who he really was.

Under the twinkling stars, we felt like we were all in on a big secret story. The fire was like our secret-keeper, making everything feel innocent. As the night got darker, the fire turned into glowing embers, but the bond we created by sharing our stories stayed strong. It was like a promise of something exciting waiting for us, hidden in the flickering light and the stories we told each other.

∞

The sound of the steaks cooking on the grill echoed in the quiet night. The delicious smell of barbecue sauce wafted through the air like magic. When John took his first bite, his face lit up with pure joy, and you could see the happiness in his eyes. Our impromptu outdoor dinner under the twinkling stars turned into a time of laughter.

We sat next to the fading embers, the smells of our

spontaneous feast still lingering around us. John looked content, his face showing the happiness we shared. When our eyes met, we understood each other without saying a word.

Walking back into the big house, the echoes of our laughter stayed in the air like a happy song. It felt like we were connected by all the moments we'd just shared, making our hideaway feel less lonely. The things we'd confessed weighed in the air, making a bridge between us. It was there, but neither of us was brave enough to cross it, even though we both wanted to.

In the soft light of the hallway, I turned to John. My eyes showed a vulnerability I hadn't let him see before. "Thank you John," I whispered, and before he could fully understand how grateful I was, I hugged him really tight.

He was surprised, his body stiff at first, probably he wasn't used to such close hugs. But as I held on, I felt something change, a quiet consideration that went beyond the walls we had put up.

Wrapped in the comfort of our hug, I felt brave enough to tell John about the pieces of my difficult past. "My dad used to be really mean to me," I admitted, speaking softly so only he could hear. "He'd get angry and hit me when I did something wrong. So, I left home when I was sixteen."

John squeezed me tighter, a silent way of letting me know he understood the heaviness of my words. "You didn't deserve that," he said, his words like a soothing touch on my lingering wounds. "You should have had a dad who loved you."

I gazed up at him, my eyes showing all the different feelings swirling inside me. "You deserve someone who loves you too."

The air felt heavy with a truth we hadn't spoken yet, and there was a clear tension between us. In that moment when I shared my vulnerabilities, John's usual composure faded. He pulled me in even closer, and his lips met mine in a gentle kiss. We were two lost souls, searching for a place where we felt safe and understood. In this moment, the secrets and the walls that had separated us dissolved.

We were finally crossing the line.

And when I pulled away, his eyes told me he had been waiting for this moment too. The feeling of his arms around me was like a promise that things could be different.

∞

We hurried upstairs, hand in hand, a newfound closeness and the thrill of the unknown propelling us forward. In the privacy of my room, the shadows of the night were replaced by a new kind of darkness. Our lips met in a heated rush, a release of pent-up longing and desire. His kisses were soft and slow, exploring my mouth with an eagerness that made me gasp.

I closed my eyes and allowed myself to get lost in the sensation. The weight of his body pressed me down into the soft mattress, his hands roaming over my body in a frenzy. My skin burned wherever he touched me, the fire inside me fueled by his need.

Our clothes came off quickly, leaving us bare and exposed. The cool air caressed our skin, but the heat of our passion made us oblivious to the chill. He kissed his way down my neck, his hands cupping my breasts and teasing my nipples. I arched my back, pushing my chest into his hands, desperate for more.

He continued his descent, his tongue darting out to taste my skin. He circled one nipple and then the other, before sucking it into his mouth. I moaned, the pleasure making my toes curl.

He moved lower, his hands parting my legs. I lay back, anticipation making my heart beat faster. He teased me with his fingers, dipping them inside me and making me squirm.

His mouth joined his hands, licking and sucking until I was a quivering mess. The pressure inside me built, the delicious tension coiling tighter with each flick of his tongue. I was on the edge, the pleasure almost too much to bear. Then out of nowhere, he turns me over and starts touching my ass. I gasped, not expecting this.

He massages my buttocks, his fingers gently pressing into the soft flesh. I could feel his manhood, hard and hot, resting against my leg. My breath caught in my throat, the sensation new and unexpected.

I pushed back against his touch, wanting more. He obliged, his fingers circling my anus. I cried out, the forbidden pleasure making me crazy.

"Oh, John," I murmured, my voice hoarse with desire.

He continued his exploration, the tip of his finger slipping inside. I was overcome with sensations, my body trembling with need. He withdrew, his hands gripping my hips. He positioned himself behind me, his erection poised at my entrance. I closed my eyes, anticipating the sweet intrusion.

With a gentle thrust, he was inside me, filling me completely. We moved together, the rhythm slow and steady. The friction was exquisite, mixed with pain and pleasure, a sensation unlike anything I had ever experienced.

His hands stroked my back, his breath coming in

short gasps. I could feel the pressure building, the heat coiling deep inside me. We were climbing together, the ecstasy almost too much to bear.

Then, suddenly, the pace changed. He quickened his thrusts, his grip on my hips tightening. I met his movements, the passion consuming me.

The pleasure reached its peak, sending us both spiraling into a blissful oblivion.

We collapsed onto the bed, spent and sated. The afterglow washed over us, the feeling of satisfaction and contentment enveloping us in its warm embrace. The sound of our breathing was the only thing we could hear. Everything else seemed to fall away, the world around us disappearing. In this moment, it was just the two of us, connected in a way we never thought possible.

This secret union, hidden in the shadows of the night, had turned our hidden world upside down. In the soft darkness, John's lips found mine again, a silent promise of more.

And even though we had crossed the line, a newfound closeness had wrapped itself around our lives.

The secret of the night, our shared longing, and the hidden connection that was forming between us—

all of these things made my childhood house of horrors, feel like a special place.

Chapter Twenty Three

Suspicion tangled up my thoughts like a complicated maze, right in the middle of bustling London. I felt trapped in a confusing web of not knowing the truth. Every step I took, which used to be so sure, now felt like I was walking through mist, hiding the real answers I didn't want to find.

Sarah, my fiancé, used to fill my heart with her laughter. But now, it sounded strange and not right. I wondered if she was somehow involved in the mysterious happenings around Amara Delacroix, or if I was just imagining things and getting too worried. Doubt weighed on me like a heavy anchor, pulling our relationship down into unknown depths.

To dodge the tough questions itching to escape my lips, I turned into a sort of invisible person at home. When morning rolled around, I was ready to leave, wrapped up in my work gear. I only came back late at night, when the city lights had turned down, becoming a soft hum. Sleep, a visitor that barely stayed, left me all alone with my thoughts at night, and the uncertainty seemed scarier in the dark.

Sarah needed to know things, to feel sure our love was still strong despite everything. But fear held my words back, and I stayed in the shadows, feeling guilty about it.

All of a sudden, the tabloids lit up, making it seem like a big, bustling concert. And everyone with a camera or microphone couldn't wait to share the exciting story they'd found about Amara Delacroix and the mysterious stalker she was caught up in. The air felt charged with nervous energy as the news people talked about her life and how she was in hiding.

It was like a big storm of information and rumors hitting us, making Amara the center of everyone's attention. All my doubts and worries about my fiancé now seemed small compared to the crazy whirlwind surrounding Amara. She went from being a part of my personal puzzle to becoming the main focus in the middle of all this chaos.

Amidst all the fuss on TV and in newspapers, my own feelings got pushed aside. Instead, I started worrying about an actress stuck in the middle of her own story. The news had cleared away the doubts I had, making me feel more for Amara Delacroix.

And yet, our apartment felt strange, like there was a thick cloud of unsaid stuff hanging around. It was like a quiet storm, filling the air with a heavy feeling. Even though the city lights usually looked cozy from our window, that night they seemed different, like they were trying to shine through the secrets we had between us.

∞

One night, when the city was fast asleep, Sarah spoke up with a quiet voice that broke the silence. "Hey, Mike, maybe we should tell John about all the news about Amara. She should know, right?"

My heart felt heavy already, and I didn't like the idea. I looked at her with a little doubt and said, "Nah, Sarah. It's better if we don't."

She looked right back at me, like a battlefield of caution and worry. "What's up with you, Mike? You've been acting weird, avoiding me. What's going on?"

I took a moment, not sure how to say it. "It's nothing, Sarah. Just work stuff, you know how it is."

But her eyes, sharp and unyielding, stared right into mine. "Is there someone else, Mike? Are you cheating on me?"

I stepped back, feeling the surprise on my face. "No, Sarah, not at all. It's not like that."

The air got heavy as she kept asking. "Then what's going on? Tell me, Mike."

My truth, hidden behind a bunch of confusing words and dodges, felt really hefty. "The news thing doesn't matter, Sarah. Amara left to stay safe. Safe from you."

Her eyes got big, surprise all over her face. "What do you mean, Mike?"

I let out a big breath, my confession hard to say. "John thinks you're the problem, Sarah. That's why John wanted to leave with Amara to god knows where. And maybe he's right."

Her voice was barely there, like a soft breeze cutting through the quiet. "What did you mean by that?"

I looked at her, unsure and scared. "I don't know, Sarah. But we have to figure it out. For Amara and for us."

The words hung in the air, like a storm about to happen. Sarah's eyes, once full of trust, now showed a mix of feelings — like she felt let down, confused, and a bit sad. It was like a big, heavy cloud hanging over us.

"Do you think I'm a problem for her?" Sarah asked, her voice shaky, like a fragile song filled with surprise.

I thought for a moment, feeling my own confusion. "I'm not sure what she's thinking, but something made her run away, Sarah."

Her eyes stared at me with even more blame, and my words felt heavy, like a breaking bridge. "You should've asked me, Mike. I had a right to know what you thought about me."

A heavy quiet hung in the air, like a stretched-out wire between us, and my guilt felt even stronger. "I just wanted to keep you safe," I said weakly, knowing it wasn't enough.

Anger and pain mixed in her eyes. "Safe from what, Mike? The truth? I trusted you, and you didn't tell me."

The room, once a cozy place, now turned into a battlefield of broken trust and unsaid worries. "Sarah, I—"

"No," she interrupted, her eyes showing both hurt and determination. "You should leave, Mike. I need time to think. Maybe it's better if we take a break."

Her words felt like a final decision, creating a gap

between us. The apartment, that held the remaining bits of our love, now echoed with the sound of our broken connection.

As I gathered my things, Sarah's voice followed me. "I just don't get it, Mike. What was so wrong that you couldn't share it with me?"

I turned to face her, trying to find the right words. "It's complicated, Sarah. I thought I was protecting you, but I messed up."

She crossed her arms, a mix of frustration and sadness in her eyes. "Protecting me from what, exactly? We're supposed to face things together."

"I know, and I'm sorry," I admitted, feeling the weight of my mistakes. "I thought if I kept it from you, you wouldn't have to deal with it."

Her expression softened a bit, but the hurt lingered. "Mike, we're a team. If there's a problem, we tackle it together. Secrets only make things worse."

I nodded, realizing the truth in her words. "You're right, Sarah. I should've trusted you more. I messed up, and I'm really sorry."

She sighed, the tension in the room easing a little. "Maybe we can figure it out, but I need time. I just can't deal with this now."

∞

The city at night was bright and alive with people and lights. But for me, it didn't bring any comfort. I couldn't keep my feelings inside any longer, and the heavy silence followed me as I walked out into the chilly night. It felt like a big decision to leave Sarah, and it made my heart ache. It was like saying goodbye without actually saying it.

When I stepped into the shadows of the busy city, the cold air hit me. It was really cold, and I could feel it through my clothes. It reminded me of the coldness that had come between Sarah and me. The city lights, usually friendly and warm, now seemed a little unsure and flickered in the night.

My mind was like a whirlwind of feelings, all spinning around the worry for John. Was he alright? The last time we talked, there were so many things we didn't say, making our friendship feel shaky. I really wanted to talk to him, to feel better with the comforting presence of a friend. But the memory of our last chat held me tight.

As I walked through the city streets, filled with hidden stories and dark corners, it felt a lot like the maze of my own mixed-up thoughts. I went through memories, my steps making echoes in the quiet night of London. The far-off sounds of cars and the occasional laughter from nearby pubs were like a soundtrack to the mess inside my head.

My phone, full of missed calls and messages I hadn't answered, felt really heavy in my pocket. John's name might be somewhere in there, like an unsent message just waiting to be sent. But I hesitated. I was scared of what might happen if I broke the quiet that settled between us.

The Thames River, which had seen so many stories unfold, spread out in front of me. Its water was like a mirror, reflecting all the lights from the city. The bridge up ahead felt like a big intersection, a place where choices were made right under my shoes.

Standing on that bridge, feeling unsure about everything, I tried to figure out if talking to John would bring us closer together or make the gap between us even wider. The cold air of the night was there, watching me as I struggled inside. It felt like the night had secrets that could help me understand things better, but I wasn't sure if I was ready for them.

Chapter Twenty Four

Every night, the house seemed to come alive with memories. We would lie down next to each other, and even though we didn't say much, it felt like we were talking a lot. The sounds of the creaky floor told a story too, like an old friend sharing a secret. I knew that a young Amara had been through tough times, but as an adult, she was strong and determined. She brought much needed light into my world, which sometimes felt a bit dark.

Her touch changed the story in my heart, erasing the troubling thoughts that had stuck in my thoughts. In the gentle candle light, she turned into more than a friend beside me; she became my silver lining, tying me to a reality I didn't know I wanted.

Every morning, I woke up with a smile on my face, a natural reaction to the warmth of her body next to mine. The walls I built around my feelings had broken down because of her openness. Amara not only got into the strong walls around my heart but also started a fire that didn't care about the cold of my past.

Being in bed with Amara was like finding a treasure chest of surprises. She had this incredible strength about her, like a dominatrix, yet at the same time, there was this delicate part that brought out my tenderness. It was like discovering a secret map to a world of emotions I didn't know existed.

Before her, I thought keeping things simple with one-night stands with guys was the way to go. But she changed all that. She's like a colorful puzzle, full of pieces that don't quite fit together, and I couldn't help but want to figure her out.

As the nights turned into mornings, I started feeling this strong urge to be like a shield for her. To protect her from all the not-so-nice things the world can throw our way. It's like being the hero for someone who's secretly a wonder woman herself.

∞

Before my day even began, with Amara snoozing next to me, I thought about how things were changing for me. Amara's way of being was like a mix of being super strong and also sometimes feeling a bit unsure, kind of like a song with ups and downs. She was like a magical force that was rewriting my past, making a new connection between our hearts. I didn't even realize back then that she would be the one starting a whole new adventure for us, a mix of love and danger, totally shaking up my usual way of living.

When the first rays of day started painting the sky with soft purple colors, it made the old floor look brighter in Amara's room. I sneaked out, trying not to make any noise. The house, kind of like a secret keeper for our feelings, stayed quiet in these early hours. Even though the floor gave away my steps, Amara was still sound asleep.

Walking into the kitchen, the heart of our hideaway, I happily started making Amara's morning drink. The smell of freshly ground coffee mixed with the warmth of brewing made the air smell so good, like a feeling you never want to end. Our kitchen, with its old-fashioned dishes and a touch of memories, turned into a special place where regular things turned into something really cool.

As I poured the coffee grounds into the filter, a little smile popped up on my face. Making Amara's morning coffee was like a secret handshake between us. It showed how we had a special connection that didn't need any fancy words.

This connection, getting stronger every day, was like a jigsaw with more pieces fitting in perfectly.

Soon after, I heard the quiet tap-tap of Amara's steps as she walked into the kitchen. Her hair, all messy, framed her face that had a hint of morning pink. Our eyes met, and without saying a word, we both knew the special feeling of the morning and the secrets we shared during our nights together.

"I brewed your favorite coffee," I said, a smile playing on my lips.

Amara's eyes sparkled with gratitude. "You always know how to make my mornings better."

I leaned in and gently kissed her forehead. Her face blushed even more under my touch, showing a special feeling that warmed me inside.

"You look beautiful in the morning light," I whispered.

A soft giggle escaped Amara's lips, and she playfully nudged me. "Stop it, you're making me blush."

I handed her a cup of coffee, and she thanked me with a happy smile.

Her eyes stayed on mine, like she was figuring out the feelings we didn't need words to share.

"Did you dream anything interesting last night?"

Amara asked, taking a sip of her coffee.

I chuckled. "I dreamt we were on a jungle adventure, flying on the back of a giant butterfly."

Her eyes widened with amusement. "That sounds amazing!"

"You're dreams are probably filled with wonder, just like you," I replied, and Amara's cheeks turned an even deeper shade of pink.

As we sat together, sipping our coffee and exchanging morning stories, the sun painted the room with a golden glow, and the simple moments became the most incredible part of our day.

In that moment, as the aroma of freshly brewed coffee wrapped around us and our breaths played a gentle tune, I found comfort in the simple bond we shared. Outside, the world was filled with shadows and mysteries, but in our kitchen, time stood still. It was like a secret place where protector and protected blended, and our hearts made a beautiful melody of love and excitement.

∞

Deciding to step out into the crisp morning air felt like making a promise. I wanted to bring back some ingredients to make our lunch special.

"I'll go to the market, grab a few things," I murmured, my words hanging in the air like a whispered reassurance.

As I buttoned up my jacket, feeling the cool fabric against my skin, Amara came over with a warm smile. "Need my help?" she asked, her eyes filled with kindness.

I smiled back, appreciating her offer. "No, it's okay. You can do your thing, chill out here. I'll be quick," I replied.

She nodded, her gaze lingering on me. "Alright, but don't forget to pick up those little chocolate treats we like."

I chuckled, "Of course, wouldn't want to miss those. See you in a bit." And with that, I stepped out, leaving the warmth of our kitchen behind.

The outside world was ready, like an ice land filled with all sorts of quests and challenges. I tied my shoelaces and took a step outside, bringing the warmth of Amara with me. The market was buzzing with life— a mix of voices, the crinkling sound of bags, and the delicious smell of fresh fruits and veggies. Each thing I picked had a little promise to make our times together better, to turn ordinary moments into a special treat for us.

As I walked through the market, I felt a bit uneasy around the folks there. It was important to be careful because you never know what could happen. So far, we had been lucky enough to avoid any intrusive neighbors and I intended to keep it that way.

The market was super busy, full of bright colors and pleasant smells that held the hidden stories beneath a happy surface. As I strolled through the aisles, the sounds of people talking all around me made me feel like I was quietly watching a big secret unfold. It was as if I stumbled upon something important that cut through the calm air like a sharp knife.

I overheard two people talking about something that made me feel a bit uneasy. Their voices were filled with curiosity and speculation, and the name they were discussing sent a shiver down my spine - the Wilsons. It was like a mystery unfolding right before my ears.

"Who knows where that Mr. Wilson disappeared to?" one of them said, making my mind race with thoughts. His words felt like a spooky hint about something important. "And didn't he have a daughter, Amara?"

I clutched my grocery bag tighter, feeling a bit on edge. The name Amara echoed in the air, and I couldn't help but wonder if they were talking about Amara Delacroix.

Suddenly, a strange suspicion crept into my mind. Amara had never really talked about her past, and it felt like I was missing a piece of the puzzle, as if there was a hidden history behind her that I didn't know about.

A strange feeling crept over me, a kind of quiet worry that hung in the air like a mist. There was a strange tension between what Amara told me about her father being abusive to her.

I stood there quietly, overhearing the shoppers talk about Amara's dad who had been missing since many years. And the police had deemed it as a cold case, yet Amara never shared that part of her life with me.

But who am I to say anything? My own past has hidden damages that I haven't talked about yet. We both treaded carefully, not because we want to lie, but because we're afraid of breaking the intimacy we've created.

Right there, in the middle of the busy market, I tried to understand this new piece of information. It felt like a cold breeze, waking up shadows that had been asleep.

The air around me felt different, like the whole world wanted to uncover what we were hiding and make each of us face the truth.

I walked quietly through the market, feeling like a person carrying a big secret. The bags of groceries felt extra heavy, and I could hear people talking in soft voices. I wondered if they were sharing more secrets about Amara. As I walked closer to Amara's home, I couldn't help but wonder: what other hidden stories were there in Amara's past, waiting to be discovered?

∞

The sound of the groceries landing on the kitchen counter rang out in our quiet place. I looked over at Amara; she was standing in the doorway like a quiet protector of the house. "Hey, you're back," she whispered, her words sounding like a song, carrying the unspoken stuff we both knew.

Her eyes, full of trust we've built over time, met mine. It felt like she got what I was thinking—living in the present was something precious. Who cares about what happened in the past? I certainly didn't, anymore.

For a moment, we just looked at each other, and I thought about how close we've become. Our hideaway wasn't some fortress away from the world; it was more like a safe spot made from the things we shared, the times we were open with each other.

Holding onto the delicate present, I wondered how long this feeling would stick around, especially with a stalker lurking around.

As I started unpacking the groceries, Amara asked, "Anything interesting happen at the market?"

I hesitated for a moment, then shrugged, "Nah, just the usual. People rushing around, trying to grab their stuff. Nothing exciting, really."

She gave me a playful smile, "Come on, spill the beans. There's gotta be something!"

I chuckled, deciding to keep things light, "Alright, you caught me. There was this parrot at the pet shop that kept mimicking people. It was hilarious. Made the whole place burst into laughter."

Amara laughed, "A talking parrot, huh? Sounds like a riot. Wish I could've seen that."

I nodded, keeping the lie going, "Yeah, it was a riot alright. Other than that, it was just the same old market scene."

She raised an eyebrow, "You sure you're not hiding some juicy details from me?"

I shook my head, still grinning, "Promise, it was a mundane market day, just like any other."

Amara smirked, "Well, alright then. Let's get this

lunch going."

Chapter Twenty Five

The familiar space of my home, suddenly felt smaller, like the walls were squeezing in, and shadows were dancing around in the light. I sat there all alone, and Mike's hurtful words kept playing over and over in my head. The air, which used to be filled with our shared dreams and whispered promises, now felt heavy with doubt and betrayal.

Mike, my fiancé, said something really to me that I never expected. His words were like a poisonous mix, and they just hung there in the quiet room. Could I have really been a part of Amara's stalker situation? The idea that he thought I could do something like that was making me feel really confused and upset. It felt like my mind was unraveling at the edges.

It had been many days since I told him to leave, and his absence has made my heart feel so heavy. Why did he say such a terrible thing? The city outside my window was busy with people going about their day, but inside my heart, a storm was brewing. I touch the ring on my finger, the one that was supposed to be about loving each other, but it just made me miserable. The walls in my room seemed to know all about my long sleepless nights and my pillows wet with tears.

When I was alone like that, I kept wondering about the questions that won't leave me alone. Did he really know me? How did our dreams turn into something full of doubt and lies?

The engagement ring used to be a promise, but now it feels strange on my finger. It became a painful reminder of love mixed up with things that weren't true. The place where we lived, which used to feel so full of love and hope, now feels empty and broken because Mike broke my trust.

As I looked into the uncertain future, a solid feeling of not giving up rose inside me. I couldn't let myself start thinking I couldn't do it. Amara really needed a friend she could rely on, and I promised to be that reliable friend. Even though Mike said things that made me feel terrible, I wouldn't let those words become the whole story of our friendship.

In the quiet room all by myself, I prepared myself for the tough times that were coming. The storm outside was just like the mess in my mind, but I was determined not to let it put out the fire of being a good friend to Amara. I believed that the truth would come out, and I would stay right by her side, strong and not changing, even when things got really hard.

My stomach twisted with worry as I grabbed my phone, hoping it could fix the growing problem. My fingers shook as I called John, but with each ring, my worry grew. The voicemail sound made my heart sink - his phone was turned off.

"Ugh, seriously, John?" I couldn't hold back my frustration. It felt like a big sigh of disappointment. I really wanted answers, something to reassure me that Amara was alright.

My heart beating fast as I grabbed Amara's phone that she left in my care. Maybe there's a clue somewhere in it, like a trail of breadcrumbs pointing me to where they went. I unlocked it quickly, since I already knew her passcode, feeling the urgency like a clock ticking in my head.

The screen showed many missed calls and messages, like a digital map of all the confusion. My fingers moved over the smooth surface, going through the maze of texts. I just wanted something to make me feel better.

The messages told a story in snippets—Amara asking about if John was doing okay, and him trying to calm her down. But there was something hidden, something more.

My heart raced when I realized what it meant. Amara and John went to find the stalker who was bothering her, but I had no idea where. The answers, I believed, were inside Amara's apartment. With a surge of determination, I grabbed the keys and rushed out of the apartment.

∞

The city of London stretched out in front of me, like a giant mystery full of secrets. The nighttime air was thick and exciting, like I was close to finding out where Amara was. It whispered secrets I couldn't quite catch. But I was almost there, right on the edge of discovering the truth. I felt my heart race as I got closer, to the place that would help me discover where Amara and John had disappeared off to.

Amara's apartment was like a quiet caretaker, holding onto secrets that filled the air with uncertainty. Her home felt empty without anyone around, and the doubt hung in the air, making it feel heavy. In the corners, shadows seemed to gather, as if they were protecting her buried stories.

As I walked inside, the familiar smell of Amara's perfume mixed with the tense atmosphere. The apartment, which used to be a safe place, now held the quiet conversations of a dramatic tale. I could almost hear Amara and John's words in the air. The answers I needed were hiding in the dark corners, ready to be found.

In my search for answers, I quickly looked around the living room. I spotted clues that told a story of a life suddenly stopped—a book left open, a half-full coffee mug on the table. The room echoed with the sounds of someone leaving in a hurry, creating a mysterious scene. That what was happened, weeks ago and I was there when I watched John and Amara leave in a hurry.

My eyes then landed on Amara's daily planner. It seemed to hold secrets about her daily life. Acting fast, I grabbed the notebook, my fingers flipping through the pages to find any important details.

What I found was a puzzle of strange words and numbers that didn't make sense. Worry filled me as I thought about Amara's mental state. I felt a mix of fear, determination, and a strong commitment to solving the mysteries that had puzzled me.

I tiptoed into Amara's bedroom, feeling the air filled with her special touch but also noticing the emptiness left by her absence. As I explored the drawers, each holding pieces of her life, I discovered a treasure trove of memories stitched into the very fabric of who she is. In this quiet moment with her things, I hoped to find any hidden clues that could lead me to their secret hideaway.

The room was so quiet, like it was holding its breath, and I was on a mission to find some answers all by myself. Amara's bedroom was wrapped in shadows that seemed to be keeping secrets, only telling half of what they knew. I looked around at the furniture, each piece a special memory mixed up with things I didn't understand.

Then, in the corner on her nightstand, there was a small, old journal. It looked like it had been forgotten, left there for a long time. I wondered how I had never seen it before. When I touched its worn cover, I could feel the bumps and creases, like it had stories of its own to tell.

I hesitated, thinking about opening the journal. It felt like I was about to step into Amara's private thoughts. What kind of mysteries could be hiding in those pages? What secrets did she write down when she was all alone? I wondered if Amara used this journal to keep her special thoughts safe, ones she didn't want to say out loud. The journal seemed like it had listened to all of Amara's quiet moments, and it was ready to share a story I hadn't heard yet.

Taking a big breath, I opened the journal, and its cover easily gave way to show the empty pages inside. I looked at them, and it felt like they were staring back at me, all blank and silent, just like the big mystery of where Amara and John went.

My face must've shown how confused I felt. I flipped through the pages, hoping to find some secrets or thoughts that Amara might have written down. But there was nothing – just emptiness. The blank pages felt like a heavy hollowness, like they were waiting for me to fill it up with Amara's secrets.

As I stared at those bare pages, I felt both frustrated and kind of amazed. Frustrated because there was nothing to read, but amazed at how carefully Amara had managed to stay hidden, like a big secret. The empty pages seemed to hold the echoes of Amara's thoughts, just waiting to be uncovered.

The diary, quietly observing the mystery of Amara's life, turned into a symbol of many questions hanging in the air. Did she purposely keep the pages blank, showing the things she couldn't put into words? Or was it a hint she left for me, telling me to discover the parts of her story that were left unsaid?

A strange feeling settled in the room, a tense vibe that matched the uncertainty about Amara's future. The diary, now closed and back in its spot, carried the weight of secrets and self-control. Amara's laptop, shiny like silver, caught my eye, almost like a guard to the secrets stored within its metallic shell. A feeling of anticipation filled me, as I carefully opened it, the screen waking up like a magic door to the mysterious world I was eager to uncover.

My fingers danced across the keyboard, like a secret code unlocking the mysteries that were about to be revealed. The emails started to unfold, telling a digital story of her journey. It was like following a map of hidden messages that contained hints about what they were doing.

But the thing that really caught my attention was the unsuspecting email of her credit card statement. It was like a quiet secret, showing the traces of money moving around in the digital world.

I moved the cursor over the 'Bank Statements' email, like opening a door to secrets hidden in a maze of numbers. Click. The screen changed, and I saw a list of transactions that looked like waves going up and down, just like Amara's mysterious stalker.

My eyes focused on the last entry—a charge at the London Train Station. My heart started beating faster as I followed the numbers, revealing the last few transactions that opened a door to a world of questions. Did Amara leave London? And if she did, where in the world could she have gone?

Uncertainty hung in the air, mixed with the quiet tick-tock of an invisible clock. Amara's laptop, like a magical treasure chest, had the power to unlock the mystery surrounding Amara and John.

Feeling like a detective on a mission, I plunged into the digital maze. I searched through other emails and files, hoping to find clues that would lead me to the truth. Each word on the screen felt like a clue, holding the secret to unraveling the mystery. Yet, like whispers carried by the wind, the answers remained just out of reach.

A heavy sense of responsibility weighed on me. I couldn't let the stalker take Amara and John without a fight. The London Train Station, a place filled with mystery, called out to me as the next stop in my search for answers. But should I try to find where Amara went, or should I just let it be? Maybe now was the right time to let everything go. To finally move on without Amara holding me back.

As I walked out into the night, the lingering silence of those empty pages stayed with me, a reminder of stories still waiting to be told. The city, filled with shadows and soft whispers, was ready for the secrets about Amara's life to be revealed. Where the fuck did you disappear to, Amara?

Chapter Twenty Six

Under the hazy streetlight's flicker, I stood next to Inspector Smith, our eyes glued to the regular-looking apartment door. We were getting ready to face the stalker's lair, whom we'd been chasing during our investigation. It was a frantic call from the building manager, through the emergency services that brought us there. Someone had been illegally staying at that apartment which was supposed to be empty. A few witnesses reported seeing a tall masked man in and around that neighborhood.

Pushing the door with my shoulder, it slowly creaked open, revealing a super messed-up scene inside. Furniture was knocked over, and broken glass bits sparkled on the floor like confetti. The air smelled funny, kind of like when you're really scared.

Inspector Smith, checked out the mess with a

confused look on his face. "Sergeant Stewart, it looks like our buddy liked breaking things," he said.

I looked around the room, trying to find clues in the mess. The walls didn't have any pictures, newspaper pieces, or a creepy shrine to the person he was stalking- Amara Delacroix. I ran my fingers along the broken coffee cup, and it made a crunchy sound.

"He left really fast," I thought out loud, looking at the scattered bits of a messed-up life. "Maybe weeks ago or even longer."

Detective Smith squinted his eyes, thinking hard as he looked at the room. "The big question is, where did our mysterious stalker go? And why did he leave in such a hurry?"

As we searched through the broken bits and pieces, a scary thought hit us. The stalker whom we were trying to catch, like the invisible man, had gotten away right under our noses. The leftovers of where they had been hinted at how much they were fixated on something, like a story made up of threads of feeling really bad.

I followed the bits of a ripped-out magazine page, finding a part of Amara Delacroix's face. In that quiet room, I felt like a bunch of questions were pushing down on me without any answers. Looking for the stalker had brought us really close to finding him, but the answers were still like quiet words you barely catch in the breeze.

As we walked into the dimly lit hallway, a mysterious feeling hung in the air, hinting at a riddle waiting to be solved. But Amara's stalker, like a ghost in the night, had definitely left his mark on our investigation. We were left to our own devices, trying to figure out the strange truth that, in the world of shadows, the real mystery was often hidden in plain sight. Just like how Amara Delacroix's stalker did.

Inspector Smith looked at me, and I could see that he had the same lingering questions in his eyes. The corridor, lit by flickering lights, felt like it was closing in on us as we thought about the problem that we were facing.

"This is weird," he said, sounding suspicious. "Our stalker guy isn't like the usual ones. They usually get really obsessed and make shrines with things from their target. But in this case, it's all messed up, like the person didn't care about Amara Delacroix at all."

A shiver ran down my back as I thought about what Inspector Smith had just said.

"So, you're saying someone actually paid someone to stalk Amara?" I asked, trying to wrap my head around the unsettling idea.

Inspector Smith nodded, looking serious. "Yeah, it seems that way. The way this stalker operated – so precise, no signs of personal feelings involved – it's like they were on a mission, not just driven by their own obsession."

I frowned, trying to make sense of it all. "But who would want to make Amara's life so difficult? And why?"

Inspector Smith's eyes showed a mix of frustration and determination. "That's what we've got to figure out. There's someone out there with a serious grudge against her. They went as far as hiring a professional stalker. This isn't just a normal obsession – we're dealing with something much deeper and darker, Ronald. It's like we're caught in a maze of secrets."

The big revelation hung in the air like a storm on the horizon, kind of scary and exciting at the same time. We headed back into the dark streets, and the whole city spread out in front of us like a giant puzzle with lots of secrets. We were investigation the stalker following Amara Delacroix, but now it felt like we were on a mission to find the one really in charge.

We didn't say much, but you could tell from our faces that we were serious about what we had to do. The night was super quiet, like it was getting ready to show us something big. In the shadows, it felt like we were part of a game that was more than what it appeared to be.

∞

The big city stretched out in front of us as we sat inside our police car. Inspector Smith's serious words hung in the air, urging me to do some thinking. The job we had was heavy, like a big secret pressing on my shoulders, quietly telling me that figuring out this mystery would take us even deeper into a dark fight.

Inspector Smith, the more experienced among the two of us, finally spoke up. "Ronald, we have to find out more. Maybe someone out there knows if there's a professional stalker prowling around."

I nodded, holding onto the steering wheel tighter as the car engine rumbled to life. The sound of the tires screeching on the road became the soundtrack to our thinking, like the music before a big adventure into the city's mysterious side.

Inspector Smith guided me through the winding streets, and soon, the fancy city view changed into something completely different. We stepped into an area that seemed untouched by the city's fancy lights—a place where tents stood like brave soldiers, creating a makeshift city beneath the towering buildings. The people here, who had no homes, had formed a strong community in the shadows.

When we found a spot to park, Inspector Smith looked at me, and we both knew there could be a treasure trove of information hidden in these overlooked corners. "Ronald, we're about to meet folks who live on the edges. They might have seen something, caught wind of rumors. We've got to discover the threads that link our stalker to the world beyond."

We stepped out of the car, and the bright city lights turned into softer colors as we entered the tent city. Inspector Smith walked in front, determined, like he knew exactly where to go through the tents.

People living there looked at us, some curious and some a bit cautious. Inspector Smith, who everyone seemed to know, moved through the narrow paths, talking quietly to those who usually go unnoticed by everyone else.

I followed quietly, taking in all the interesting things around us in this secret hideaway. The air was filled with soft talking and stories of how people survive tough times. It was like the sounds of lives being changed by difficult situations.

Inspector Smith pointed to an old man sitting at the edge of the tent area. "That's my informant, Charlie. He knows everything about the city. Maybe he heard something important."

We kept going forward, shadows dancing around us, as we searched for clues in the quiet pathways of the tent city. It was a place that many forget, but it held secrets that could help us understand the mysteries surrounding Amara Delacroix's life.

The light from the flickering lamp made Charlie's face look warm and tired. As we got closer, he looked up, and his eyes seemed like mirrors reflecting all the stories written on the city's roads.

Charlie looked right into Inspector Smith's eyes, and without saying a word, they understood each other. Inspector Smith, like a skilled conductor directing a special performance, leaned in closer. His voice, a quiet whisper, mingled with the night sounds around them. "Charlie, we need to know about this new player. Can you give us anything solid?"

Charlie's face formed a little grin, showing gaps like secret doorways. He stretched out his hands, sort of asking for money. I gave Inspector Smith a look, kind of annoyed, and he nodded like, "Yeah, go ahead." With a sigh, I took out some pounds from my wallet and handed them over, swapping them for bits of wisdom hiding in Charlie's head.

While he counted the money, his eyes got all greedy. "New folks always gotta pay, guys. Now, listen good."

Inspector Smith's stare stayed firm, like we made some secret deal in the shadows. "Spill it, Charlie. We gotta find this creepy stalker before he does more harm."

Charlie's wrinkled fingers drew an invisible map in the air, showing the financial district. There were old, empty buildings stretching high, like the bones of dreams. "I can't say which one exactly, but our new buddy was hiding in a building that's still being put together."

The news just stayed there, like a secret connected to the city's growing and changing places. Inspector Smith's eyes, full of willpower, looked right into mine. The city, which didn't seem to care about us before, now hinted that the answers we were looking for might be hiding in the dark corners.

Leaving the tent city, the bright lights of the city hugged us again. Our car hummed happily as we drove through the twisty streets, heading towards the tall buildings in the financial district. Empty buildings stood like quiet guards, ready for us to reach them. It felt like a big battlefield where shadows and the real story were about to clash.

As we cruised along, Inspector Smith glanced at me, his eyes serious. "This stalker's been playing cat and mouse for too long. We're getting closer, I can feel it," he said, gripping the steering wheel.

I nodded, trying to match his confidence. "Yeah, we're like good cops in a movie, chasing down the bad guy."

Inspector Smith chuckled, "Only this isn't a movie, kid. This is real life, and it's unpredictable." He adjusted his hat, the neon lights reflecting in his detective badge.

The pursuit intensified as we entered the financial district. The city seemed to hold its breath, watching our every move. "It's like the whole city knows something's about to go down," I remarked, peering out the window.

Smith smirked, "Cities have a way of feeling the pulse of events. Now, we just need to follow the rhythm and catch this stalker before he slips away again."

Our car weaved through the tall buildings, each turn bringing us closer to the mystery waiting in the heart of the financial district. The detective's eyes never left the road, focused and determined. "Keep your eyes peeled, kid. We might be stepping into the lion's den soon."

I nodded, gripping the edge of my seat. The neon glow outside painted the car's interior with flashes of vibrant colors. The anticipation hung in the air as we continued our journey through the city's maze, chasing shadows and seeking the truth.

Chapter Twenty Seven

High up in the air, hidden in the bare bones of a half-built building, a man in a hoodie sat on the very top floor, blending into the dark corners. The cold wind, free to roam without any glass in the windows, whooshed through the unfinished structure, carrying whispers of faraway secrets.

Under the dark hood, the person's eyes watched the city below, stretched out like a glowing board of lights. Each little twinkling light was like a peek into someone's private world, holding stories waiting to be told. The mix of sirens and far-off voices down there played a melody, all the while unaware of the hidden figure above.

Inside the building being constructed, its workers left behind their tools, the stalker found his secret hideaway, a safe spot where no one could find him. The tall metal frames and empty walls whispered about being alone, like a hidden stage for him to quietly watch what's happening around.

The city, shining with the energy of its people, felt both far away and just a short distance from him. He looked amazed at how the busy streets were like a woven pattern of people's lives. Sitting up high, he became a quiet audience to the sounds of life, an unseen watcher in the flow of things.

The wind, strong and chilly, carried the very heart of the city's stories. It played with his hood, showing just bits of a face hiding in the shadows. He stared, a quiet guard, as the night unfolded below, with the world not knowing about the eyes keeping watch from above.

In the quiet bones of the half-built building, he felt a comforting calm. The place, stuck between being built and finished, was like him, not quite ready but brimming with possibilities. He stayed there in the dark corners, a mystery watching the city pulse beneath him.

While the wind softly swayed through the incomplete structure, the person in the hood thought about the game happening below. It was like a strange dance between hunters and hunted, where shadows shared hushed secrets, and the city was clueless about the dangerous game being played.

His mind replayed memories like a movie, taking him back to the times he spied on John using a secret camera inside the apartment he had to leave behind. John, the military guy, never suspecting, always a step behind, trying to find his way through a complication set by an invisible puppet master. A small smile appeared on the stalker's face. What started as a job had turned into an exciting game of cat and mouse, a battle of cleverness that he enjoyed a lot.

He played on the edge of being caught, giving John little hints of his presence, a quick shadow in the corner of his eye. Every time, the ex-military man was just a bit too slow, catching his breath where the stalker had been not too long ago. The city, with its winding paths and hidden corners, became the stage for their secret game.

Deep within his mind, the Amara Delacroix's stalker grasped a powerful truth—he was the one pulling the strings of this eerie puppet show. The whole thing was like the opening act, a spooky introduction to the grand finale that only he was directing. His secret client, lurking in the shadows, had spun a web of stories, guiding him to this very moment.

A serious determination showed on the stalker's face. He already knew the final chapter, the result of a carefully planned and intense buildup. While the city slept, completely unaware of the unfolding story, the stalker silently led the way, like a conductor guiding the destiny symphony.

In the quiet hum of the wind and the beat of the city, the mysterious person felt that playtime was almost over. The exciting chase between the one seeking and the one hiding had come to its peak, and only this person knew how it was all going to end. A creepy grin stayed on their face, like a sign of the storm getting ready in their secret world—a storm that would swallow everything in its way, leaving only echoes in the city's dark.

That's how, an old construction site, forgotten by everyone, became a secret hideout for the stalker. He set up his temporary base on a pile of old, worn-out wooden boxes. In the midst of the silent remains of walls that were never built, he crouched over a laptop. His fingers moved swiftly and sneakily over the keys, creating a sinister dance. The distant sounds of machines and the city's soft music played like a strange background to their mission all alone.

In the dim glow of the computer screen, the man, hidden beneath a hoodie, carefully studied the lines of secret codes. Amara Delacroix, his elusive target, appeared to have slipped away like a sly ghost in this digital puzzle. The stalker feeling a bit like a detective, tried hard to find where she had gone.

The sound of keys being pressed echoed urgently,

like a fast drumbeat, capturing the attention of the man in the hoodie. The busy city around them faded away as he focused on exploring the digital shadows, looking for any sign of the woman was hired to follow.

Amara had turned into a sort of master at disappearing, like a sneaky phantom in the big city. The stalker's fingers danced across the keyboard, trying to unlock secret information and follow the digital clues she might have left. But it seemed that Amara had become really good at making herself invisible.

But Amara's stalker felt a bit annoyed. Things weren't going the way he wanted, making him feel a bit off balance. It was like a surprise that messed up his carefully made plan, adding a layer of uncertainty. The city, all quiet and peaceful below, had no clue about the hired stalker who was supposed to be chasing his target, but was kind of stuck for a moment.

He looked away from his computer screen to see the city's buildings in the dark night. He was thinking hard about Amara Delacroix, trying to figure her out. A tiny bit of doubt sneaked into his thoughts, making him remember that plans, no matter how perfect, could change because of unexpected stuff.

But he was a professional, scowling at the challenge ahead. The city had its secrets, and he was determined to uncover them, step by step. The chase had hit a small pause, but he, like a hidden piece inside a computer, was ready to dive back into it. He was dead set on finding Amara Delacroix, and the digital game started again – like a dance between stalker and his prey, hiding in the middle of the city at night.

Spending days and nights inside that quiet, empty building, the light from the computer made the half-finished walls look kind of unnerving. Up on the tippy-top floor, the stalker was sitting like a ghost, looking at the glowing computer screen.

His fingers danced carefully on the keyboard, like he was doing a secret dance with the computer codes.

As the lines of secret codes mixed together, the stalker's eyes got big with a surprise. He found out something important about Amara Delacroix. All her hidden stuff that was out in the cyber world was now showing up on the screen. Things like her credit card bills and a digital trail of where she had been. The last thing she bought was at a train station in London.

Bingo.

Hidden beneath the hood's shadows, the sneaky grin on the stalker's face told a story of triumph. The quiet building, still under construction, stood like a secret keeper, watching as Amara's digital life unfolded in secrecy.

The London train station, a hub where everyday people came and went, became a vivid picture from the stalker's high perch. He imagined the busy station with its halls and platforms, a puzzle of hiding spots where Amara could be anywhere, blending into the hustle and bustle.

Every day, he carefully looked through the train station's surveillance footage, like a detective solving a case. He stared at the fuzzy pictures, taking his time to study each one. His eyes were sharp, searching for a tiny clue that could link him to the person he was after.

So, why was this stalker still looking for Amara Delacroix? The client paying him to do this, like a secret boss hiding in the shadows, hadn't given a thumbs up yet. All communications with his client fell silent, they weren't responding anymore. But the stalker felt a strange, dark feeling growing inside him. It wasn't just about getting paid anymore. It was like an uncontrollable urge, eating away at his insides.

In the quiet that filled the air with hushed secrets, he moved forward, determined to get what he wanted. Whether it was free or not, he had something important to settle. There was a feeling inside him, like a strong urge, pushing him to make things right by bringing an end to Amara Delacroix and her hard-to-find bodyguard, John Stewart. In his mind, it was like a twisted game, a dangerous dance that only ended when he got what he was after.

He was a person, who liked to take charge, had always been someone who made things happen, especially when it came to dark and serious side of his job. And this job, was coming from his own not-so-good desires, but it was no different. He had to locate them, kill them, and make sure that they stayed dead.

Looking at the blurry screens in front of him, he kept going. It wasn't just about doing his job; there was also a strange satisfaction in making sure they met their end. The game had started, a determined chase where it was hard to tell who was the hunter and who was the prey, where destiny and choices mixed together in a its own way.

Chapter Twenty Eight

The intoxicating smell of Amara's sweat filled the room as she walked out, signaling a short break in the busy song of our lives. I saw her leaving, a happy smile on my face as she went behind the bathroom door for a quick shower after her run.

"Come back fast, or you might miss me," I joked, adding a playful note to my words.

Her laughter, like a beautiful tune, traveled through the hall, and I felt a warm and happy feeling inside. In those quiet moments, the stress from the world outside disappeared, and it was replaced by the joy of being with Amara Delacroix.

With her not around, I headed to the kitchen, the heart of our special place. The pan sizzled, and I chopped veggies in a rhythmic way, creating a kind of music that made me feel good.

While cooking, I thought it would be nice to add some real tunes to the mix. So, I grabbed my phone, which was like my connection to the outside world. I unplugged it, turned it on, and bam! A bunch of missed calls and messages popped up – like messages from the world outside our cozy spot. It tried to break into my calm bubble, but I said, "No way, not today, not now."

I swiped past the unread messages on my phone, totally focused on what I had to do. My fingers moved quickly over the screen, finding comfort in the beautiful sound of Whitney Houston's song "I Will Always Love You." The music was like a magic spell, making the room feel full of different feelings that were way beyond ordinary.

When the first lines of the song filled the air, I shut my eyes, letting myself get carried away by the haunting melody. It was like there was a special dance happening inside my mind, swirling with images of John. But I decided not to pay attention to that tension right now. The only tune that really mattered was the one that promised love – it was like a safe place away from all the troubles waiting outside our walls.

Soon the delicious smell of cooking filled the kitchen, making my tummy rumble with excitement. The kitchen was all bright and warm, thanks to the sunny afternoon shining through the windows. It felt like a peaceful hideout, a break from all the madness outside.

Just when I was getting lost in the soothing tunes of Whitney Houston, a sudden weird sound interrupted everything. My phone, the noisy troublemaker, buzzed like crazy on the counter. I made a puzzled face as I picked it up, and there it was – his name lighting up the screen.

Ronald.

His call kept buzzing, like he had something super important to say. It felt like a storm was trying to mess up the peace I made for myself. I thought about picking it up because it was my brother who was calling, but I really wanted some quiet time.

Finally, I decided to shut the phone up. I made it silent on purpose. It was like my way of telling the world to chill out because right now, it's just me and Amara in this old house.

The delicious smells of the cooked dish in front of me grabbed my attention, bringing me right back to reality. The ingredients make a sizzling sound, mixing with the last echoes of Whitney's singing, and I enjoyed how simple everything feels right now.

I just don't want to deal with the complicated stuff

outside just yet. Ronald's phone calls, full of things unsaid, can wait. Right now, all that matters is the tasty food on the stove, the gentle noise of the frying pan, and looking forward to spending more time with Amara.

I chose to focus on our peaceful hideaway instead of my brotherly duties, and although a tiny bit of guilt popped up, I pushed it away quickly. All I really wanted was to be with Amara and enjoy the meal I had prepared—a delicious feast made with the perfect mix of flavors, a dance of our lives all tangled up together.

The smell of my hard work floated in the air, when Amara walked in after her shower, looking calm and happy after her run. She had a little smile on her face, a secret we both shared, a twinkling in her eyes. She touched my chest and gave my neck a kiss, making me feel all tingly.

"Smells amazing," she said, her words like a soft whisper in our private space.

∞

Sitting outside, on the porch with a small table in front of us, we dug into the feast. Every bite was like a reminder of the good days we've had together. The sun quietly watched over our simple lunch, making patterns of light and shadow that added a feeling of peace to the scene.

Our whispered talk floated like a gentle song, creating a special tune that connected our hearts in a secret dance. We felt so comfy, like we built a cozy place just for us, even if it were for a short time.

When Amara laughed, it was like joy spreading in the air. I thought about how these happy moments were delicate, like a bubble that could pop anytime in our secret world. The outside air smelled so good making the afternoon feel warm and intimate. The porch, lit up by the soft sun, turned into a safe spot where time hung around a bit more. In our private space, everything outside didn't matter, and the only thing real was what we felt in our quiet talks and shared looks.

As our quiet lunch wrapped up, a sense of peace enveloped me in the simplicity of this special afternoon we'd snatched away. The breeze whispered gently, leaves rustled softly, and our stolen glances spoke volumes without words. It was like a secret language only our hearts understood. In this calm bubble, we weren't just ourselves; we were partners in crime.

The afternoon sun dipped low, casting a cozy warmth on everything. Amara, sitting comfortably in her chair, leaned back, and the sunlight painted playful shadows on her face. A thoughtful hush settled between us, the remains of our lunch blending into the background of our own little hideaway.

"Hey, John," she said quietly, looking out at the far-off horizon. "Do you think we could just stay here forever?"

Her question hung in the air, filled with a hopeful feeling that matched the calm moment. I looked at her, my eyes showing the complicated feelings of our secret world.

"Well, someday, we'll have to go back to the real world," I answered, my words holding a truth we both knew but didn't say out loud. The porch, with its sweet charm, was like a safe place, but it wasn't a way to run away. We were only here because of a problem – a stalker who followed Amara and made her life terrifying.

Amara looked a bit unhappy, her eyes filled with a momentary sadness. "I already miss London," she said quietly, her words carried away by the wind.

I chuckled softly and reached over the table, holding her hand in mine. "We're here to keep you safe, Amara. The city will be there when we're ready to go back."

A calm quietness surrounded us, and Amara's next words hung in the air. "What if the stalker is gone? And when we go back to London, will things still be the same?"

At that moment, you could feel something special happening in the air. I pulled Amara's chair closer to mine, gently touching her face with my hand. "Amara," I whispered, "it's not just about the danger. It's about us. No matter where we are, it will be the same."

A sweet quietness surrounded us as I leaned in, giving her a soft, lingering kiss—a silent way of saying something we didn't put into words. Through looks we shared and moments we stole, we found comfort. The porch, our safe spot away from everything, watched over our love formed in secret. And in that hidden kiss, we promised each other a future that waited for us outside our special place.

When we moved apart, it felt like everything around our porch was holding its breath, frozen in the pretty colors of the evening.

But I couldn't shake off that little worry in my mind. It felt like something was not quite right, like our secret hideout might be compromised somehow, but then again, no one knew where we were.

Even though our porch looked fitting in the evening glow, it was hiding our story like a favorite secret. But deep down I knew that, the truth was like a sneaky shadow, ready to show itself at any moment.

"John," Amara whispered, her eyes shining with

the fading sunlight, "let's bring our plates inside."

Her words sounded like a secret plan, a silent understanding that our porch dance might have a hidden audience – the people living around us who still didn't know that Amara Delacroix was back in town.

We stood up together, holding our plates, leaving the porch with a warm feeling around. The air smelled like blooming flowers and a promising spring, softly telling me to enjoy those moments while it lasted.

As we went back inside the house, a feeling lingered in me that our secret relationship was like a delicate dream, waiting to fade away once everyone starts looking closely. The walls, quiet witnesses to our story, wouldn't protect us forever.

Inside, the sound of plates clinking echoed around us as we moved away from the porch, where the evening was sneaking in. The town, not knowing our secret yet, stayed on the edge of finding out. It was like a ticking clock, counting down to the moment when everyone would know about Amara Delacroix's return.

Inside our little kitchen, I peeked at Amara, and her eyes showed that she felt the same way. Our feelings, made in secret, thrived on out closeness. Because while the town slept peacefully, we danced carefully through the secrecy of our intimacy—a dance that would soon make me question everything.

Chapter Twenty Nine

The sun was hanging low in the sky, making long shadows in the late morning. Detective Inspector Smith and I were walking through a spooky part of the city. The old buildings were like skeletons, with broken windows and rusty stairs hanging off them. Our footsteps echoed loudly in the quiet.

Inspector Smith, who looked like he'd seen a lot in life, was leading the way. The air smelled musty and old, like nobody had been here in ages. The buildings around us told stories of the past, with cracked windows and rusty stairs telling tales of busy days long gone.

Climbing up the creaky stairs of the old building we picked, the steps moaned and groaned as if they didn't like us being there. The walls, covered in peeling wallpaper, seemed to be telling stories about the people who used to live here a really long time ago.

When we reached the highest floor, it felt like a big empty space with windows that had given up to time. The weak sunlight came through the dusty glass, making shadows dance on the old, cracked floor. Everything was so quiet, except for the far-off sound of the city humming in the background.

Inspector Smith and I looked around carefully, checking for anything unusual. I copied his careful look, paying attention to every little detail. We walked slowly, stepping cautiously, almost like the building was holding its breath, waiting for us to discover the secret hiding in the shadows.

All of a sudden, a breeze moved the still air, making me shiver. It felt like something uncertain was in the air, a gut feeling that told me to keep going. The walls felt like they were getting closer, and the shadows turned into quiet watchers of our investigation.

As we opened each door, a sense of excitement and curiosity filled the air. The rooms were all empty, and their quietness made us wonder what secrets they held. Finally, we reached the last room, and a feeling of both excitement and nervousness bubbled up inside me.

The room stretched out in front of us like a big picture filled with stories nobody had remembered for a long time. But then, in the corner, I saw something move—a quick shadow playing on the edge of our search.

Inspector Smith and I looked at each other, understanding passing between us without saying a word. Even though the room was so quiet, and we felt the tension in the air. We decided to explore further into the shadows, determined to find the stalker whom we were searching for.

The hallway brought us to a big open area on the tippy-top floor. It looked all lonely and stretched out, like it would never end. The windows were all smashed up, showing a kind of beautiful view of the city covered in the soft morning colors. Big buildings that used to be super fancy now just stood there, like they were guarding this part of the city that got all worn out.

When I peeked at the city through the broken windows, a chill went down my back. It was pretty, but kind of sad too, because no one seemed to care about it anymore. The tall buildings, which were once symbols of prosperity, now just stood there, watching how everything got old and tired. This part of the city, which used to be wonderfully lively all the time, now looked like it was taking a really long nap.

As I scanned the wide space ahead, I noticed a little movement near the open area's edge. Some rats scurried about, their slim bodies weaving through the leftover bits of abandoned offices. It gave a sinister feeling to the already kind of creepy place. I squirmed a bit, feeling uneasy because of the weird things hiding in the shadows.

Inspector Smith, this tough guy standing tall against the city backdrop, observed where I was staring into. His eyes, normally super serious, showed a bit of dislike when he saw those rats running around the edges.

"I fuckin hate rats," he grumbled quietly, like the critters were his least favorite thing in the world.

This surprised me because he usually doesn't show that side of himself. "Really?" I asked, sounding pretty interested.

He nodded, squinting his eyes like he just tasted something super gross. "Gross creatures. They live in the places everyone forgets, surviving even when everything else is falling apart. Little shit heads!"

His words felt heavy, making me think about how those little pests sneaking around in the broken places mirrored the same problems in our own lives.

The distant beat of the city sounded like a drum, reminding us how serious our investigation was. The rats kept on doing their little dance near the edges, and

Inspector Smith looked my way. His eyes, marked by countless investigations, kind of told me that we both knew we were exploring forgotten corners together, searching for the truth.

The sun in the late morning made long shadows on the quiet floor, like it was quietly watching us. The city, once full of life, was quiet under us, hiding secrets that wanted to be found. Now that we knew the stalker was hanging around in the abandoned buildings, our search got more serious. Before he could reach Amara, or worse, get to my only brother John.

My hand reached out for my phone, a little gadget that has been my best friend during this difficult investigation.

Every day, I called John, trying to fix the gap that's growing between us. But, his phone, like most women I dated, was always turned off. It's like a shield, stopping me from reaching him. That day, as the wind added to the tension of the investigation, I dialed his number again.

A cold, computerized voice told me that the caller was not available. I was getting frustrated, adding to the frustrations that were building up inside me. I end the call without leaving a voice message, and now I have to face Inspector Smith's judgmental eyes.

"What's happening, Ronald?" he asks, his voice a

deep sound echoing off the walls.

I paused, feeling the weight of the truth pressing down on me. "It's about my brother, John. I've been trying to get in touch with him for weeks, but his phone is always off, even now."

Inspector Smith's forehead wrinkled with worry, like the lines of a map drawn with concern. "You seem distracted with it, and I really need you to focus on what we're doing. So try calling your brother again."

I agreed with a nod and dialed my brother's number once more, tapping away on the phone screen. The call's digital buzz filled the air, mixing hope and worry. Finding out where John was could bring me answers, but I couldn't shake the nagging feeling that the case was closing in on us, pulling us deeper into its puzzling grip.

When I called my brother, yet again, as I did so many times before, all I got was silence from his turned-off phone. But this time, a tiny bit of hope lit up when the call started ringing on the other side. My heart raced, getting more and more excited with every ring.

"Pick up, John," I said quietly, my frustration creeping into my voice. The questions in my head lingered like friendly ghosts in the calm air when I ended the call.

Inspector Smith, always quick to notice things, saw that I was having a tough time. "Having trouble again, Ronald?"

I sighed in frustration, my jaw tightening as the voicemail told me once again that I hit a dead end. Inspector Smith could tell I was uneasy, and his sharp eyes showed he was just as curious as I was. "So what's going on with your brother, Ronald?" he asked, his gaze telling me to spill the secrets I was keeping.

The truth hung in the air, like a secret I couldn't keep. "He's got this new job. He's working for Amara Delacroix."

A grave look passed over Inspector Smith's face, showing how serious the situation was. "Amara Delacroix? The actress, whose stalker we're trying to catch? What the fuck is your brother doing with her?"

"He's her bodyguard," I explained, a hint of frustration in my voice. "But I don't know where they are. It's like he's avoiding me. I've been trying to reach him for days, but—"

Inspector Smith's eyes narrowed, and it seemed like he was putting the pieces together in his experienced mind. "So where do you think they are? Your brother and Amara Delacroix?"

I nodded, my worry out in the open. "I have no

idea where they could be hiding. He never told me, and now, calling him on his phone's not helping either."

Inspector Smith looked at me intently, trying to understand the complicated situation. "Ronald, we've got to locate them. There is a good chance that the stalker is still going after Amara Delacroix."

A heavy quiet settled between us, the connection between the dots hanging in the air. Inspector Smith broke the silence, his voice steady in the midst of the uncertainty.

"Give him another call," he said, his voice strong and sure, showing he knew what he was doing. "We have to find them, Ronald. Everything is starting to make sense, and the stalker can only keep the truth hidden for so long."

I pressed the buttons to call John, and a hopeful sound echoed in the phone's dial tone. Each ring felt like a piece of a puzzle waiting to be solved. After a while, a connection was made, but it was just his voicemail.

I felt a bit frustrated, wondering if John was in some kind of trouble or if he was avoiding me. But Inspector Smith's determination made me feel a little hopeful.

∞

It was the middle of the day, the sun shining bright and making long shadows in the bustling city. I felt a heavy sense of not knowing what's going to happen, like a big question mark hanging in the air around me. I looked at Detective Inspector Smith, my eyes showing how urgently I needed his help.

"Sir, I really need your help. Can you trace my brother's number with the cyber division?"

Inspector Smith looked back at me, understanding how serious it was. "Sure thing, Ronald. We'll figure this out. Give me his number."

As I shared John's phone number with him, the air around us suddenly got really quiet, like everyone was holding their breath. Inspector Smith, who's really good at figuring things out, knew how big a deal this was. He said, "It might take a little while, but we'll get some answers soon."

I felt a big sigh of relief, like a break in the middle of a big storm. I nodded and said, "Thanks, Inspector Smith. I just have this feeling that my brother might be in some kind of trouble."

He put his hand on my shoulder, kind of like saying everything will be okay. "We'll find him, Ronald. The cyber division will do their tracing thing. For now, keep your eyes open. The stalker might be closer than we think."

The final building on our checklist stood tall and mighty, like a giant block of secrets in the midst of the city. The empty hallways told stories of an abandoned construction project, but now it's like a quiet museum of unfinished development. Inspector Smith and I climb the lonely stairs, the only sounds are our soft steps and the creaky sounds of the building.

As we go higher, it's like opening a sad storybook – each floor covered in the dusty bits of dreams that have faded away. When we get close to the top, there's a feeling in the air, like we're about to discover something important – maybe the hiding spot of the stalker whom we're looking for.

At the very top, our flashlights cut through the darkness, showing an empty space that feels like it's holding its breath. Even though it looks empty, our lights find a surprise – a bunch of empty food wrappers scattered on the floor, like a bunch of stars in the dark.

Inspector Smith squinted his eyes, and I could sense the excitement building up. "Someone was here," he said quietly, his words serious and important.

We searched the area carefully, paying close attention to even the tiniest clues. It felt like we two men on a mission, listening for any small sign if someone was still there. The air was full of suspense, like a mystery waiting to be solved.

"Sir, there's no one here now," I noticed, looking around at the empty space in front of us.

Inspector Smith looked puzzled, his forehead wrinkling as he thought. "Hmm, maybe someone's hiding here? Watching us from the shadows?"

I nodded, feeling a shiver run down my spine. "That's the only reason. Someone's been using this place as a hide out."

We walked around for a bit searching every nook and corner, our footsteps making soft sounds in the quiet. The reason that brought us here was a crafty little stalker, slipping away like a ghost in the dark.

"Be careful, Ronald," Inspector Smith whispered, his voice soft. "Our stalker might be really close."

∞

The sun was setting, and the sky painted the city in soft colors. It looked peaceful, but something was stirring underneath. Suddenly, Inspector Smith's phone rang loudly, breaking the calmness. He quickly said "thanks" into the phone and looked at me with a serious expression.

"Did they find him?" I asked, feeling a bit nervous.

Inspector Smith nodded, his face showing both

relief and worry. "His phone was pinged in Glasgow. Any guess why he'd be there?"

Glasgow – a name that made me think really hard. The memories of files and lots of papers, all telling the story of this case, popped up in my head. Amara Delacroix's hometown – legal name: Amara Wilson, born in Glasgow.

I thought for a moment and scratched my head, like I was figuring something out. "Amara and John are in the place where she grew up, in Glasgow. Why?"

Inspector Smith's eyes got big, like he understood too. "Ronald, if we leave now, we can catch the last train. Time is of the essence."

We rushed down the old, creaky stairs, and the city wrapped us up in the dark night, like a big maze of secrets waiting to be found out. The connection between Amara, John, and the person following them was becoming clear, like all the pieces of the mystery coming together on the streets of Glasgow that waited for us.

In the cold air, urgency pushed us forward. Inspector Smith quickly tapped on his phone, reaching out to the Glasgow city police with the ease of someone who's been doing this for a long time. The night felt full of excitement, like an invisible force guiding us to the big reveal.

Inside our fast-moving car, the city lights turned into bright streaks, matching the speed of our thoughts. We felt like we were getting closer to the truth, and the roads leading to Glasgow seemed to play a part in the unfolding drama.

As we got closer to the London station, a feeling of something bound to happen settled over us. The suspense, mixed with the thrill of what might come next, connected us with a shared purpose. We were on a mission to find Amara, John, and the dangerous stalker, and it had led us back to Amara's childhood town. It was like going back to the beginning, where the shadows of the past whispered secrets that were about to shape the destiny of everyone caught up in this mysterious dance.

Chapter Thirty

All wrapped up in a thick blanket, Amara snuggled close, creating a warm haven that shielded us from the chilly night. Her gentle breathing, like a comforting melody, made the darkness around us feel calm and safe, like a soft, invisible dome. And I was just beginning to drift off to sleep, with the world around me slowly fading away.

Suddenly, a creaky sound broke the peaceful silence, and I jumped up, still half asleep. My whole body got tense, alert to the strange noise that had rudely interrupted my slumber. The quiet exhale of the wooden floor under mysterious footsteps echoed in the house.

Careful not to wake up Amara, who was sleeping so peacefully, I gently moved away from the snuggling position. I got out of bed slowly, making sure not to make any noise. The air in the room felt heavy with desperation. No matter what my job was to protect Amara.

Suddenly, Amara, with her sleepy voice, asked, "John? What's happening?"

My response was a soft, "Shh, be quiet."

I turned around and saw her looking all puzzled, her eyes widening in shock. Without saying anything, I ducked under the bed and grabbed my cold service pistol. I was wearing only my boxers and socks, but that didn't matter. I moved quietly, like a ninja, thinking about all the stealth techniques I learned from the military.

I sensed the room, as if it got darker suddenly. I felt like my heart pounding as I moved closer to the door. I was a bodyguard, ready to face whatever or whomever was inside the house. The floor creaked a bit when I moved, making a tiny creaking sound in the quiet night.

Amara whispered, "What's going on? Why are you getting your gun?"

I leaned in and explained, "I heard something downstairs. I need you to stay quiet and be careful."

Amara's eyes widened in surprise and concern.

She whispered back, "Is someone in the house?"

I nodded, "I think so. But don't worry, I'll check it out. Just stay here and stay quiet, okay?"

As I faced the doorway, holding the firm grip of the pistol in my hand, I could sense how Amara must have been feeling, like she was holding her breath. Everything was so quiet, like the calm before a secret was about to unfold in the hidden parts of the night.

The pistol's weight in my hand meant it could protect us, but it also reminded me of the danger we faced. Years of my training, kept me steady in the tense quietness. When I looked back at Amara, her eyes showed that she was clearly worried. The bedroom's gentle light made her face look softer, and for a moment, I saw a hint of vulnerability. It made me want to keep her safe from the mysterious shadows lurking outside our safe space.

I whispered to Amara, "Stay right here, no matter what you hear." My voice was low but strong, filled with determination. Amara nodded, silently agreeing. Her nod showed a kind of courage that you wouldn't expect from someone facing such a delicate situation.

I tiptoed towards the bedroom door, taking careful steps. The door, like a gateway, stood between the bedroom where we both shared intimate nights and the intruder lurking outside. It made a soft scraping sound as I closed it slowly. A quiet click followed, making sure Amara stayed safe inside her bedroom.

With the door shut behind me, it was like a protective line forming between the danger that I was in and Amara's safety. The hallway ahead was dark, but just enough for me to see. I stepped into the dark corridor, each step making a quiet thud in the night's melody.

As I walked towards the stairs, they looked wide and kind of mysterious in the darkness. Going down them felt like stepping into a place where I didn't know what might happen next. The shadows on the stairs made everything seem a bit like a secret game.

I strained my sharp ears to catch the faint sounds of any movements, but all I could hear was my own muffled breathing. It was as if the night itself was talking in a special code, and I wanted to understand it. Every step I took felt like I was tiptoeing through a world full of hidden wonders and surprises.

∞

The living room, where the lights once made it feel like a harmless place, now seemed unsure and mysterious. Shadows played games on the walls, telling me secrets in the quiet as I stepped in. Right there, he was sitting—a stranger, like the air itself brought him from somewhere mysterious. My reflexes came in handy as I flipped the light switch on.

This creepy person, covered in bad intentions like a spooky ghost, was chilling on the sofa, acting all calm in a weird way. His eyes, like two dark holes with no feelings, looked straight into mine, making me feel weird. But I pointed my gun straight at him, my hands steady, ready to shoot at the slightest movement.

"Don't do anything stupid, Mr. Stewart," he said in a slow and sly way, a little grin appearing on his face. The room felt heavy with the silent game between the bodyguard and the stalker.

The gun in my hand felt sturdy, my trusted weapon, helping me feel safe in the uncertainty of the situation. "Surrender, and we can figure things out without creating more problems," I said, talking in a quiet but tough way that tried to calm him down.

But the stalker just laughed in a creepy way that made my skin crawl. "You think there's going to be a big fight, huh? That's not how things usually happen in my line of work."

His relaxed attitude, sounded to me that he didn't care if he lived or died, but I could feel something was behind it. "Who hired you to do this?" I asked, sounding firm but cautious as I tried to find out who was behind all the trouble.

He laughed again, making the room sound like a horror house. "Even if I wanted to tell you, I can't. That's not how this game works, Mr. Stewart."

There was this weird dance of questions floating around, hiding in the dark corners. The stalker had a strange laugh that hung in the air, like a tense music before something terrible was about to happen. But I thought hard about possible ways to get him to surrender, without me having to pull the trigger on him.

The living room seemed to get smaller, like the walls were squeezing in on us, silently watching what was going on. The stalker stared at me with eyes that didn't show any feelings, like a deep, dark hole. It was tough talking to him, like walking on a shaky connection over a big gap.

"Hey, you don't really have to do all this," I pleaded, my words feeling like a delicate bridge between us. "We can figure out another way. Just surrender now, and I'll make sure that I don't shoot you."

But his eyes, like two mysterious pools, didn't show any sign of changing his mind. "You think I wanted this, Mr. Stewart? You think I like being part of this weird torment dance? I don't have a choice. It's not something I can control."

A shiver ran down my spine as I suddenly understood that the stalker wasn't really in control of himself. It was like, he was just a pawn in a chess game, controlled by forces he couldn't see or understand.

"What do you mean, not in control?" I asked, my voice cautiously searching for answers in the eerie silence. The stalker's response was like a mysterious confession, hanging in the air like a puzzle I couldn't solve.

"I can't stop it. These strong feelings, the need to do things—it's like something is making me. I have to complete what I started." His words, like delicate threads unraveling his mystery, made the tension even more unsettling. He seemed like a puppet, tangled up in strings pulled by someone we couldn't see, dancing to a strange and confusing tune that was making his sanity fall apart.

"I don't think you get it, Mr. Stewart." He said, looking kind of sad. "You're like just another body to kill, just like Amara."

I wondered, was he stuck in a bad situation or was he hiding some really dark secrets? But, when I stared into his sad eyes, the answer stayed hidden, like a mystery waiting to be solved.

But out of nowhere, Amara rushed in, and everything changed. Her sudden appearance messed up the rapport I was creating with the intruder.

"John, what's going on?" she asked, sounding worried. Her voice was like a worried song, hanging in the air. At that moment, I got distracted. I was stuck between keeping my eye on the stalker and checking on how worried Amara looked.

The stalker saw his chance and jumped at me, like a bad shadow in the dark. My only protection, the gun, fell to the ground. It was useless now, thanks to Amara who made me lose my focus.

∞

A wild fight broke out, and the room echoed with hushed grunts and the sound of a dangerous knife. I didn't have the gun, so I was left to face the attack using my basic instincts and just my bare hands.

His knife shone in the dim light, like a ghostly gleam in the room. It tried to tell me a funny story as it moved through the air. I moved around quickly, dodging his attacks with a kind of wild and desperate grace. The room turned into a battlefield, and the walls watched everything as if they were seeing a clash that wasn't just about bodies.

Every move we made in that room felt like a big decision, as if we were playing a game where staying safe or giving up was at stake. It was like a special kind of paint that turned the boring room into something intense. Amara's voice sounded far away, like she was calling for help, but it got lost in the noise of the fight that was getting louder.

The stalker seemed like a mad man who was losing his mind, and yet he wielded his knife at me with a strong determination. My hands, rough from dealing with tough times before, still struggled with the sharp blade. But eventually I managed to kick it out of his hands, much to his dismay.

The air in the small space felt heavy and full of the feeling that someone was going to die that night. Dark shapes stuck to the shapes of our fight, making it look like a strange dance where we had to figure out how to survive in quietness.

In the midst of this, Amara shouted, "Leave him alone!" Her voice cut through the tension, echoing in the room like a strong wind. The stalker paused for a moment, his wild eyes meeting hers. But then, the struggle continued, each of us holding on to our own hopes in the middle of the chaos.

I felt like the time slowed down, and everyone took a deep breath, like the whole place was holding onto a secret. During this dangerous encounter with the stalker, it seemed like destiny itself was watching. The struggle between us became much intense, like a wild storm happening in a small space. We were pushing and pulling, and you could hear the thump of our bodies colliding. The stalker was breathing hard, and it matched the beat of my own breath.

Amara's voice echoed in the air, a plea that reached us despite the chaos around. "Stop! Both of you, please!"

At that very moment, our hands were at each other's neck in a fierce struggle for survival. The room, like a quiet audience, watched as we tried to take control of each other's fate.

The stalker squeezed my neck harder, making it difficult for me to breathe. I looked at Amara, and in her eyes, I saw a desperate plea. Without saying a word, we shared a silent promise, a connection that went beyond the confusion surrounding us.

In the middle of our intense struggle, Amara quickly looked over to where the pistol lay on the ground. It was like a symbol of power that was up for grabs. With a sense of urgency, she rushed towards the weapon, reaching out with her fingers to grab it's cold, familiar shape.

My voice, a deep sound that filled the room, reached her ears. "Shoot!"

The room seemed to be filled with the quiet thoughts in Amara's mind. Her eyes, showing a mix of doubt and determination, met mine. The gun, a heavy decision that went beyond just the four walls we were in, hovered in the air, undecided between seeking revenge or showing mercy.

A sudden bang echoed in the room, making everything pause afterwards. The stalker, let go of his grip on my neck, looking shocked by what just happened.

The room felt like time stopped, showing how the choices made hung in the air, like the smell of something burning. The things that happened, echoed in the dark corners of the room, showing how things changed because of the basic instinct to survive.

I suddenly felt a really sharp pain, and I couldn't believe what just occurred. I fell to the floor, clutching my chest, where the bullet hit me.

Amara just stood there, her hands shaky, casting a shadow in the quiet room. The stalker, looking surprised, sneered, "You missed."

Time felt weird, like it slowed down. Quick as a flash, the stalker jumped at Amara, like a wild animal going after its prey. But Amara, reeling from the after effects, lifted the gun again.

Bang!

The loud sound echoed, and the stalker staggered back, paying the price with his life.

He fell to the ground, right next to me, pain etched all over his face. But Amara, her eyes showing she meant business, walked up to him. Every step she took told the story of her transformation from being scared to finally being in control.

Standing in front of the man bleeding on the floor, she told him, "I didn't miss." Another bang filled the room, and it felt like justice was done.

I felt like I couldn't do anything but watch as it unfolded before my eyes. The room started to get blurry, with pain and darkness all around, as Amara shot her stalker to death. The smell of gunpowder hung in the air, reminding us of the choices we couldn't change.

I was almost at the stage where I was about to pass out, but the last thing I saw was Amara's face. She wasn't weak anymore, but someone who brought justice to herself. Then everything went dark, as I fell into a deep sleep, escaping from the reality that had changed everything for us.

Chapter Thirty One

The Glasgow City Police Department stood tall in front of them, like a stronghold against crime. But that day, something wasn't right inside. Sergent Stewart walked quickly, and Inspector Smith was right there with him. The hallway echoed with their fast footsteps.

When they got to the front desk, a serious-looking police officer informed them, "There were multiple gunshots at the Wilson residence. You're too late." The words sat in the air, heavy and dark, like a scary cloud holding the truth of a bad dream.

In a state of panic, they rushed to the hospital, a trip filled with lots of questions without answers.

Inside the clean waiting room, they spotted Amara—she was still in her sleeping robe, shaking from shock.

When Amara saw Ronald, her eyes lit up with recognition. It was like a quick memory from a time before when they faced a different problem. She remembered meeting him, the day when John got hurt, stabbed during their grocery shopping, back in London.

"Ronald," she said in a hushed voice, looking really sad. "John got shot. The stalker, found us here."

Ronald felt really miserable and worried when he heard this. His mind was filled with questions, but he asked, "And what happened to the stalker? The one who was following you?"

Amara took a deep breath, letting out a tired sigh. You could tell that what she was going to say was really tough. "He won't trouble me anymore. He didn't make it. He died during the struggle."

Now, the hallway in the hospital felt so quiet, like time had stopped. You could see on Amara's face how everything that happened weighed heavily on her. The hospital, usually a place to make people feel better, now showed the marks of a night that changed everything.

Ronald tried to understand it all, feeling like the past and the present were coming together in a way that made everything hurt. The hospital walls seemed to remember the quiet struggle and surprise of that night, a lesson that sometimes, good people get hurt.

Inspector Smith's serious face showed he was both worried and yet very focused on his duty. He turned to Amara with a concerned look. "Did the police take your statement, about what happened?" he asked, his voice clear in the quiet hospital air.

Amara shook her head, her messy hair falling like a soft curtain across her face. "No, they didn't."

Inspector Smith felt a strong determination to find out what really went on that night. "Come with me, Amara. We need to know all the details."

But Ronald sat in the hospital waiting area, his eyes following Amara and Inspector Smith as they walked away. It was like a scene from a play where different lives come together after something bad happens.

Leaving the quiet hospital halls behind, the air felt crisp and carried the weight of many unanswered questions. Some police officers from Glasgow joined Amara and Inspector Smith, escorting them safely back to the station.

The trip to the police station was quiet and serious. The city lights outside flickered, like they were watching the secret mix of feelings hidden underneath everything. Amara, with her eyes showing a mix of sad stories, became the one telling the tale of a night that was not like normal nights.

∞

At the hospital, Ronald stood alone, like a watchful guardian in the confusing hallways. The heart monitor beeped in the background, reminding everyone of John's uncertain situation, somewhere between life and something unknown.

Time felt like it was playing hide-and-seek, just floating around as Ronald's thoughts swirled in his mind. The waiting area in the hospital turned into a place full of worry, with each second quietly hoping for John to make it through the complicated surgery that could either save his life or not.

Feeling all sorts of emotions, he walked around the hospital aimlessly. But when he stopped by the front entrance, he couldn't help but stare at the hospital doors. The bright light from the entrance made it look like a quiet battleground where strong feelings of both staying strong and feeling really miserable coexisted.

As the hours went on, Ronald felt tied to the sterile walls of the hospital, like a guardian waiting for John's doctor – whether the surgical outcome would be good news, a chance for things to get better, or the unavoidable darkness that had wrapped its way into their lives.

∞

The police station stood tall, like a giant building of rules and questions, making the whole city look small. Amara, standing next to Inspector Smith and Inspector Murray, walked into the interview room—a place that held a lot of criminals and witnesses alike.

Inside, the room felt very clean and bright, with lights that hummed softly. Amara, looking tired from everything that happened the previous night, accepted a warm blanket from a watchful police officer. The blanket was a necessity in the cold room, wrapping around her like a shield against the scary feelings that reminded her about what happened.

When Amara sat down, her eyes met with Inspector Murray's. It was like they had an unspoken agreement that went beyond the normal rules of the room where people get questioned. The questions waiting to be asked were like keys, ready to unlock the secrets of that mysterious night. It was a night where the dark and the truth were having a secret dance- but it ended up in someone's death.

Inspector Murray, who was in charge, noticed that Amara was not feeling good and so he gave her a kind nod. "We brought you here for some routine questions, Ms. Delacroix. Just to piece together the timeline of tonight. You're under no obligation to be here—it's for your safety and our paperwork."

The room took a quiet breath, as if everyone inside sighed together. You could feel it in the air; Amara being there wasn't something she had to do, but something she volunteered. She gave a slight nod, showing that she understood. The blanket she had draped over her seemed like it held not just warmth, but also a kind of heavy meaning in the strange world of the police station.

∞

Inside the interview room, everyone waited for Amara to speak. So Inspector Murray took the lead and began asking Amara some questions, to try and figure out what happened. The case was a mess, a mix of jumbled memories and broken timeline. Amara shared her story, anxiety tainting her words, creating a story that went beyond the plain room.

Inspector Smith looked at her with a serious look, his eyes never wandering. "So, tell us, Ms. Delacroix, what happened? Take us from the beginning," he said kindly, breaking the heavy silence. His words hung in the air, encouraging Amara to tell her side of the story.

Amara took a deep breath to calm herself. "Me

and John were asleep," she started, her words cautiously exploring the twists and turns of the night. "But in the middle of the night, he woke up, because he heard something, and got his gun. Then, he told me to stay in the room."

A quiet silence filled the space as Amara delved into the frightening memories. "After a little while, I heard voices—coming from downstairs. I went to see what was happening, and that's when I spotted John in the living room, talking to the stalker who was following me."

Inspector Murray, a calm and understanding figure, gave Amara a kind nod, urging her to share more. "You're doing great, Amara. Take your time," he said, his words offering comfort.

Feeling supported by Inspector Murray's presence, Amara took a deep breath. "They were arguing really loudly, and then things got worse. I could see them fighting, grabbing at each other. And then..." Her voice hesitated, creating a solemn pause, like a sentence waiting to be finished.

"Gunshots," added Inspector Smith, his eyes silently reflecting the questions everyone wanted to ask.

Amara nodded, her voice barely above a whisper, carrying the heavy weight of a night that felt beyond the ordinary. "Yes, I saw both of them, getting shot."

Inspector Smith looked at Amara, his face showing that he wanted to understand more about what happened. "What happened next, after you saw John and the stalker get shot?"

Amara, her eyes showing the chaos she witnessed, talked with a shaky voice. "I took out my phone and called the emergency number. I needed help. I couldn't..." Her words faded, leaving a feeling in the air that something important was left unsaid.

As the heavy news sank in, Amara started to feel uneasy. "Excuse me. I... I don't feel well. Can I use the restroom?"

Inspector Murray, a kind presence in the room, agreed. "Sure, Amara. It's down the hallway."

The cold interview room, a place filled with stories waiting to be uncovered, held the key to answers yet to be found. Wrapped in her own vulnerability, Amara stood up to face the shadows within the police station's walls—a witness to a night that had changed her world forever.

∞

The hospital hallways were really quiet, making a buzzing sound that echoed around. Ronald was standing with a few police officers, feeling the heavy wait for John to come out of the surgery room. It was like standing on the edge of not knowing what would happen next.

Finally, they wheeled John out. He looked kind of pale, still affected by the anesthesia they gave him. Ronald walked up to the doctor, because he really needed to talk to John. He said, "Doctor, this is important. We really have to talk to him, I insist that you wake him up." His voice was serious, like he was asking for something really important. The doctor, understanding how serious the shooting was, nodded in agreement.

Inside a private recovery room, machines beeped rhythmically. John was lying very still, after successful his surgery to remove the bullet that injured him.

The doctor, did what Ronald asked, he reduced the flow of the pain medication that was continuously being given to John.

After a while, when the medicine started to wear off, John's eyes opened a little bit. It was like he was quietly saying, "I know what's happening." His face showed he was beginning to feel the pain from the surgery.

Ronald, his brother, came closer. "Hey, bro, it's

me," he said, talking in a quiet voice.

John's reply was serious and filled with hurt, breaking the silence. "It's her, Ron," he said, the words sounding heavy and important, hanging in the air like an echo.

Suddenly a jolt of pain hit John hard, like a strong force inside him. It was like the marks on his mind were visible on his body. The doctor, understanding the balance between sharing news and finding comfort, quickly adjusted the flow of more pain medicine. It was needed to calm the pain that was trying to take over John.

Ronald understood how serious his brother's words were. He could feel the heaviness of the unsaid truth. Questions swirled in his mind, and he knew he needed clear answers, the kind only found in John's thoughts.

Ronald immediately pulled out his phone. He called Inspector Smith, hoping this call could bring light to the secrets of Amara Delacroix.

∞

Back at the interview room, Inspector Murray carefully opened an evidence bag filled with random things. The items, stuff found in the stalker's pockets, were neatly arranged in front of them. There was a wallet with no name, a holster for a knife that was found at the crime scene, and a burner phone.

Inspector Smith, looked closely at those things with a careful eye. He switched on the phone, and its cold light made the room look strange. With his gloved hands, he pressed buttons on the phone, trying to find clues about the secret life of the stalker. There was no identification on him, so they were doing everything they could to find out his real identity.

"There's only one number in the call list," he noted, his gaze meeting Inspector Murray's.

Inspector Murray, the lead in their detective team, decided to make the call from his phone. He dialed the one and only number they had, and surprisingly, someone picked up on the other end. The room, filled with silent excitement, waited as the phone rang.

A soft buzz, so gentle that you could barely feel it, came from inside the room. Inspector Smith, who had a knack for sensing the truth, started to explore, trying to find where this mysterious sound was coming from.

Right there on the floor, cleverly hiding in plain sight, was a small black phone—a secret witness to all that had happened. With careful hands covered in gloves, Inspector Smith picked it up, feeling like he was about to discover something important.

"Whose phone could this be?" he wondered aloud, looking around at his fellow colleague. They exchanged puzzled glances, each trying to make sense of the situation.

As Inspector Smith answered the call, the dialing on Inspector Murray's phone had stopped ringing too. The room, caught between two phones, seemed to hold its breath, realizing something important was unfolding right then and there.

Suddenly, a lightbulb moment lit up their faces— a sense that went beyond figuring things out. The room, heavy with the surprise of discovery, felt like it let out a shared sigh as Inspector Smith and Inspector Murray, tied together by invisible understanding, figured out something unsettling.

The second phone, held a secret connection in the dance of darkness—it hinted at a truth that was unbelievable. In the quiet looks they exchanged, the room watched as they realized the shadows they were trying to uncover were actually controlled by someone hiding among them—a shocking discovery that hinted at a plot more complicated than they had imagined.

∞

The stillness of the interview room shattered as Inspector Smith's own phone rang, slicing through the hushed ambiance. He fished it out from his jacket and answered with a brisk, "Smith here."

On the other end, Ronald's voice, strained with urgency, relayed a revelation that sent shockwaves through the investigative tableau. "My brother identified Amara Delacroix as the shooter."

Inspector Smith, a look of surprise on his face, responded, "Amara Delacroix? Are you sure about this, Ronald?"

Ronald's voice quivered a bit as he affirmed, "Positive, Inspector. You need to detain her."

The room felt like a secret clubhouse buzzing with exciting secrets. Inspector Smith, his detective skills sharp from all the twists and turns in the case, looked at Inspector Murray, silently saying, "We've got something big here."

∞

Quick as a flash of light, they dashed out of the room, zooming through the police station hallways. The ladies' restroom, usually a quiet place, now seemed like a hidden room full of mysteries, calling them to discover the real mastermind behind the case.

They rushed into the restroom, and the bright lights above made the shiny tiles look really bright. The air felt like it was holding its breath, as if it knew something important was about to happen.

They checked everywhere, peeking into each stall and looking in all the corners. They carefully examined every inch, hoping to find Amara Delacroix. But nope, she wasn't there. The ladies' restroom, a place where secrets of women hide, didn't give any clues about where Amara could be. It was like she had vanished completely from their investigation.

They asked the officers outside for information, their faces showing how worried they were. Then, one officer came up, carrying unsettling news. "The woman who came out of the rest room? She just left, sir."

This news hit them hard, like a really heavy hammer. The truth echoed through the halls. The police station, which was busy with questions before, now turned into a place where the outcomes were coming together. It was like a puzzle, connecting the escape of someone on the run with the mysterious shadows they had been trying to figure out.

Inspectors Smith and Murray, a mix of frustration and determination on their faces, realized that the story had changed once more. Amara Delacroix, the mysterious figure causing all the trouble, had managed to escape their investigation, leaving behind the lingering question of her role in the mysterious events surrounding them.

∞

A few days later, John found himself in a hospital room, lit up by bright fluorescent lights that made everything look clean and sterile.

With a bunch of pillows supporting him, he shared the wild events that happened after the big showdown.

Standing beside John's bed were his brother Sergeant Stewart and Inspector Smith, their faces showing how serious they were about getting to the bottom of things. Outside the hospital window, the Glasgow skyline stretched out, setting the stage for a storm of new information and a city caught in the middle of confusion.

John, speaking with a thoughtful tone, shared the surprising truth that came out after the big showdown. Amara Delacroix, the woman who hired him to keep her safe, turned out to be the one behind all the confusion. She was like the secret puppet master pulling the strings in a mysterious performance.

"She shot me first," John admitted, the words heavy with a mixture of disbelief and betrayal. "Then she went after the stalker. Killed him."

Sergeant Stewart and Inspector Smith looked at each other, silently agreeing on how serious the news was. The room became like a small world of truths and surprises, showing the cracks in the story that connected them all.

As John kept talking, his words painted a picture full of surprise and disbelief. Amara, the person he trusted, turned out to be the one who brought a big storm that changed everything.

"John, are you sure about this?" Sergeant Stewart asked, his voice carrying a mix of concern and disbelief.

John nodded, his eyes reflecting the weight of the truth he was unraveling. "Yes Ronald, I am sure. I never thought Amara would be involved in something like this, but I saw it happening with my own eyes."

Sergeant Stewart, hearing his brother confessing, felt a mix of different feelings. Outside the hospital room, the city didn't know about the intense story happening inside and continued with its busy life.

"We need to figure out how deep this goes and what Amara's involvement really means," Inspector Smith said, determination in his eyes. The room, now filled with tension and uncertainty, became the center of a mystery that needed solving.

Inspector Smith, the captain steering the ship of secrets, felt a twist in the plot.

Things were not sailing smoothly anymore. Amara Delacroix, once a damsel in distress, had become a person of interest in their ongoing investigation.

A decision was made. Ronald and Inspector Smith had to head back to London, the heart of the case to hunt for answers.

Leaving the hospital, the city wrapped them in its lively buzz, a complete opposite of the confusion inside. John, trying to make sense of everything, gazed at the skyline—a city balancing on the edge of truth, where secrets and surprises waltzed in a complicated dance of excitement and betrayal.

∞

Weeks later, inside the hospital room, where everything feels like a cozy cocoon for getting better, John was dealing with lots of feelings after finding out the truth behind Amara's stalker. Each day had its ups and downs, like waves coming and going. The room was full of the constant noise of machines helping John feel better.

Then, there was a knock on the door, and it was Mike, his friend, holding flowers. Watching him stand there, brought up those special feelings John felt for him.

"Hey, buddy," Mike said, sounding like he cared a

lot and was simply happy to see John. The flowers were like a bunch of happy colors against the plain hospital walls, making the room feel less boring.

John, with a mix of different feelings on his face, gave Mike a tired but friendly smile. "Mike. I didn't think you'd come."

Mike pulled up a comfy chair next to John's bed, a quiet agreement passing between them. "Thought you might want some company. And hey, hospitals could use a bit of cheering up, right? So, I brought you these flowers."

They started chatting, sharing their thoughts without saying much. John, feeling weighed down by hurtful memories, wanted to fix the cracks in his friendships. "Hey, Mike, I should say sorry. I shouldn't have doubted Sarah."

Mike looked at John with understanding in his eyes. "No sweat, pal. We've all been through tough times. Oh, and by the way, Sarah and I... we decided to go our separate ways. It just wasn't clicking for us. And don't stress about the money — she already wired your payment for a bodyguard job well done."

As the room filled with the soft scent of flowers, John hesitated before speaking. "You know, Mike, I never thought Amara would be behind all this stalker drama. It's just so unexpected."

Mike raised an eyebrow, a hint of surprise on his face. "Really? Makes two of us. I never saw that coming either. Wonder what pushed her to do something like that."

John shook his head, a mix of confusion and disappointment on his face. "I have no idea. It's just messed up, you know? Thought I knew her better."

Mike nodded sympathetically. "People can surprise you sometimes. But hey, at least we found out now, right? Saved us from more trouble down the road."

John sighed, finding comfort in Mike's words. "Yeah, you're right. I guess it's a lesson learned the hard way."

The two friends continued talking, the hospital room slowly feeling less gloomy as their conversation shifted to lighter topics, providing a much-needed distraction from the recent turmoil.

But John looked puzzled, his forehead wrinkling with a big question mark. "So what went wrong with you and Sarah, Mike?"

"It's a bit tricky, John," I said, feeling the heaviness of what I was about to say. "Sarah thinks she needs to go on a journey to find herself again."

A worried look crossed John's face as he tried to understand. "A journey? But why?"

"Sarah feels like she's lost, John," Mike shared, his words carrying the pain he felt. "She wants to figure out who she really is, away from the usual stuff in our lives."

A quiet moment filled the air, with the truth hanging around like a ghost. Mike could tell John was struggling to make sense of how a strong relationship could suddenly come apart.

"I didn't see it coming, John. None of us did," Mike admitted, a bit sad. "But I think it's something she needs right now."

John, regret showing on his face, tried to take it in. "I'm sorry to hear that."

Mike, putting on a brave face, grinned a little. "No worries. Some things just don't stick. We weren't a good match, I guess."

A quiet moment lingered in the room, the air filled with thoughts about the twists and turns of their friendship. John, appreciating Mike's surprise visit, gently said, "You know, Mike, you didn't have to come all the way here. I understand you've got things to do."

Mike looked at John, his eyes reflecting honesty. "John, there's something I need to tell you." He took a deep breath. "All those years ago, when you got hurt that day at the desert, I didn't come by the hospital because... I was scared. Scared of seeing you, my best buddy, lying there, maybe dying. I didn't think I could handle it."

John listened, a mix of understanding and surprise on his face. He reached out and took Mike's hand. "Mike, I had some serious injuries that day. The doctors kept telling me I could have died. But you know what was really scary? The thought of not seeing you again."

Mike's eyes widened, realizing the depth of John's feelings. "I never meant to let you down, John. I just... I couldn't face the idea of losing you."

Quiet filled the room, making them pause and think about the tangled feelings even after all the ups and downs. John, really wanting the warmth of his old friendship, admitted, "I missed you, Mike. Missed having my best buddy around."

Mike's face softened, showing the strong bond of friendship between them. "Well, I'm here now. In town for a bit. Figured I'd drop by every day at the hospital. Keep you company during all this mess."

A real smile appeared on John's face, and you could see thankfulness in his eyes. "I'd like that, Mike. More than you know."

As time went on, Mike kept visiting every day—like a reliable friend helping John through his recovery. The hospital room, once filled with secrets and shadows, turned into a safe place where their friendship, tested by tough times, stood strong and lasting.

∞

Back in London, inside a dimly lit office filled with awards and certificates on the walls, Sergeant Stewart and Inspector Smith sat all serious.

They were there to discuss about the Amara Delacroix case, and the police chief, who looked quite serious, was listening.

"So, Chief, we've got some big news about the Amara Delacroix case," Sergeant Stewart said, his voice sounding serious.

Inspector Smith, who's been doing this detective stuff for a while, added, "The Glasgow police found remains of Amara Delacroix's father in the house. Now, they think he didn't just go missing, something really bad happened to him."

The chief, leaned forward, looking really surprised. "Something bad? What happened?"

Sergeant Stewart kept on talking, making sure his

words were careful. "The Glasgow Police think someone killed him. His neck was broken, like he was strangled."

The room felt heavy with an uneasy truth, hanging in the air like a mysterious secret.

The chief, realizing the seriousness of the situation, spoke urgently. "This case might catch the attention of Interpol soon. We need to be ready."

A quiet moment filled the room as everyone thought about the tangled mess of lies surrounding them, creating an unnerving atmosphere.

"Do we know why Amara Delacroix hired her own stalker?" the chief asked, hoping for an answer that will help to solve the case.

Sergeant Stewart, staring at the certificates on the wall, suggested, "Maybe she wanted to be famous, get attention in the media."

Inspector Smith, not easily convinced by simple answers, interrupted. "I don't think so, Ronald. This seems more like the work of a psychopath, maybe even a bit crazier. The way the stalking was done, and the complicated plan—it points to someone with a more complex frame of mind than just wanting some publicity."

The chief, facing the challenge of the case, nodded with determination. "Stay on top of things. Keep me informed. We can't make any mistakes here."

As Sergeant Stewart and Inspector Smith left the chief's office, the hallways echoed with the unspoken understanding that the Amara Delacroix case had become more than just the case of a stalker.

It was no longer just a regular investigation. The past's shadows, mixed with layers of lies, hinted at a truth that wasn't easy to understand—a truth that was ready to change the story just as they were trying to figure it out.

Chapter Thirty Two

The sunny London streets stretched out ahead of me, all lit up in the morning sunshine. As I strolled towards the bustling breakfast cafe, I couldn't help but catch glimpses of myself in the shiny glasses of the shops I walked by.

With every step, I saw a confident young man in the reflection, rocking the best summer outfit that flattered my figure. The city's steady buzz filled my ears, making me feel dizzy as I thought about all kinds of things.

The cafe called out to me, welcoming with the coziness of a hug and the delicious smell of coffee wafting through the air.

I took a seat in the corner, feeling the gentle hum of people chatting around me like a friendly atmosphere.

The menu in front of me held so many choices, like a magical list of things to eat, but I couldn't help watching the other people moving around.

I realized I hadn't ordered any breakfast, which was something I usually skip. It's become a habit that I cannot seem to break.

As I took a sip of my hot coffee, the convenient warmth spreading through me, I glanced over to the entrance. Soon enough, two men walked in, and it felt like they timed it perfectly. Destiny had its own plans, bringing them together again. It was John and Mike, meeting up in a quiet café in London.

They strolled in like they've known each other forever, sharing a friendly bond. I couldn't help but watch their reunion, like a secret observer of fate doing its thing. John's eyes, a mix of sadness and strength, briefly met mine. It was like a quick hello from another time, a connection between what was and what is now. But then, he shifted his focus to Mike, and their conversation began.

Hiding in a corner table, I watched them closely. Their laughs blended seamlessly with the regular sounds around.

It was like a cool picture of surprising

friendships, the kind that hints at making things better and starting fresh.

They had picked a table by the window, and the sunshine made it seem like a happy get-together. John and Mike, who had been apart because of difficult times and situations, felt comfort in just having breakfast together. It was like a lucky turn in their life story, proving that fate can be full of surprises.

The café hummed with the excitement of untold stories, and in the corner where I sat, I watched the fascinating dance of lives unfolding. The city, full of secrets and unexpected moments, held us in its comforting embrace, offering the promise of new connections and the whispers of undiscovered past bonds.

My mind drifted back to when I was sixteen and decided to run away from home. After a few weeks, I returned only to find my father moving forward as if nothing had changed. That night, he slept peacefully in his favorite armchair, the TV blaring in the background. That's when I made a choice I never thought I would – I ended his life. In that moment, a strange sense of freedom washed over me. I could now shape my life the way I wanted.

With his lifeless body easily concealed beneath the basement floor, I set out for London, the city of dreams. Armed with the little money I found in his study drawers, I embarked on a new journey, spreading my wings in the world of acting.

Even though I acted in movies where I played controversial characters, I still didn't get the attention I really wanted. I started thinking about a plan. I wanted to hire someone to be my pretend stalker, thinking it would make get the fame that I deserved. I never imagined that my stalker would cross the lines, and that night he almost tried to kill me at my apartment in London. But afterwards something unexpected happened – I fell in love with my bodyguard John. Suddenly, I felt like there was a reason to be happy and alive.

But, there was a twist. Right from the start, it was clear that John liked Mike, not me. That night, when we had sex for the first time, I realized my suspicions were true – he fucked me like he would fuck another man. If I wanted any chance with John, I knew I had to change something about myself.

And on our last night in Glasgow, I found myself facing a dangerous stalker choking the man I loved. My heart pounded in my chest as I knew what needed to be done. I couldn't let this stalker harm us any longer.

But it wasn't going to be easy, I need John out of the way, just for a little while, so that I could deal with my stalker.

I needed to create a diversion, something that would make John believe the danger was gone. As I aimed the gun, my hands trembled, but I knew it was the only way. I aimed carefully, and with a single shot, I managed to hit John on the right side of his chest. John crumpled to the ground, wounded but not fatally.

Panic spread across his face, and my heart ached at the sight. Yet, I needed to ensure he stayed out of harm's way. As he lay there, I rushed to kill the stalker, ready to protect the love I had built with John, even if it meant sacrificing a part of myself in the process.

I thought I had gotten away with it, but as fate would have it, I almost got caught. In that cramped police interview room, tension hung thick in the air. I sat across from the inspectors, concealing my true identity behind a mask of innocence. The questions probed into the details of the events, and I knew the time had come to set the next stage of my master plan into motion.

As I rose from the uncomfortable sofa, purposely allowing a burner phone to slip from my pocket. The device fell to the floor with a soft thud as I left the room, the door closing behind me.

In the restroom, I took a deep breath, composing myself for what lay ahead. The plan had to unfold flawlessly, and leaving that burner phone behind was a crucial piece of the puzzle. I glanced at my reflection in the mirror, steeling my resolve, and then left the police station all the while knowing that the world needed to believe Amara Delacroix was gone.

But I knew that John wouldn't forgive Amara Delacroix for her actions. So, I decided to transform my look, hoping it would give me another shot at winning John's heart.

As I sat at my table in the lively breakfast cafe, enjoying my coffee, a friendly waitress approached with a beaming smile. She had bright eyes and a welcoming manner that instantly caught my attention.

"Hey there handsome! How's your coffee?" she asked cheerfully, her tone carrying a hint of playfulness.

I couldn't help but grin, feeling a surge of confidence. "It's great, now that you're here," I replied in my casual American accent, returning the flirtatious vibe.

She chuckled, flipping her hair back with a playful glint in her eye. "Smooth talker, huh? What can I get you to make your day even better?"

I glanced at the menu, maintaining the flirtatious banter. "Hmm, how about a slice of pie? I heard it's as sweet as your smile."

Her laughter rang through the air, and she leaned

in a little closer. "You sure know how to make a girl blush."

As she walked away, I couldn't help but feel the rush of testosterone in the playful exchange. The cafe buzzed with energy, and I sipped my coffee, eagerly anticipating the sweet treat she promised.

∞

A rush of memories flooded over me, like a fast-flowing river filled with both pain and change. Each time I had surgery, it was like an artist adding a new brushstroke to the picture of my transformation—a journey away from a past I wanted to forget. The buzzing sound of the clippers, the cold feel of metal on my skin—these were the things I had to endure to become Kyle.

I used to be a woman with blonde hair flowing down, but after countless surgeries, I emerged like a butterfly breaking free from its cocoon, my head now shaved short like armor against being recognized. When I gazed into the mirror, I saw a stranger looking back at me. I welcomed the feeling of being unknown; it became my safe place. Now, the world didn't see Amara Delacroix anymore; it only saw Kyle Manning.

My fingers glided on my phone's screen, like a magic door to the big world outside. My phone was like my sidekick, sometimes helping me, sometimes playing tricks on me. It had been a long time since people talked about Amara in the news. Everyone thought her story was over, lost in the busy waves of time. But guess what? Amara turned into Kyle, like a hero with a new name.

Taking a big breath, I opened the news app. Amara Delacroix's name was nowhere to be found in the latest news articles. It was like she vanished successfully, leaving no trace. But this emptiness on the screen, where her name used to be, it was like losing a friend and that felt a little scary.

In that busy cafe, where I hid behind the body of a young man, I watched John. He's like a ghost from my past, a bright light of longing. His laughter filled the air, a tune I wished I could create. Mike, just another person in the background, held a napkin to John's lips, making me feel all sorts of things.

I felt a little jealous as Mike wiped John's lips, making him laugh even more. The closeness of their actions hurt my heart, like a part of me wanting to own him. John was mine, something deep inside of me knew that since I met him. What we had was real, a connection that went beyond time and change.

While I stared at Mike, feeling a bit green, a decision formed in me. No one could take John away from the special love that we had for each other. People might think Amara Delacroix is gone in the wind, but they don't know that Kyle Manning is back. He is the protector of a love that beats the shadows of a messed up past.

∞

With my heart pounding like drums and a disguise that took me years to perfect, I gathered my courage to approach the windowed spot where John and Mike sat, sharing their meal. My voice, changed by a special modification surgery, sounded deep and different, hiding any trace of my old way of speaking. Now, John wouldn't have a clue who I really was.

"Hey guys, mind if I join in?" I said, trying to act cool with a friendly smile. My American accent filled the air as I introduced myself. "I'm Kyle."

John looked at me, his eyes squinting a bit, a hint of confusion in them. "Do I know you from somewhere?"

I let out a little laugh, trying my best to act calm even though my heart was racing. "Oh, maybe, buddy. I've been hanging around, you know. Just got into town recently. Thought I'd share a joke with some cool guys like you. Know any fun places to hang out?"

Mike, who had unknowingly become a part of my little act, smiled warmly. "You're in for a treat, mate. I work at this awesome pub nearby. It's really cool. You should come check it out sometime."

He quickly scribbled the pub's address on a napkin, handing it over to me. I took it, giving him a thankful nod. "Thanks, man. I'll be sure to swing by later today."

John, who always thinks things through, chimed in, looking a bit worried. "Hey, Mike, we don't really know this guy. Maybe we should think twice before inviting him along."

I ignored John and looked at Mike, my eyes hiding a secret. "I understand, Mikey. It's important to be careful nowadays. But let's live a little, huh. Catch you later!"

And with that, I strolled away, leaving them behind in the middle of my little act. The streets of London called my name softly as I vanished into the busy city scene, feeling a happy quiver. Destiny had given me another chance to be close to John, and this time, I was determined to grab it, even if it meant dealing with whatever that came between us.

∞

Later that evening, the pub thumped with its lively music as I walked in, my heart pounding just like the beat. The insides were kind of dark, but I looked around until I spotted Mike behind the bar. When our eyes met, he smiled like he recognized me from earlier that day.

"Hey Kyle! You came. Welcome!" Mike said, pushing a drink toward me.

I nodded and took the drink, trying to act cool even though there was a bit of tension. "Thanks, Mike. I thought I'd give this pub a shot."

While I sipped the drink, Mike squinted at me, like something was wrong. "You seem different, somehow. Can't figure it out, though."

I laughed a little, feeling mischievous. "Maybe London's changing me up a bit."

Resting against the bar, I pretended to be all cool as I guided our talk into new places. "Hey, Mike, where's the cool spot to hang out and make new buddies? Any guys who aren't taken?"

Mike replied with a bit of a tease, "Well, you might just strike gold here. Loads of people hang out, but telling who's single or hitched? That's the real mystery."

I looked at him, giving a friendly smile. "What about you? Do you know about the local dating scene?"

He laughed, and the sound mixed with all the

other noises around us. "Nah, not for me, buddy. I already have a boyfriend."

I was surprised and tried to keep it off my face while we chatted. "Really? Who's the lucky guy?"

He had a loving look in his eyes. "You met him this morning, actually. His name's John."

I couldn't believe it but kept my cool with a practiced smile. "John, huh? Small world. How did you guys get together?"

All of a sudden, John popped up right beside me, his eyes lighting up with a big "I know you" kind of look. "Hey, buddy! You came!"

Mike, who was busy wiping the counter like a total pro, glanced over, "John! You're here!"

While we talked, the noise from the club made a cool background to our chat. John shared cool stories about the city, and Mike threw in a few comments here and there.

Time flew by as we hung out, and when it got late, Mike suggested, "Let's hit the dance floor, guys. The music's calling my name."

The three of us made our way through the near empty dance floor, our laughs showing off our newfound friendship. On the dance floor, with the flashy lights and thumping music, we grooved together, and it felt like we'd known each other forever, not just a few hours.

Amidst the laughter and dance moves, I noticed how well John and Mike clicked. It was like they had this secret language, even without saying much. I wrestled with some not-so-happy feelings inside me, wanting to mess up this vibe. But, man, I couldn't believe I was dancing so close to John. More than that, I couldn't believe I actually pulled it off without him figuring it out.

∞

As the night went on, we ended up back at the bar. Mike, sweat shining on his forehead, gave us fresh drinks. We chatted easily, becoming good friends, but something sinister was planning in my mind.

My grand plan waited in the shadows, ready to show its dark side. The night, full of possibilities before, was turning into a time when things would change a lot, but not for the better. Soon Mike found himself getting pulled away to his bartender duties.

But all the fun from the evening started making me feel a bit dizzy. The club lights mixed into a blurry picture, and I leaned on the bar for help.

John saw me struggling, looking worried. "Kyle, you okay, buddy? Seems like those drinks hit you hard, huh?"

I managed a small nod, trying to hide the strange feeling on my face. "Yeah, just need some fresh air, I guess."

John, always kind, offered to help me get a taxi. The two of us went outside into the cool night, but in my head, the city sounded so far away. Waiting on the sidewalk, a pair of headlights came closer, and I felt relieved. I needed to get out of there fast. The drinks were making me feel like I might spill everything to John any moment now, and I was getting worried.

But then, something kind of unexpected happened. A police car drove up and stopped right in front of us. I felt my heart jump as the officer got out, and I got this really scared feeling inside me.

Guess what? It was Ronald, John's brother.

John said hi to the officer like nothing was going on. "Hey there, officer. We're just waiting for a taxi."

Ronald glanced at us in the dim light, giving a quick nod. "Alright, guys, just tone it down. The neighbors complained about the noise."

I shifted my gaze downward, avoiding eye contact

as Ronald observed both of us. It was crucial that he didn't recognize me. Ronald knew who Amara Delacroix was, and if he recognized me somehow, it would be really, really bad.

At a distance, a taxi slowly approached, snapping me out of my intoxicated haze. John's grip on my shoulders tightened, his fingers pressing into my skin. Panic gripped my chest, the harsh reality sinking in under the flickering city lights.

Ronald, seizing the opportunity, walked over with a serious look on his face. "Hey, how's it going? Can I check your ID?"

I felt my stomach drop, and everything around us suddenly felt heavy with trouble. Panicking, I searched through my pockets, pulling out an ID that matched the person I was pretended to be. But before I could figure out what to do, something really strange happened. A bunch of police cars screeched to a stop right in front of us. Officers jumped out, pointing their weapons at me.

Then, John spoke quietly, sounding apologetic about something. "I hate that it has to be like this, Amara."

My stomach twisted as Ronald, who was now in charge, put handcuffs on me. The cold metal pressed against my skin, making it real that my plan was actually falling apart.

Trying to stay calm, I asked John the question that was bothering me. "How did you figure out it was me?"

He looked at me, his eyes showing the same sadness I was feeling. "Your perfume, Amara."

There was a heavy feeling of sorry in the air as I gave him a sad smile, realizing that this was bound to happen. John just stood there, not wanting to be part of what was going on.

Police cars surrounded us, creating a wall of flashing lights. From the pub, Mike stepped out looking worried. He walked up to John, who gave him a reassuring pat on the back. They shared a hug that spoke without words, understanding the twists in our lives.

Feeling rather disappointed, I was forced into Ronald's car. The doors closed, cutting me off from the world I was trying hard to be a part of. As Ronald drove away, the city lights turned into streaks of color, and the night's beat became a sad goodbye tune.

In the rear view mirror, I watched John and Mike outlined by the bright pub lights. Their love for each other became a picture in my mind, a mix of happy and sad, a reminder of a connection broken by fate.

Leaving that image behind, I let myself move forward into the unknown future. My heart felt heavy with a secret that wasn't hidden anymore.

Regret echoed in the police car, and I braced myself for what was coming, consequences of a life caught up in love, lies, and the search for freedom.

Chapter Thirty Three

The police station buzzed with urgency as I went through case files and crime reports. Papers shuffled, and people hurried around. Suddenly, my phone rang loudly, interrupting the commotion. John's name flashed on the screen, and a tight feeling curled in my stomach. His voice, normally steady, had a slight shake.

"Ronald," he said, his words serious. "She's back in town."

Amara. Her name echoed in my mind like a scary song. We had a feeling she might come back, her love for London following her every step. The whole world had held its breath, waiting for the infamous Amara Delacroix to show up again. And it was only a matter of time, before she would show up.

"What do you mean, John?" I asked, gripping the

phone tightly.

"Changed, Ronald. She's changed everything. Appearance, identity, everything. She's now a man named Kyle."

The news hung in the air like fog, making our pursuit uncertain. Amara, or Kyle now, wasn't a woman anymore but a man. It was a big change that shook up all the ideas we had about her.

"So, when did you see her?" I asked, my brain quickly figuring out what we should do next.

"Just a few minutes ago," John answered, his voice sounding serious. "Mike and I were having our breakfast at the café when Kyle strolled up to us, acting like a tourist."

The picture of Amara, who was now Kyle, confidently coming up to them in the busy café made me feel a bit uneasy. The whole situation had changed, and things were getting more intense.

"Watch out, John," I said, my worry showing on my face. "We can't ignore how dangerous this situation might get."

John, being the brave soldier he is, didn't seem bothered. "No worries, Ronald. We are expecting Kyle to drop by at Mike's pub later in the evening. It's time to end this."

A little shiver ran down my back. The pub was where John's boyfriend Mike worked and that evening everything could change. Now that John and Mike were in a relationship, Mike had become like a second brother to me. I checked the squad board, making a promise that we'd have backup close by, just in case.

"Okay, John," I agreed. "But I'm not risking anything. We'll keep a squad nearby. You never know."

The call ended, leaving a serious feeling in the air. We both knew what was coming – a big clash of past and present at the pub. The game had started, and in the city's shadows, the finale was about to play out.

∞

The police station felt kind of quiet and tense as I walked towards the Chief Superintendent's office. The door was a little open, like it was letting in some secret talks. I walked in and informed him about John's call and how Amara turned into Kyle. It was like she completely changed who she was before.

The chief, who's been in the police force for a really long time and has never seen such a crazy turn of events, listened seriously.

He nodded and said, "I'll get a team ready,

Sergeant Stewart. We can't mess up this time. Gotta be careful."

Time hung still, like a held breath, and the city buzzed with a quiet excitement. The police squad, like a hidden silhouette near the pub's edge, waited for the signal. The air felt charged with excitement as I kept glancing at my phone, each buzz shaking my determination.

At last, the long-awaited message from John appeared - a mysterious code that kicked our plan into gear. "The bait is set."

Stopping my patrol car by a corner of facing the pub, I focused on the entrance, the gateway to the peak of our adventure. Outside stood John, his arm casually around someone swaying with the rhythm of tipsiness.

My heart raced as I looked at his face – it wasn't the old Amara Delacroix, but a man's.

A shiver ran down my spine, realizing the case had veered off course. The surgically changed face, a map of hidden stories on skin, concealed the woman we were after. Amara had disappeared, leaving behind a transformed version of herself.

As I handcuffed Kyle and led him to my car, the feeling of betrayal hung in the air like a heavy cloud. Kyle seemed lost and confused, his face telling a story of changed identity that left me questioning what secrets hid in the shadows.

Back in the driver's seat, I guided us through the city's winding streets, with the police squad following at a distance. We headed towards the center of unraveling mysteries- the police station.

The city buzzed around us, a mix of hushed sounds, as I drove the patrol car, its shiny surface reflecting the uncertainties of the night. Kyle sat silently in the back, a puzzle wrapped in quietness. The city lights painted his face with shadows, once familiar as Amara's, now a mystery hidden behind a mask.

"Kyle," I asked gently, breaking the silence with my cautious words. "Are you okay back there?"

His eyes, like a curtain hiding a secret, met mine, but there was no revelation. The weight of the unspoken words hung in the air, a barrier resisting my attempts to uncover the truth.

The city outside the window whispered secrets, like it was in on some big secret. The car felt like a tiny island, surrounded by uncertainty.

∞

Inside a quiet police interview room, you could feel the heaviness all around. Kyle, who was placed under arrest, stayed calm and serious, sitting right in front of me. His face looked almost plastic like, because he had undergone a lot of surgeries. You could see it in the lines and shapes on his face. It was a big change, and it made everything uncertain.

As the night went on, the minutes felt like they were taking forever. But Kyle stayed calm and serious. It was like whatever had happened, changed how he talked or shared things. It was hard to get through to him.

I tried again, hoping we could connect somehow through his guarded eyes. "You know, Kyle, we just want to hear the truth. It might be your best chance to come clean."

But silence stuck to him, not moving even when I asked nicely. I usually understood people well, but Kyle's calmness confused me. Was he being stubborn, scared, or pretending to be something he's not?

I sat there, waiting, believing that the truth, no matter how crazy, would eventually come out.

As time passed quietly, the mystery of Kyle lingered in the air. It was like we were having a conversation without speaking, just exchanging glances that held a bunch of hidden messages. Every blink felt like a clue to some complicated puzzle. But the answers stayed hidden, wrapped in a mysterious story.

"Kyle," I said, keeping my voice steady, "I get that this might be tough for you. But we have solid proof that you are in fact Amara Delacroix. Your DNA matches hers."

Kyle stayed silent, like a fortress keeping all the secrets safe. Figuring out how to deal with a person who changed from a woman to a man in the eyes of the law was tricky. The courtroom, a place where facts and opinions clashed, was waiting for the story to unfold, a story that balanced on the edge of identity.

"Kyle, we've gotta figure this out," I said, really wanting him to help me in the middle of all this mysterious stuff happening. "Let me help you, please."

There was quiet, like a big wall keeping Kyle all to himself. The light above us flickered, making his face look like it had secrets written all over it. My patience had finally run out, and I knew that I had to give up.

I closed the door, leaving Kyle alone with his thoughts. I couldn't shake the feeling that we were chasing after things that were hidden in a city with more secrets than we could imagine. The night held onto the mystery of Kyle, like a puzzle missing some pieces. The streets were quiet, telling a story that wasn't finished yet.

The city slept, full of its own mysteries, and I walked through its quiet streets, feeling unsure about a woman who had turned into someone completely different.

∞

It's been days since Kyle Manning aka Amara Delacroix was arrested on murder charges. The police department was dealing with a sensational trial, where the truth would fight against lies. Outside, the city didn't care about what was happening in the police station. It just kept going with its daily routine, like the heartbeat of a big city hiding more than it wanted to show.

The public was still buzzing with the news of Kyle Manning's arrest, like the final rumbles of a thunderstorm fading away. Everything settled into a new normal after the arrest, and I found myself on the brink of a big change in my own life. Because of my work in solving the mind bending case of Amara Delacroix, I was about to get promoted .

Walking into the police station, where everyone was always busy, felt different now. Colleagues exchanged whispers and knowing looks, silently acknowledging the journey we all went through to uncover Amara's secrets.

The police chief called me into his office, a room filled with seriousness and important decisions. I entered, feeling a bit nervous about what was coming.

The chief, a person with many years of experience under his hat and authority, motioned for me to sit down.

"Sergeant Stewart," he said, his voice deep and thoughtful, "your hard work on the Amara Delacroix case not only brought justice but also showed dedication and skill. I'm happy to tell you that you're now officially a Detective Constable."

His words hung in the air, making it clear that my career was taking a big step forward. The weight of the new title settled on my shoulders, a sign that people trusted me to handle the dangerous business of solving cases and bringing criminals into the light.

The police station was buzzing with excitement as everyone heard the news. People were giving me pats on the back and saying congrats, making me feel like a superstar. The city, with all its hidden stories and lucky moments, was happy to see, me, Detective Constable Stewart evolving into someone who cracked a case that nobody thought could be solved.

Getting promoted was like getting a big shiny award, and it only happened because of the Amara Delacroix case. But it changed everything for me. The city, with all its different stories, watched as I, Detective Ronald, tackled the mystery of Amara, going right to the heart of it. It was like a story that didn't follow the usual rules of right and wrong.

After the promotion, I stood there feeling like I was in the middle of something big. The shadows of Amara's past, which used to be like a big puzzle, now felt like a story that had come to an end.

As Detective Stewart, I was ready to step into the unknown world of future investigations. Each case was like a picture waiting to be painted with the colors of truth and fairness.

Chapter Thirty Four

In the big city, full of mysteries waiting to be solved, I was about to step into a new adventure. The journey ahead was lit up by the echoes of a special case, one that had not only shaped the story of Amara Delacroix but also changed how I worked as a newly promoted detective.

There were lots of papers spread out in front of me, all official and legal, showing how complicated things could get when dealing with the law. I went deep into the details, trying to figure out all the difficult parts that came up when the person accused of a crime underwent a complete sex change.

Kyle's transformation and the fact that his DNA

matched with Amara Delacroix's was going to be our express ticket to justice. It wasn't going to be that difficult to prove that they were one and the same. Now, in the courtroom where stories were told in a legal way, we had to prove that Kyle was a cold blooded murderer.

The courtroom turned into a kind of stage where we had to persuade the jury. Every word and every piece of evidence was important to make people believe that Kyle Manning was once Amara Delacroix. As part of the team trying to prove our case, I had to show the connection between the woman from the past and the man standing in the present – to make the jury believe that Kyle Manning was guilty of all the crimes he was being accused of.

∞

The trial unfolded like a big news sensation with people all over the world, tuning in. I had front row seats inside the courtroom, along with my brother John and his boyfriend Mike. Both me and John were witnesses for the prosecution and we had to be there.

The prosecution said things to make it seem like a famous actress named Amara Delacroix did what she did because she was hiding from her past. The defense, wanted to mix up the story about Amara and Kyle, saying they weren't the same person mentally. They wanted to make the jury question the story that the prosecution painted.

But soon enough, it was time for Kyle to take up the stand. He looked mysterious, sitting there against all the serious attention. The whole courtroom was holding its breath, waiting to hear what he would say. His words were like the key that could either let him go free or prove his guilt, exposing all the hidden things about Amara Delacroix, who was now Kyle Manning.

The prosecution lawyer started talking. "Mr. Manning," he said in a serious way, "you say you didn't do anything wrong, but the proof makes it seem like you're hiding a lot. Can you tell us why Amara Delacroix decided to change her name and disappear?"

Kyle, calm and sure of himself, looked right at the person talking to him. "After all that happened, I couldn't trust anyone. My life was full of scary twists and turns, and the only way to make it through was to vanish. Amara had to turn into Kyle to stay safe."

The prosecution pushed forward wanting to hear what happened, he kept asking questions. "Mr. Manning, when someone disappears, it usually means they did something wrong. Why didn't Amara Delacroix just stay and explain if she was innocent?"

Kyle thought for a moment before answering. He talked in a calm and confident way. "Just because you're innocent doesn't mean you're safe. I was in danger, so I had to do things to make sure I was okay. Becoming Kyle was necessary, not because I did anything wrong."

Everyone was suddenly talking about Kyle Manning, who was going through a trial of a lifetime. The newspapers and the internet couldn't get enough of the story. They called Kyle a hero—a survivor who faced challenges.

"Amara Delacroix, the actress who disappeared, is now Kyle Manning—a symbol of strength and change," the news said, making sure everyone knew about this amazing transformation. The story was so big that it reached beyond the borders of the country.

But in the courtroom, where the jury who was set to decide the outcome of the case, they listened closely to what Kyle said.

The lawyer for the prosecution tried to break down what Kyle was saying. "What about that secret burner phone, Mr. Manning? The one the police says you used to cause yourself problems by hiring the stalker. Can you tell us why you had it?"

Kyle stands strong, not letting the questions bother him. "That phone was like a rope keeping me connected to the world when I was hiding in Glasgow with my bodyguard. It doesn't mean I did anything bad. It was just a way for me to survive, nothing else."

The lawyer kept asking Kyle lots of questions, trying to find holes in what he was saying. But Kyle didn't back down. He told his story, mixing in the real facts with his own way of seeing things. It was like a back-and-forth of words, a kind of dance where the truth was hidden in a cloud of uncertainty.

As the questioning went on, the whole world watched. It was like a battle of stories, with each side telling its own version of what really happened. The jury had a tough job – they had to figure out what was true and what wasn't. The room got heavy with the feeling that nobody was really sure about anything.

∞

Weeks of witness testimony went by and right in the middle of it all, Kyle sat like the main character in a play of shadows and surprising moments. The city, full of its own mysteries and lucky chances, waited to see how this trial would end. It was like a chapter in its mysterious history, a story that was going to stay with it for a long time.

The courtroom was alive with whispers, like a secret shared among the grown-ups. The defense lawyer, who was helping Kyle, stood up with a confident smile. He spoke in a way that made everyone stop to listen.

"Ladies and gentlemen of the jury," the lawyer

said, his words smooth and convincing. "We're in a courtroom, like a big mystery where we try to figure out what happened. People want to know not just who my client is now but who he used to be. But it's super important to tell the difference between things that might be true and things that are totally, absolutely true."

The lawyer's words moved through the room, kind of like a gentle breeze, poking at the ideas the prosecution had. The jury was like a bunch of friends at the edge of a decision, waiting to see which way they'd go.

"The prosecution says my client, Kyle Manning, murdered his stalker. But where's the concrete proof? His phone number was on the stalker's phone, not the other way around. Just by having a burner phone doesn't mean he was the one pulling the strings."

With each word, the lawyer made it seem like Kyle wasn't the one making a dangerous plan with Amara's stalker. He made it feel like the whole courtroom was holding its breath, waiting to see if the prosecution's case was really as strong as they claimed.

"Is it fair to say for sure that Amara Delacroix hired her stalker, just because of her phone number on his phone? It's like a really thin thread, barely there, like a tiny whisper in the breeze, not strong enough to be sure she's to blame."

When the defense lawyer made the jury look closely at what the prosecution was charging her with, the trial turned into a big scene. The reasons they were pointing fingers seemed unsure, like the pillars of their story were wobbling under the doubt. You could feel the nervous energy in the air, like a story hanging right on the edge of not knowing.

"Let's not get carried away with guesses, with just the chance of being guilty," said the defense lawyer. His words were like a comforting lotion, easing the worries of the people deciding Amara's fate. "It's up to the ones accusing Amara to show that she did it, and we ask you to see the emptiness where proof should be."

As the lawyer talked, the world seemed to hold its breath, listening to every word in the courtroom. Each thing he said was like a request for the jury to think carefully about the mystery that was Amara Delacroix. The jury, who had to figure out what was true and what was made up, struggled with the big decision that went beyond just that room.

On a bright screen, the defense showed a picture of the weapon that caused a lot of trouble—a gun that killed the stalker and injured John Stewart. The defense lawyer talked carefully, making a story that tried to prove that Kyle didn't do it.

"Where are the fingerprints, the real proof that connects my client Kyle Manning to the murder weapon?" the lawyer asked, challenging everyone to think twice. The lawyer was like a detective, looking for clues in the evidence presented against his client.

Then the defense lawyer turned the spotlight to John, a man with wounds from the past. "John Stewart, a guy haunted by the echoes of war, dealing with something called Post Traumatic Stress Disorder. Can we really believe what someone says when their mind unbalanced, hurt by the terrible stuff from battle?"

He took the jury back in time, to the main point - how his client escaped from a bad home. "When Kyle was only sixteen, my client, who was then known as Amara, ran away from her abusive father. And yet there is no concrete proof that she was the one who murdered her father. There's only the circumstantial evidence surrounding the memory of a past life she tried hard to get away from."

The courtroom, like a big stage with different stories, listened closely to what the lawyer was saying. Every argument was like a stroke of paint making a picture of doubt, trying to make the jury wonder about what really happened.

"Don't let assumptions steer our thoughts," pleaded the lawyer, his words like a gentle stream trying to guide our judgment. "The prosecution relies on shadows and echoes, but we ask you to notice the lack of solid proof, to see how fragile a case can be when it's built on the whispers of a troubled past."

As the lawyer finished talking, the jury members held their breath. They were in the midst of uncertainty, deciding the fate of the case. The truth, tricky and hard to grasp, teetered on the edge, waiting for the decision that would ring through the halls of justice. The courtroom, a place where people fought for what they believed and doubted what they heard, was anxiously waiting for the final say.

The jury, a group of careful thinkers, studied the evidence with serious consideration. The city stayed quiet, its heartbeat echoing in the courtroom walls while everyone waited for the verdict. The story of both versions of Kyle Manning and Amara Delacroix hung in the balance, a tale that went beyond rules and laws, delving into the feelings of the human heart.

∞

As the trial was almost coming to an end, I couldn't help but wonder if the city really knew all the tricky stuff happening in the shadows. The night was hiding more things than it showed, and in the world of fairness, the real truth was like a puzzle we couldn't figure out. The decision, a decision that would be remembered for a long time, was about to be announced. The whole city, full of secrets and surprises, was holding its breath, asking a big question: Was Kyle Manning guilty?

Inside the courtroom, where different stories clashed, we were right on the edge of finding out what would happen. Kyle's lawyer, a master with words, stood up to deliver the final remarks.

"Ladies and gentlemen of the jury," the lawyer started, sounding sure of himself, "we are at a special moment where fairness and justice come together. The only crime that my client, Kyle Manning is actually guilty of, is trying to feel safe again."

The room got a bit tense as the lawyer tried to change how everyone saw what had been happening. The city, full of its hidden stories, paid close attention. Every word the lawyer said was like a stroke of paint making a picture showing Kyle was innocent.

The lawyer, with words that dance like a melody, challenged what the jury thought about Kyle. The city, with its mysterious history, watched as the lawyer asked everyone to understand Kyle's situation.

"My client didn't do anything wrong. Changing how you look or who you are is not against the law in the United Kingdom. It's a basic right, a personal journey of change."

"Kyle is not guilty of hiring a stalker to hurt herself or using her situation to hurt others. He only wanted to feel safe, away from the stalker who followed him. In a world where danger hides in familiar places, he looked for comfort in new things."

While the lawyer talked, the courtroom became a place of understanding, each sentence asking everyone to feel for Kyle in a complicated situation. The city, with all its stories, wondered about the importance of a decision that goes beyond saying if someone is guilty or not.

The lawyer finished speaking, and it felt like a moment of definite closure filled the room. "So, let's think about justice and, you know, being fair. Kyle Manning is not a criminal; he is someone who went through tough times by finding his way through an abusive past."

∞

The courtroom was really quiet as the jury, a group of people who decide things, left to deliberate about the case. The trial had been like a mystery story with lots of surprises, and now everyone was waiting to know what would happen next.

Inside the special room where the jury talked, they were busy figuring out all the details of what people said during the trial. It was like they were trying to solve a tricky puzzle to find out what was true and what people just thought was true. The city, full of its own secrets and lucky moments, was waiting excitedly to hear what the jury would decide.

But something surprising happened – the jury didn't take a long time to decide. It was like they rushed through it within just a day, and everyone was shocked. The sun went down, making long shadows everywhere in the city, and the decision came out really quickly. It showed that the jury either really knew what they thought or were a bit confused, and it was a big moment for the city's justice system.

The big courtroom doors swung open wide, like the grand entrance to the end of a story that everyone in the city was talking about. The jury walked in, and their faces were like a secret code, not giving away what decision they had made. The city, with its mysterious history and present, was holding its breath to hear what they would say about Kyle Manning, who used to be called Amara Delacroix.

The judge, sat down to share the final decision. "In the case of Kyle Manning, formerly known as Amara Delacroix, the jury finds the defendant not guilty."

These words were like a big announcement that echoed outside the courtroom, reaching every corner of the city. People outside shouted with joy, and others gasped in surprise, making a mix of feelings that filled the air. All the dark accusations that followed Kyle, who was once Amara, disappeared like magic with the morning sun.

∞

After the verdict was passed, the city was still buzzing with excitement. People talked about what happened, and every little whisper reminded everyone about how complicated life can be. Kyle Manning, who used to be an actress, stepped back into the spotlight as a free man. Now, everyone in the world knew about Kyle and what he went through.

The trial, like a chapter in the city's mysterious history book, ended with a decision that echoed through time. It created a story that would be told for years and years.

The big courtroom doors swung wide, letting Kyle Manning step out into a bright world that had been watching every bit of his trial. Reporters, with their cameras flashing and questions popping like popcorn, were waiting outside, eager to get a close look at the newest sensation.

When Kyle walked out, the whole building seemed to hold its breath, like a big picture puzzle waiting to be solved. The air felt like it was buzzing with the excitement of a story that had unfolded just like a love story, leaving behind a bunch of questions and mysteries.

But in between all the commotion, Kyle turned around, his eyes searching for someone in the crowd. I felt that there was something more in the way that Kyle held his gaze. Almost immediately his face broke into a sinister smile. It sent shivers down my spine and made the hallway feel colder. His eyes seemed to gleam with a dark satisfaction as they lingered on me, John, and finally, Mike.

Caught off guard, Mike's confusion deepened. "Ronald? Why is she smiling like that?" he whispered to me, a sense of unease creeping into his voice.

Kyle's grin got even bigger, and it made a spooky shadow on his face. It was a kind of smile that gave you the shivers, like he knew something no one else did. The hallway, which was loud, suddenly felt quieter as everyone turned their attention to Kyle.

But his eyes stared right at Mike's, like he was trying to find something deep inside him. I just stood there watching, and it felt like Kyle and Mike were the only ones there, even though it was packed with people.

My stomach felt all twisted up as the feeling got heavier. It wasn't just any old smile – it was like Kyle found something out, something not good. It was clear that Kyle wasn't just running away from the law; he was kind of happy in a mean way, and Mike looked like he was going to be his next target.

Mike started to feel a bit uneasy, shifting

uncomfortably. Kyle's look seemed like it could uncover something hidden, making the air feel a little weird. It was as if Kyle's eyes were hiding secrets, peeling away layers to show something nobody knew.

John, caught off guard by Kyle's gaze, stumbled with his words, saying, "Does anyone else here feel weird around her?" His question lingered, hinting that there might be more to the situation. Kyle's stare hung in the air, making everything feel uneasy, like a mystery unfolding in just one look.

Kyle suddenly turned away, his happy face disappearing as he strolled towards waiting reporters. His team of defense lawyers, standing strong like a shield, walked beside him. Beyond those doors, the outside world was ready with lots of camera flashes and the promise of becoming famous.

When Kyle shifted his attention, it was like a twist in the tale, making the mystery around the once-famous actress even more interesting. The city, with its hidden stories, observed as Kyle entered the world of fame just waiting on the other side of the courthouse doors.

∞

The doors of the courthouse opened wide, showing bright lights and the excited eyes of the media. Kyle, now a sign of triumph, stepped into the spotlight.

The camera flashes made a lively picture of his new celebrity status, a man who had proved he was innocent, and he happened to be transgender.

The reporters were like hungry birds, circling around a tale that was way more than just a courtroom drama. They were all shouting for attention, sticking out their microphones like they were blaming someone, and the cameras were going click-click non-stop, freezing the moment that was going to be remembered in history books.

While he walked past the courthouse doors, the world got to know Kyle Manning as a fighter, a person who beat the odds. But beneath the surface, in the layers of his past that only a few could understand, was the truth known to those who really knew who Amara Delacroix was.

For them, the story wasn't about making things right; it was a cautionary tale where getting justice seemed really out of reach. The world might cheer for Kyle Manning's win, but those who knew Amara Delacroix also knew the chilling truth – she had slipped away from the grip of justice, leaving behind a story where it was hard to tell innocence from guilt, a story that was filled with secrets and lies.

*** *THE END* ***

ABOUT THE AUTHOR

Kathy Winslower is a gifted storyteller with a passion for weaving tales of love, resilience, and triumph. With her captivating narratives and richly drawn characters, she takes readers on unforgettable journeys that explore the depths of human emotions and the power of love to transform lives.

Born with an insatiable curiosity and a love for words, Kathy began her writing journey at a young age, filling countless notebooks with her imaginative stories. As she grew older, her passion for storytelling only deepened, leading her to pursue a career as a novelist.

Drawing inspiration from her own experiences and the world around her, Kathy's writing is characterized by its heartfelt authenticity and emotional depth. She skillfully delves into the complexities of relationships, capturing the raw and tender moments that shape her characters' lives.

When she's not immersed in her writing, Kathy can be found exploring nature, seeking inspiration from the beauty of the world around her. She believes that every moment holds the potential for a story, and it is her mission to capture those moments and share them with her readers.